PRAISE FOR
I WISH YOU ALL THE BEST

"Heartfelt, romantic, and quietly groundbreaking. This book will save lives."
—**BECKY ALBERTALLI**, *New York Times* bestselling author of
SIMON VS. THE HOMO SAPIENS AGENDA

"Tender and bursting with humanity, *I Wish You All the Best* tells
a heartwarming queer love story without compromise."
—**MEREDITH RUSSO**, Stonewall Award-winning author of *IF I WAS YOUR GIRL*

"This is the sort of novel that goes beyond being important;
it has the potential to save and change lives."
—**KACEN CALLENDER**, Stonewall Award-winning author of
HURRICANE CHILD and *THIS IS KIND OF AN EPIC LOVE STORY*

"*I Wish You All the Best* reminds us that, when we open up to love,
we have the capacity to become our most authentic selves."
—**ADIB KHORRAM**, Morris and APALA Award-winning author of
DARIUS THE GREAT IS NOT OKAY

"A beacon of hope in a broken world. We all need this book."
—**NIC STONE**, *New York Times* bestselling author of *DEAR MARTIN*

"A truly unique and beautiful debut."
—**ADI ALSAID**, author of *LET'S GET LOST*

MASON DEAVER

I WISH YOU ALL THE BEST

PUSH

This book was originally published in hardcover by PUSH in 2019.

This book is a work of fiction. Names, characters, places, and incidents are either the product of the author's imagination or are used fictitiously, and any resemblance to actual persons, living or dead, business establishments, events, or locales is entirely coincidental.

ISBN 978-1-338-60835-9

10 9 8 7 6 5 4   25 24 23 22 21

Printed in Mexico   189
This edition first printing 2020

Book design by Nina Goffi and Stephanie Yang

For Robin, who was there from the beginning

ONE

"Ben, honey, are you feeling well?"

Mom plucks the plate from in front of me, with most of my dinner still on it, untouched. I'd taken maybe one or two bites before it fell into my stomach like a rock and what little appetite I'd had to begin with was gone.

"Yeah, I'm fine," I tell her. Always easier to just tell her that. It's better than having her pull out the thermometer and every bottle of medication we have in the cabinet. "Just a lot on my mind."

There. Not a *total* lie.

"School?" Dad asks.

I nod.

"You aren't falling behind, are you?"

"No, just a lot going on." Again, not a total lie. Is it really even a lie if I'm just withholding certain information?

"Well," Mom starts. "As long as you're keeping your grades up. When does your report card come in?"

"Next week." It'll be all As, except in English, which will probably earn me a "We're not angry, just disappointed."

"Are you sure you're feeling okay? You know these temperature changes have always gotten to you." Mom walks back over to me and brushes the hair away from my forehead. "You do feel a little warm."

"I'm fine." I shake her hand away. "I promise, just tired."

And I think that's enough for her because she gives me this little smile.

"All right." She's still staring at me as she walks away. "We should schedule you a haircut, it's getting too long in the back."

"Okay." I sip some water to give myself something to do. "Did I tell y'all that Gabby Daniels had to drop out as Art Club president?"

"No, did something happen?" Mom asks.

"I think it was just too much for her, she's in like every other club at school. But that means that I get to take over for her!"

"Oh, honey, that's great!" Mom says from the sink, washing off the plates before she slides them into the dishwasher. "Are you going to have to do anything extra for the club?"

"It's mostly organizing events and trips. I was already covering for Gabby most meetings, so it won't be much different."

"You sure that won't interfere with studying?" Dad chimes in, a grimace on his face. "Remember our agreement: If your grades slip, you have to quit."

"Yes, sir." I can feel that light pressure in my brain, like something's getting tighter against my skull. I look at Mom, hoping she might say something, but she doesn't. She just stares at the floor like she normally does when Dad gets like this. "I know."

Dad sighs and walks into the den, while I grab the last of the dishes on the table and take them over to the counter, before pulling out the Tupperware to pack the leftovers.

"Thanks, honey." Mom doesn't look up from the dishes.

"No problem," I tell her. "How was work?"

"Oh, you know." She shrugs. "Dr. Jameson keeps handing off his paperwork to me instead of doing it himself."

"Doing his own paperwork?" I tease. "What a concept."

"Right?" Mom chuckles and gives me this wide-eyed look. "One day I swear I'm going to tell him off."

"Don't you tell me to never burn bridges?"

"Yes, that's true. But I'm the adult here, and I can do what I want." Mom giggles to herself and sets the dishes aside. "So, what did you do today?"

"Nothing really. Drew a little bit, worked on a few projects that are due after break, nothing too exciting." Again, just withholding information.

Mostly my day comprised absolutely freaking the fuck out about what I was about to do, rewatching videos on YouTube about how people did this, rereading old messages from Mariam, and almost throwing up the peanut butter sandwich I'd made for lunch.

You know, typical, everyday stuff.

Mom sets the last of the dishes on the drying rack just as I'm stacking the Tupperware in the fridge. "Are you sure you're okay? You didn't eat anything weird, did you?" Mom reaches up to touch my forehead again, but I manage to avoid her.

"I promise, I'm totally fine."

Liar.

"If you say so." Mom carefully folds the dish towels by the sink. "You still up for the movie?"

"Yeah, sure, I'll be there in a minute."

"Maybe he won't make us watch *Home Alone* for the twentieth time," Mom mutters, mostly to herself I think.

"It's a classic," I tease, and she smiles at me, grabbing the little baggie of peppermint bark she made a few days ago, before she disappears into the living room.

When she's gone, I drape over the sink, bracing myself in case my dinner comes up. I can do this, it's going to be fine. Everything is going to be okay and this is most definitely the right thing to do. I know my parents, they know me, they deserve to know this thing about me as well.

And I want to tell them, I really, really do.

So that's exactly what I'm going to do.

"Ben, bring me the popcorn," Dad calls from the den, and I feel my insides clamp up again. I grab the huge tub from the counter, the kind with the four different flavors that Dad always buys at Christmas, and migrate my way into the den, except it's like my feet are covered with cement blocks.

It still looks like Christmas in here. Mom and I actually agree that people don't appreciate the holiday nearly enough, so she tends to leave the tree and decorations up until the first of the year. I'm not really sure if that's how other families do it, but it's my favorite of her mom-isms.

She's already decided that *Elf* is the movie for tonight, except we don't own a copy of it, so it's my responsibility to find somewhere we can rent it.

"We can watch *Lampoon* next." Dad crunches on a piece of popcorn.

After a little exploring, I find it, enter Mom's credit card information, and settle in. It's weird, I usually love this movie to death, but tonight? It's almost irritating. But I don't think that's actually the movie's fault. I feel uncomfortable, no matter how I sit, it's like I have to escape my body somehow.

And then the movie gets to the weird scene where Will Ferrell's character is singing with Zooey Deschanel while she's in the shower, and I get that his character is supposed to be naïve or whatever, but it still creeps me out a little.

"Now, that's a woman." Dad chuckles, feeding himself another piece of the chocolate-covered popcorn. "Right, Ben?"

"Right." I try my best to act like I'm in on the joke, even though that couldn't be further from the truth. I wonder if they've ever seen through that disguise, if they've ever entertained the idea that I was anything other than their perfect son.

I don't like lying to him.

Or Mom.

I'm basically always living a lie. They don't really know everything about me.

And that's what I've been working up to tonight, or really, the past few weeks. It's the reason I didn't have an appetite, the reason why I couldn't really focus on anything over the past week. Christmas break seemed to glide by at a snail's pace because I promised myself it'd happen now, at some point over the break. Tonight feels like the right moment, even though I can't really explain why. Maybe I'm riding some magical Christmas high.

'Tis the season, I suppose.

Too bad I don't feel very jolly right now. Maybe I should've donned some more "gay apparel" to lighten the mood.

Some commercial starts playing, and a car company is running a sale for the "Ho-Ho-Holidays," and out of the corner of my eyes, I see Dad shake his head.

"Ain't right," I hear him mutter.

Mariam walked me through this half a dozen times; I just have to wait for a good moment, a lull in the night, when we're all feeling pretty good.

It was going to be fine; Mariam kept telling me that.

Everything was going to be fine and I was finally going to get this huge thing off my chest and it was going to be great and they'd respect what I was telling them.

And it was all going to be fine.

I keep telling myself that *now* is the right moment. Over and over again as the movie keeps playing and commercial breaks keep coming. But every time I open my mouth, the words fail me, and I can't force them out.

I shouldn't be scared.

But for some reason I am, no matter how much I've willed myself to not be. I can't get over this feeling. Maybe it's an omen or something. A sign that I shouldn't do this. Except I *have* to do this. I can't explain it; I just feel it inside me. And underneath all that, I really do think it'll all be okay.

It's cheesy, but I wait until the end of the movie, when everyone is together and happy and I see a smile on Mom's face.

Dad looks indifferent, but he pretty much always looks that way.

It has to be now. I can actually feel it.

"Hey, I wanted to talk to you two about something," I say, my voice really dry.

"Okay." Mom leans back on the couch, tucking her legs underneath her and balancing her head in the palm of her hand. "What's up?"

Dad reaches for the remote and turns the volume on the TV down.

"I . . ." I can do this. Just keep breathing.

There's that tightness in my stomach, like something is just twisting and twisting and it won't let go until the moment is over. And everything will unravel, and I'll feel free.

"I wanted to tell you two something."

Dad looks at me now.

This is it.

It's kinda funny actually; the script I wrote for myself, the one I typed in Word so I'd cover everything I wanted to, it's just totally gone from my memory now. Like someone zapped it all away.

Maybe that's for the best; maybe this is how I'll be the most honest with them.

If it just comes from *me* and not some rehearsed version of myself, maybe that will help; maybe that'll be better?

I tell them. Slowly.

At first, relief floods over me. I think I can actually feel myself relax.

I just wish that feeling could've lasted longer.

TWO

"Please pick up. Please pick up," I whisper into the receiver of the pay phone, bracing against the sharp chill of the night, watching the glow of Christmas lights still hanging in shopwindows, even though it's New Year's Eve.

Just an hour, that's all it'd taken for my life to crumble around me. And now I'm here, walking around downtown without any shoes, calling collect to a sister I haven't seen, let alone spoken to, in a decade.

"Hello?" Hannah's voice sounds tired, but it isn't even that late yet. At least, I don't think it is; I don't have a watch. And my phone is sitting at home on my nightstand, charging, because the battery is total crap.

"Hannah, it's me."

"Who is this?"

"It's me," I whisper. Of course. She wouldn't know my voice, not anymore. Hell, she probably wouldn't even recognize me. "It's Ben."

There's a slip, or noise, or something on her end. "Ben? What are you—"

I cut her off. "Can you come get me?"

"What? Why? What's going on?"

"Hannah." I look around. The sidewalk is totally empty, probably thanks to the sinking temperatures. Everyone else is inside, somewhere nice and warm. And here I am slowly losing the feeling in my toes, trying my absolute hardest not to shiver from the sharp gusts of wind.

"Ben, are you still there? Where are you?"

"Outside Twin Hill Pizza." I tuck my hands under my armpits, balancing the phone between my cheek and shoulder. There's some more rustling on her end, and the sound of someone else talking.

"What in the actual hell are you doing there? It's like thirty degrees outside."

"Mom and Dad kicked me out."

The line goes silent, and for a second, I think the call dropped without warning. Oh God, I don't know if calling this way will work a second time.

"What?" Her voice almost seems emotionless, the way it'd get when she was truly, needlessly enraged. Usually with Dad about something that didn't call for it. "Why would they do that?"

"Can you please just come pick me up?" I try to breathe on my hands. "I can . . . I can explain everything later."

"Yeah, of course, just wait for me. Okay?"

"I'm going to the Walgreens down the street." I can see the bright red sign from here, just a block over. I give Hannah the address, listening closely to whatever is going on in the background.

"Okay, I'll be there as soon as I can."

Hannah lives in Raleigh, an hour drive at least, maybe forty-five minutes if she speeds. So I'll be waiting for a while.

At least no one inside the drugstore seems to care that I'm no longer abiding by the "no shoes" part of their two most basic rules. The cashier behind the counter doesn't even look up as I weave my way into the farthest corner of the store and take my seat in one of the chairs near the pharmacy waiting area.

My legs ache, and I've already torn a hole in one of my socks. I wrestle the filthy, soaked things off my feet, and start rubbing at the numbed skin. I hope I can at least get some of the feeling back. None of my toes are blue, so I'm taking that as a good sign.

At first, I don't even notice I'm crying. Maybe it's because my face already feels raw from the wind outside, or because crying is something I'd been doing for nearly two hours straight before I made the phone call. My vision goes blurry as I start to cry again, staring at my naked feet. I try my best to wipe the tears away but the skin under my eyes stings so badly.

Jesus. I'm a fucking disaster.

I felt so numb on the walk over here, trying my best to get to the one place I knew had a pay phone. Everyone at school liked to joke it was probably the last one in the country. Because who needs pay phones anymore, right?

I pull my knees in tight, trying to keep quiet. If any of the employees notice, or see me, they don't say anything.

"Get out of this house."

I didn't even know it was possible for Dad to look at me the way he had, it was . . .

Terrifying.

At first, it was calm. Almost like they wanted to hear me out. They let me talk, and then I was done. Mom never took her hands off her necklace, the cross, the one she told me Grandma gave her when she was seven.

Dad spoke up first. *"That's a good joke, son."*

Except the way he said it told me he didn't think it was a joke. His voice was flat, like there was nothing to it.

"Dad . . ."

"You should take it back," he added, to pretend like nothing had ever happened, that the conversation was dust that could just be wiped away.

But it couldn't.

And even if that was possible, I wouldn't want to.

I don't think I would at least.

"Mom." I looked at her, and she kept looking from me to Dad and then back to me, not saying anything. *"Please?"*

But she didn't say anything. And Dad kept getting angrier. He never actually yelled at me. Dad's voice was that scary sort of calm. We all just sort of sat there. *"You're our son, Ben. This just doesn't make any sense."*

"Dad, I can—"

"Get out of my house, just get out of here."

"What?"

"You heard me."

"Please." I begged them both. *"Don't do this."*

Dad led me to the door, and Mom followed on his heels. I just kept begging and begging, but they never did anything.

"Mom! Please!"

"God doesn't want this for you, Ben."

I begged her not to say that, and then I started crying. But that must not have been enough. The door closed, and I wanted it to open back up. I wanted this to be some cruel joke on their part. One I could forgive them for later. I tried the knob, but it was locked, even the spare key they hid under this fake rock didn't work because they'd locked the dead bolt too.

I stop myself from rocking back and forth in the stiff chair, hoping, praying that Hannah can find me.

What could I even do now? They wouldn't take me back, would they? Would I even go back? Would Hannah have some answers? I don't even know what the hell I'm supposed to tell her, or if she'll even be able to help me. God, what if she's as bad as Mom and Dad? She can't be, can she?

If only I'd just kept my goddamn mouth shut.

I don't want to believe that, but it's been ten years. Since she graduated, since we last talked to each other, since she left me alone with them. She could be a totally different person. The kind who hates who I am. But then again, I thought Mom and Dad might not either.

"Ben?"

I jump at the voice, not daring to look up.

"Benji?" It's been forever since someone called me that. "Come on."

It seems impossible for Hannah to already be here, but who knows.

"Hannah?" I murmur. My throat feels like it's full of something. It's harsh and prickly.

"Come on. These are your socks, right?" She picks them up carefully. The disgust on her face is humiliating.

I nod. "They're ripped."

"They're wet too." She balls them up and throws them in her purse. "Let's get you home."

I shake my head. "Don't want to." I feel like a child, but the thought of going back there—I can't go back there.

"I meant my place. Come on." Hannah puts her hand on my shoulders so she can grab under my arm and help pick me up. I guess I have been sitting here for an hour, because all the blood starts rushing into my legs again, filling them with that television-static feeling I hate. We walk out slowly, each step sending a sharp sting up my spine. I'm silently praying that the cashiers have found something else to do so they won't see us.

Hannah's car is still running, thankfully. When she's

finished helping me into the passenger's seat, buckling my seat belt for me, she bolts across to the driver's side. "I should've turned your seat warmer on, sorry."

At least the car is warm.

"You feeling okay?" Hannah puts the car into reverse and backs out of the parking space, glancing between me and the rear windshield.

"Yeah," I say, even though "okay" might be the thing I'm furthest from now. What the fuck am I supposed to do now? Everything is . . . it's gone.

"Are you hungry?"

I don't reply. I'm not though. Mom had made chicken for dinner, but since I'd been planning this for weeks now, months even, my stomach had been churning all day, so much that I knew I'd never keep down whatever I ate. Even now on an empty stomach, my appetite is nonexistent, and the thought of any sort of food makes me feel sick.

"Ben?" Hannah says my name again, except this time she feels a thousand miles away. Then I hear her mutter, "Taking you to the hospital."

"No." I grab her arm, as if that'll stop her from making the U-turn. "I'm fine, I swear."

"Benji."

"Just, can we go back to your place? Please?"

She looks at me with the same brown eyes I have, the ones we both managed to get from Dad.

"Okay." She finds another turn lane, her blinker clicking in the deadened silence of the car. "You don't want to talk about it, do you?"

I shake my head. "Not right now."

"Okay, try to get some rest or something. I'll wake you up when we get there."

———————

We ride in silence, the only real noise the low volume of the radio playing Top 40 songs. I try to sleep, or to ease my mind, to relax, to not think about what I've done. But it's impossible. Because I said those three little words.

"I am nonbinary."

Mom and Dad both sat there speechless for a few seconds. Dad was the first to react, asking for an explanation. That was fair, and maybe a good sign. I wasn't quite sure but was willing to take whatever was thrown my way at that point.

Dad used the T-word, and it came like a slap to the face. I'd never heard him use that word before. That was the moment my stomach sank. I tried to explain the differences, what being nonbinary meant, but it was like every time I tried to speak, the more I wanted to cry. Then the yelling started, and everything was moving so fast. I couldn't talk or make any sense of what they were saying.

"You need to leave." Dad pointed right at me.

"Ben?"

I must've fallen asleep at some point because my eyes are heavy, my mouth groggy and gross, and my limbs tight.

"We're here." She puts the car in park but leaves the engine running, vents still spewing hot air.

I stare at the house. The brown bricks and the green siding. I've seen it before, never at night, but in Facebook photos and posts. The only way I'd been able to keep up with what was going on in Hannah's life.

"You can sleep in the guest room, okay?"

I nod and follow her through the garage, my feet going frigid at being exposed to the cold of the pavement again. Hannah unlocks the door quickly and leads me up the steps, flipping on the light switch of the guest room. "Bathroom is across the hall, if you want to take a shower or anything."

I stare at the bedroom: There's a huge queen-sized bed, plenty of pillows. Definitely nicer than my room at home, but emptier too. There aren't any pictures on the walls, or little toys on the dresser.

"Here." Hannah folds back the mirrored doors of the closet and grabs a stack of blankets. "Get some sleep. We'll figure things out in the morning, okay?"

I nod again and stare at the bed. Hannah looks like she wants to add something else, or hug me, or tell me it's all going to be okay. But she doesn't do any of those things.

Guess even she knows it won't be.

She closes the door behind her, leaving the room even emptier.

I undress down to my boxers and pull back the sheets, crawling into the soft, unused bed. I toss and turn, but after a few minutes it's obvious I'm not going to be sleeping tonight. Every time I close my eyes I see their faces. So vivid, right there in front of me, yelling. And when I open them, there's nothing but the dark loneliness of the bedroom. I reach over to the remote on the nightstand and flip through a few of the channels on the TV, my eyes settling on a rerun of *The Golden Girls*.

Because I can't be alone right now. Not tonight.

Thanks for being a friend, Betty White.

THREE

Yesterday *actually* happened.

It takes me more than a few minutes to realize it wasn't some super vivid nightmare, or a fever dream or something. It was really real.

I came out to my parents, and they kicked me out of the house.

To think I'd been ignorant enough to believe it'd go well. I really did. I thought that we could still be this happy family, no secrets between us. I could actually be *me*. And I should've known better than that.

And now everything is over.

Everything.

I don't know whether to cry or scream or do both. It feels like I've done more than enough of both. And it feels like I haven't done enough.

And at some point, I know I'm going to have to crawl out of this bed and pick up the pieces, but right now it can be just me. Just me, these four walls, and this bed.

The universe doesn't have to exist outside this bedroom, and that's perfectly okay.

———

"I still can't believe them." I hear Hannah's voice echo through the house as I make my way down the stairs, because there was only so long I could stay in my own little universe.

"He just called from a pay phone?" That voice I don't recognize, but it's deep and gruff. I'm guessing that's her husband. Thomas?

There's only so much you can learn about someone on

Facebook without actually friending them. That probably sounds a little creepy, but I couldn't risk Mom or Dad going on my profile and seeing "Hannah Waller" on my friends list.

"When it was thirty fucking degrees outside." Hannah drops something into the sink so hard that I'm guessing she's broken whatever it was. I rub my eyes, unsure of what time it is as I try to guess where the kitchen might be.

"Hannah?" I call out, glancing around the hallway filled with pictures. There are a few I recognize from Facebook. Some from what looks like their wedding day, others while her and Thomas are out on a boat. They look happy together.

The door at the far end of the hallway swings open, Hannah pushing through, dressed in an oversized sweater and dark jeans. "Good morning." She smiles, crossing her arms.

"Morning." I run a hand through my hair, trying to make the curls in the back lie down.

"We made breakfast." She leads me through the swinging door into the kitchen. The white guy from all the photos is at the table, empty plate pushed to the side. He's sporting a beard and a shirt with a logo for a sports team I don't recognize.

"Good morning. Sleep okay?" is all he asks me.

"Yeah," I lie. My body must've finally shut down, because one minute I remember trying to laugh at something on TV and the next the sun was shining through the thin curtains of the bedroom. I'm guessing this is what being hit by an eighteen-wheeler feels like.

"Oh, Ben, this is my husband, Thomas." Hannah nods to the guy at the table. It's weird to think there's this brother-in-law I have now, one that I've literally only ever seen pictures of.

Thomas raises his mug to me. "Nice to finally meet you. Hannah's told me a lot of stories."

No doubt I was a kid in all of them. Hannah offers me a seat at their super tall bistro-style table that sits in the far corner, the windows letting in way too much light for so early in the morning. Though a quick glance at the microwave tells me it's nearly noon.

"Ben." Hannah takes the seat next to Thomas, her hands folded. "Can you tell us what happened?"

I suppose there really isn't any avoiding it, and I do owe them an explanation of some kind. The problem is I don't even know where to begin with this. I mean I know *where* to start, but it's like my mouth doesn't want to work, like it's stuffed with cotton or something, and I know whatever I say probably won't make much sense.

"I'm going to go upstairs. Maybe you two should talk alone." Thomas takes his mug and pushes his chair under the table, stretching his legs. I watch the kitchen door swing on its hinges after he leaves, back and forth until it steadily slows, and the door settles into its natural place.

"Please, Benji, talk to me."

Okay. I can do this. I did it last night. Those three words and this whole thing could be over. But do I really even know my sister? Can she even help me? Maybe this was all some huge mistake.

But she might be my only shot at some kind of normalcy, at least for now.

"I'm . . . nonbinary," I finally spit out. I even manage to make it two words instead of three.

Hannah leans back in her seat, sort of staring at me and not staring at me at the same time. This was a mistake. I'd found somewhere to go and now I've fucked it up all over again. Jesus, where could I go after this? Mom will have definitely called Grandma, probably Aunt Susan too. And I can't exactly show up at any of my classmates' houses. Besides, how would I even make it back home without paying for a taxi or something? I push back in my chair, preparing to go upstairs and get my things before I remember I don't have any things with me.

At least that means a straight shot. Right out the door. There's no way I'll remember how to get home, so I'll have to stop at a gas station or something, get directions. How am I even supposed to walk that far without shoes or socks?

"No, Ben, wait." Hannah grabs my wrist, and I almost pull away. Her grip is too tight though. "Sorry, I just wasn't expecting that." She looks at me. First at my face, then the rest of my body, as if I've somehow transformed right in front of her. "So, Mom and Dad kicked you out for that?"

I nod.

"Figures."

"I thought they'd understand." I really, really did. I mean, I'm their child. I thought that might account for something.

"I'm sorry, kiddo." She nods to the chair. "Sit back down. Please."

I eye her before I take my seat again, rubbing my sweaty palms on the knees of my jeans. I haven't showered yet, which makes me feel that much more disgusting. Like I'm covered in a film I'll never crawl out of.

"You're eighteen, right?"

I nod.

"Have you graduated yet?" she asks.

I feel like the answer should be obvious, but I have to remind myself again. She's been gone for ten years. "No."

"Okay, this is a question I already know the answer to, but do you want to go back there?"

Even at the idea my stomach clenches, like there's a fist slowly closing around it. "No. Please, no."

"Okay, okay. It's all right. We'll need to talk about some things, okay? Like school, new clothes, everything else you'll need. I've already talked with Thomas, and we don't mind you living here."

"Are you sure?"

"Yeah, kid." She runs a hand through her red hair, a dye job, I'm guessing, since no one in our family has red hair. And the chances of her hair suddenly turning red naturally seem bleak. She hasn't changed much since she left. There's still no mistaking us as anything other than siblings. Same eyes, same pointy nose, same pasty white skin, same mess of hair. I wonder how different I look to her. "Sorry, I'm trying to think. Not really sure where to start with this stuff."

I can't even look at her. "Sorry."

"Hey, don't apologize, okay? This isn't your fault."

I know that. Deep down, I do. But right now it's hard to swallow. To accept it.

"So, what are your pronouns?" she asks.

The question strikes me. Not in the bad way. It's just weird. Hannah is the first person to ask. The first person who *had* to ask. "They and them," I say, trying to sound confident, but even I can tell I'm failing miserably.

"All right. Well, it might take some getting used to, so I want you to correct me when I mess up, okay? Do you want me to explain everything to Thomas?"

I nod.

At least that way I won't have to.

━━━━━

Hannah gives me some of Thomas's clothes to change into after I get out of the shower. "He's about two sizes bigger than you, but I'll need to wash these before you wear them again." She bunches up my clothes in her arms. I drown in Thomas's shirt, but at least the sweatpants have a drawstring. "We'll go out shopping later, okay? Get you the basics," she adds.

"Thank you."

"Thomas and I talked about getting you into another school. He teaches at North Wake High School, called his principal this morning to see what we'd need to get you switched over. We, um . . ." Hannah sighs. "We also looked into therapists in the area, someone you could talk to."

On the list of everything I want to do right now, that is near the very bottom. Probably somewhere between fighting an alligator and jumping out of a plane. "Do I have to?"

"Well, no, you're an adult, technically. But I think it'd help. There's one my friend Ginger and her son saw after he came out. Dr. Bridgette Taylor. Maybe she can help, she specializes in kids like . . . kids like you."

"You mean queer kids?" I say.

Hannah acts like she's waiting for my actual reply, my agreement, but when I don't say anything else, she just sighs again. "Think about it, okay?" And then she's gone.

I sit there in the silence of the room, not sure what I'm supposed to do now. Like, what *do* you do when your parents kick you out of your house? When your entire life is upheaved, all because you wanted to come out, to be respected and seen, to be called the right pronouns? I almost reach for my sketch pad before I remember it's in my backpack, at home. I can't even do the one thing that might comfort me.

So instead I make the bed, hoping it'll give me enough of a distraction, maybe let my mind wander for a few good minutes. But it doesn't really help, so when I'm done I walk downstairs.

"What's up?" Hannah's still at the washing machine, hidden behind these folding doors in the kitchen, basket of newly dried clothes in her hand.

I offer to take something, but she shakes her head. "I got it. Something wrong?"

"No. Do you have a computer I can use?"

"Sure." Hannah leaves everything on top of the dryer and walks back into the kitchen and through another door. I'm not sure if I'm supposed to follow, but I do anyway.

Their living room is smaller than the one at home, but it looks lived in, comfortable. Hannah was always a bit on the messy side, but it seems like she's found a nice middle ground now. Or maybe this is Thomas's handiwork.

"Go ahead and set up your own account so you can log in to your texts and stuff." Hannah grabs her laptop from its spot between the end table and the couch, disconnecting the charger. "If you have any questions, just ask, but I'm sure you know more about this thing than I do."

"Thanks." I take a seat on the huge couch. I'm already at home with the laptop, since it's exactly like my old one. I type in my email address and password, so that I can read or respond to any texts I've gotten. There aren't any yet, but Mariam is probably still asleep.

I still haven't figured out exactly how I'm going to tell them about this. I almost log in to my Facebook, but I have to stop myself. Or actually, Thomas stops me.

"Ben?" he calls.

"Yeah?"

Thomas is dressed up more than he was at breakfast. Collared shirt with a dark gray sweater thrown over it and matching gray pants. "I talked with my principal. She said she wants to meet with you, get you enrolled."

"Today?" I ask.

"If you're okay with that. I'm not sure yet if we'll need to go to your old school. They should be able to send over your records no problem."

"Oh."

"We don't have to right now, but the sooner we do, the less you'll miss."

"No, I mean, that's fine." I glance down at my sweatpants. "Just, do you have anything else I can wear? I don't think Hannah's done with the laundry."

Thomas chuckles and nods toward the stairs. "Come on."

Fifteen minutes later, I'm sitting in Thomas's car, wearing the still too-big shirt, jeans that are so long I have to roll them up three times, and socks that are slowly pooling around my ankles.

But it's something at least. The hoodie Thomas gave me hides most of my discomfort, I think. And the shoes fit me, which must be some kind of miracle. Or maybe Thomas just has really small feet? He even says I can keep them.

"I can't tell you the last time I wore them."

"Thanks." We pull out of the driveway and onto the road, and immediately everything is so awkward. What do I even say to this guy? What are we supposed to talk about? Would it be too awkward to ask him a bunch of questions? Eventually I spit out: "So why aren't you at work today?"

Because that's totally normal. Really hit it out of the park with that one, Ben.

"I called out when Hannah woke me up last night. Figured this was more important."

"Oh." I fiddle with the fraying hem of his hoodie. "What do you teach?"

"Chemistry."

"That's cool." I wait a few seconds longer than I probably should. "I like chemistry."

"It's interesting, to say the least." Thomas turns on his blinker. "I guess it's weird that we've never really met."

"Yeah." I stare down at the shoes.

"Did your parents talk about your sister a lot? After she left?"

I shake my head. "They sort of had a no-talking-about-Hannah rule." I pull another of the loose strings, balling it up in my fingers. "How long have you two been married?"

"Four years last September."

"Oh, that's great."

"Yeah." Thomas sighs. "Hannah talks about you a lot. She's really missed you."

Thomas's words sit sort of heavy in the air, and for a few seconds, there isn't a word between us. "Yeah, I missed her too," I add quietly.

I don't think Thomas fully realizes what he's said, not that there's really any reason for him to.

———

North Wake High is definitely nicer than Wayne.

Wayne High was built in the sixties, with only slight updates here and there when needed. North Wake is all new, with floor-to-ceiling windows, and slanted roofs, and chrome. Even the parking lot is filled with shiny, expensive-looking cars.

Everything looks so bright and new and put together. Like everything here has a place and that's exactly where it belongs. And I'm the extra piece that doesn't fit in. Thomas pulls into the parking lot, parking near the front entrance of the school. "Here we are."

I stare at the front doors of the school. Unmoving.

"You know we don't have to do this, right?"

"Might as well get it over with," I say quietly.

"Are you sure? You don't seem too thrilled. We can look at different schools, I just thought this would be easier."

"I don't want to tell them," I blurt out. "That I'm nonbinary."

Thomas's hands drop from the wheel. "Are you sure? You know that means everyone's going to call you by the wrong pronouns?"

Like that wasn't obvious. "I don't care." I'm used to it by now.

"And you're sure about this?"

"One hundred percent certain." And I am. I don't think I can handle actually being out right now. Not unless I absolutely have to be.

"Okay. We'll have to lie and say it was something else. This sounds harsh, but if Principal Smith knows you were kicked out, that'll help."

I shrug. "Whatever."

"All right."

Thomas leads me through the huge glass doors at the front of the school. There's a group of kids hanging out near the front, and each of them waves to Thomas as he passes by. I guess their Christmas break is already over. Back home we still had another week left to go.

"Thought you were sick today, Mr. Waller?" one of them says.

Thomas waves back at them. "Nope, just had some stuff to handle."

I try to follow far enough behind Thomas so maybe the

other students won't make a connection between us, but the way their eyes drop from him to me tells me that they already have. He leads me through another set of glass doors into the front office, waving at the secretary behind the desk. "Hey, Kev."

"Hey, Thomas. Principal Smith's already waiting for you," he says.

"Thanks." Thomas turns to me. "You wait out here for a second. I'm going to explain the situation to her."

"Okay." I take a seat in one of the plush armchairs up against the glass dividers of the office. "Don't tell her. Please?" I say under my breath.

"I swear," he assures me, and something about the way he says this tells me to believe him.

I watch Thomas as he vanishes around the corner, waiting to pull my phone out of my pocket, before I remember it isn't there. I'll need to talk to Hannah about getting a replacement, though I'm not really sure how I'm going to pay for it. Maybe I can get a job somewhere, start saving up too. I don't really know what Hannah's offered. If she's only planning on letting me stay until graduation, or as long as I need to.

Then there's college, and the letters that'll decide my entire future. Letters that'll be delivered to Mom and Dad's house because that was the address I put on all those applications. I wonder if there's anyone I can talk to at the schools, ask to be sent another letter. Or maybe I'll have to apply all over again.

God, I don't want to even imagine having to pay for it. I can't ask Hannah to do that; I don't *want* Hannah to do that for me. Maybe that's some kind of blessing in disguise, Mom and Dad were definitely more excited about me going to college than I was.

Maybe now I don't have to worry about it anymore.

I guess we still have a lot to discuss, but how am I supposed to basically ask my sister when she's planning on kicking me out?

I'm getting antsy, and now isn't the time to think about this stuff, but I can't get my mind to focus on anything else. Every time I glance up at the clock above the door, it's like time slows down, which is only adding to the torture.

And then the door swings open, and a boy walks in.

He's tall—much taller than me, tall enough that his legs are the first things I notice—with a skinny frame and dark brown skin, black hair buzzed shorter on the sides so the top sticks out a little more.

"Hi, Kev," he says with a smile.

"Hey, Nathan." The secretary behind the desk smiles back. "Not in any trouble, are we?"

"I knew my street racing days would catch up with me." This kid, Nathan, laughs like it's his favorite thing in the world to do. "Principal Smith called for me."

"You specifically?" Kev raises an eyebrow. "Must be some special occasion."

"Maybe my status as a model student is finally getting recognized."

"Hilarious." Kev doesn't laugh. "Well, she's in a meeting right now, so just take a seat, shouldn't be too much longer."

"Cool." Nathan takes the seat next to me, crossing one long leg over the other, and rests his hands in his lap. It takes just a few seconds for him to break the silence. "Are you new? I don't think I've seen you around." He adjusts the way he's sitting so he can sort of face me.

"Yeah, um, just moved here." I shuffle my feet, my socks falling farther down the backs of my feet.

"Nice. I'm Nathan." He sticks out a hand.

I take it slowly but don't shake, and I don't really know why. It's like my brain is falling behind the rest of my body. "Ben."

"So where are you from, Ben?"

"Here." I answer before I realize what I'm really saying. "Or, not here, but I am from North Carolina," I sputter. Dammit, I can't even get this right. "Goldsboro, I'm from Goldsboro," I finally say.

"Oh." To his credit, he doesn't laugh at how much of a walking disaster I am. "So not too far out?"

"Yeah."

"Ben." Thomas saves me from any further embarrassment. "Principal Smith's ready to see you."

"Hey, Mr. W!" Nathan perks up in his seat. "Thought you were out today?"

"Hey, Nathan, just helping Ben with something." Thomas tucks his hands into his pockets. "What're you doing here?"

"Principal Smith called me in."

"Oh," Thomas says, looking a little confused before he glances my way again. "Come on in, Ben, she's waiting."

"Good luck, Ben, hope to see you around." Nathan grins at me.

"Thanks," I say, giving him a quiet smile back before I follow Thomas down the hallway.

FOUR

Principal Smith has a slow way of explaining things that I really appreciate, because all this information feels like it's going in one ear and out the other.

There are about two dozen documents to read over and fill out. Forms to get me back into my classes, authorization for a school ID, cafeteria account information, classes to sign up for.

It's all so confusing.

"Will Ben still be on track to graduate?" I can tell Thomas is watching his pronoun use, which I appreciate more than he probably realizes.

"We won't know until we get his transcripts and grades, but I'm guessing he will be. Our school system operates similarly to his former one."

His.

No, I can't be angry, or upset. This was my choice, and that isn't allowed, not right now.

"How soon could I start?" I ask.

"Tomorrow if you wanted, provided the papers are faxed over in a timely manner. Thankfully it's the start of a new semester, so you won't have too much trouble catching up in your classes."

"Ben's a smart kid." Thomas pats my shoulder. I want to take the compliment, but we've known each other for all of about two hours in total now.

"So, what do you say, Ben? Would you be okay with that?" Principal Smith asks me.

I nod. "Yeah."

"Good." She pulls out a manila folder and stuffs inside all the papers she's laid out for me. "If you two want to review the documents real quick, fill them out, and just sign where each page tells you."

"Come on, we'll go to the teachers' lounge, should be empty." Thomas takes the folder.

"Oh and, Thomas? Can you send in Nathan, please?" Principal Smith asks.

"Sure thing." Thomas holds the door to the office for me. "Nathan, Mrs. Smith is ready for you now." Nathan's typing away on his phone when Thomas calls for him.

He gives Thomas a mock salute and jumps out of his seat, giving me a smirk and a wink as we cross paths. Yep. He's definitely taller than me, at least a full head, and maybe more. I try to smile back, but I'm sure it comes off as creepy more than anything else. I follow Thomas down the hall to a door just outside what looks like an empty cafeteria. He types a code into this keypad, and there's a distinct *click* before he pushes it open.

A hell of a lot fancier than Wayne.

Filling out paperwork is even more tedious than it sounds. There are questions I don't know the answers to, some that make me feel totally useless, some I'm worried I'm answering in the wrong way because the wording is confusing. If Thomas wasn't here to help, I would be up a creek. But forty-five minutes later, we finish and march right back to Principal Smith's office.

"Excellent." Mrs. Smith takes the papers. "And I've contacted your old school, and they're going to fax over the rest of your papers today. I'll call you tonight if there are any problems, Thomas, but it looks like Ben is North Wake's newest student." Mrs. Smith sounds way too excited about this, but I guess I should be grateful she didn't turn me down without question.

Thomas puts a hand on my shoulder.

"Thank you," I say.

"Oh, and I've assigned someone to help show you around. Nathan Allan. He said you two met in the waiting room?"

"Yeah. Sort of."

"He's going to meet you here in the office tomorrow morning, so get here a little earlier than you normally would."

"Got it. We'll be here bright and early." Thomas moves toward the door. "Thank you, Diane."

"No problem. And, Ben, welcome to North Wake."

———

I don't talk during the drive home. Thomas wants to, apparently, but he gets the message pretty quickly.

"You can take the bus, or you can ride with me if you want."

Nothing.

He chuckles awkwardly. "You'll have to wake up about an hour earlier if you want me to take you though."

I don't answer him. Really, I don't mind either way, but I'd prefer riding with Thomas. Buses suck.

But I just don't feel like talking. Not right now. Thomas probably thinks I'm some asshole. He takes me in, gets me into a new school the day after my parents kick me out, and here I am, ignoring him.

Maybe Hannah is right. Maybe I do need counseling. I just feel so . . . drained.

By the time we make it back to their house, Hannah is gone, her spot in the garage empty. "I'm going to work on some lesson plans. You can relax in the living room or do whatever. There's food in the kitchen if you get hungry. Nothing's off-limits, so don't hesitate." Thomas drops his keys in a bowl by the door.

I retrace my steps back into the living room and take the same seat on the couch as before, pulling out the laptop. A few seconds after booting it up, the notifications start going wild. It's Mariam.

Mariam: *Benji???? What's up???*

Mariam: *Don't go ignoring me kiddo, don't tell me you got your phone taken away again???*

Mariam: *Helloooooooo?*

Mariam: *Is everything okay Benji?*

Mariam: *B E N J A M I N????*

That's Mariam for you.

Me: *Hey*

I figure out the time zones between North Carolina and California in my head; at three hours behind they'll probably be getting out of bed by now. Mariam is a total night owl, which usually means they are up by ten at the earliest.

Mariam: *How we doing today???*

Me: *Not good.*

I consider lying to Mariam, no reason to make them worry. But they'd figure it out one way or the other. If not now, then the next time we FaceTime and they don't recognize my new bedroom.

Mariam: *Are you okay? Do you want to talk about it?*

Me: *I came out to my mom and dad.*

Mariam: *Oh no...*

Me: *They kicked me out*

Me: *I'm with my sister now*

Mariam: *Fuck...*

Mariam: *The sister that your parents hate?*

Me: *The very one.*

Mariam: *Ben, I'm so sorry, I don't even know what to say.*

Mariam: *So what's the plan?*

Me: *I have no clue. I got enrolled in this other school, but other than that...*

Me: *Just trying to figure things out, get going again.*

Mariam: *Oh Ben... I feel so useless. I wish I knew what to say to you right now.*

Me: *It's fine, there's really nothing you can do.*

Mariam: *No, it's not fine. I'm so... angry, sad.*

Even trying to make a joke feels empty right now, but before I can stop myself, my fingers are typing it out automatically.

Me: *I think they call that smad.*

Mariam: *Don't make me laugh right now, please.*

Mariam: *Oh god, okay*

Mariam: *Listen I have to go get ready for a meeting. But I'll message you the second I'm out. I love you Benji. So much. <3*

Me: *Love you too.*

I close the laptop and tuck it away, ignoring the growl in my stomach. Thomas said to help myself to food, but I don't think he realizes just how awkward that'll be. I can wait.

If I have to.

I try to waste time flipping through the channels on the TV, but nothing's catching my eye. After another hour, I check my messages again, but Mariam hasn't responded, so I pull up their

YouTube channel and pick a video at random, watching with the volume low since I don't have my headphones. Doesn't matter, they caption all their videos.

I feel myself relaxing. That weird weight on my chest feels a little lighter right now. Like I can actually breathe for the first time in hours. I found Mariam's channel on a message board for trans and nonbinary teens after I'd started questioning my own identity and spent a whole night binging their videos and vlogs. Mariam talked about pretty much anything and everything. From immigrating to the United States from Bahrain, to coming out to their family, to dating as a nonbinary person.

Their videos are the reason I know what I identify as, and when I finally mustered the courage to come out to someone, it was Mariam. That was a super awkward night. In fact, I made a Twitter account just to talk to them. But they worked me through it, and we just kept talking until we realized we shared a mutual love for *Steven Universe*. Hell, they're one of the few people who I let call me Benji.

I can hear the door swing open, and Hannah comes barreling through from the garage, plastic bags hanging from her fingers and wrists. "Ben? Thomas? Y'all back yet?"

"In here," I say, but I don't think she hears me.

From the sound of it, she's moving down the hall right into the kitchen. I hear her grunt, and then something lands on the counter with a *thud*. What in the fresh hell? I slip past the still-swinging door, staring at everything Hannah's laid out.

"What is all this?" I ask, staring at the bags sporting the big red Target logo.

"I went out, got you a few things." She starts unpacking the bags. There are packs of underwear, socks, a razor, some deodorant. I can't help but notice the last two items are lacking in the

"For Men" category. I don't know if Hannah did that on purpose, but God, I love her for it.

"Oh . . ." I stare at everything laid out for me.

"I don't really know what kinds of clothes you're into." She starts balling up the empty bags. "We can go shopping together this weekend if you want, but I figured I could get you the essentials for now."

"Thank you." I can actually feel myself smiling.

"No problem, kiddo."

"You get everything?" Thomas asks, strolling in from his office.

"Close to it," Hannah says. "How'd enrollment go?"

"They'll start tomorrow." Thomas is grinning, looking at everything on the counter.

I'm still looking through the things Hannah bought for me. "Thank you," I say again. I don't want to let go of any of it, scared that it might slip away from me at any moment.

"It's no biggie." She starts rubbing my shoulder again. "You're going to be okay."

I start nodding, and I really hope I'm not crying or anything.

FIVE

"Ready for your first day?" Thomas asks me the next morning, mug of coffee already in hand.

"I guess." I look around the kitchen. "Do you mind if I have a cup?"

"Oh, yeah." He moves over to the cabinet and pulls out this mug that says "Donut Tell Me What to Do," along with a picture of a half-eaten donut. "Creamer's in the fridge."

"Thanks." I pour my cup slowly, savoring the smell of the coffee for a few seconds.

"Nervous?"

"A little."

"You'll be okay." He chuckles. "Nathan's a good kid, though I can't really speak for his tour-guide abilities." Thomas takes a sip from his mug, leaving this awkward silence. "You'll need to go to the office first thing and get your schedule."

"Okay." I wonder what classes they'll put me in. Hopefully the same ones I was taking at Wayne.

I also can't help but wonder if any of my classmates back home will even realize I'm gone. I wasn't exactly super popular there, and I didn't really have anyone I could call a friend. But someone has to notice, right? At least my teachers. One of your students can't vanish over Christmas break without you realizing it.

Thomas drives us to school with some local talk show blaring over the radio. He chuckles at a joke every few minutes, but other than that, he seems quiet. Until he isn't.

"Hey, Ben." Thomas turns down the radio.

I guess we could only go for so long.

"Yeah?" I say.

"How long has it been since you've seen Hannah?"

Out of everything he could've asked, I wasn't really expecting that. I also feel like he should already know the answer to that. "About ten years, why?"

"You don't know much about her, do you?"

"Not anymore."

"Did you even know we were married?"

"Kinda," I say, and he waits for further explanation. "I found her on Facebook. Your wedding pictures were up there."

"Oh, makes sense."

"You said that Hannah talked about me a lot?"

"Yeah." He laughs like he told a joke with himself. "She'd tell me stories about you two all the time, the trouble you'd get into."

I don't particularly remember getting into a lot of trouble with Hannah. Most of my memories of her involve loud music, slammed doors, yelling. Sometimes at Mom and Dad, sometimes at me, but okay I guess.

I want to ask Thomas if Hannah ever mentioned coming back for me, or even *wanting* to come back for me, but that feels like an inappropriate question for the brother-in-law you really just met.

My classes are almost exactly the same as they were at Wayne High: English 4, Chemistry Honors, Calculus Honors. The only difference is Art 4. I don't really know what that is though. In Goldsboro we just had normal art classes.

North Wake has different lunch times too. They're

scheduled closer to actual lunch instead of being spread between ten and eleven thirty in the morning.

"You can just wait here for Nathan, I'm sure he'll be here soon," Kev the secretary tells me. I wonder if his name is actually Kev, or if it's just short for Kevin, or maybe something else? I take the same seat I had yesterday, still wishing that I had a phone to kill time with. Hannah promised me we'd go get a replacement this weekend.

For now, I'll just have to settle for staring at the clock, awkwardly smiling at anyone walking into the office who I happen to lock eyes with, until Nathan finally gets here.

"There he is."

He.

I try my best not to let my face show anything, because this is something I need to get used to. I wanted this. It's simpler. And I can't be mad at him for it.

Nathan claps his hands eagerly. "You ready for the grand tour?"

"Yeah," I say, grabbing my backpack. Another Hannah purchase.

"Got your schedule yet?"

I hand him the folded piece of blue paper and listen to him read off the classes. "Nice, we have the same homeroom, and the same Chem class, so we'll be in the same lunch period too!"

"Oh, nice."

"Let's start with English." Nathan leads me down this sterile white hallway, with lockers against the walls that alternate between dark blue and a dull gold. "You've got Mrs. Williams. I had her last year and she's tough, but if you do your best and need some extra credit at the end of the year, she's usually good for it." He points to the empty classroom, filled with desks; hopefully I won't have trouble remembering which classroom is which.

There isn't much to distinguish it from the others, save the "Room 303" marker above the door. I repeat the number in my head. 303, 303, 303.

"Calculus?" Nathan asks. Clearly I've missed his question.

"Huh?" I shake myself out my trance. "Sorry."

He smiles again. "You're in Honors Calculus? Pretty advanced stuff."

"Oh. I like math," I say.

"Really? I have to say in all my seventeen years, that's a first." He grins.

"Well, I don't *like* it really," I correct myself. "But I'm good at it."

"You'll have to be more than just 'good' for honors classes here, even with the transfer." He adds, "We don't get too many new kids, so you're going to be a hot commodity around here."

"Really?" Great. Just what I need.

"No worries. As long as you keep your head down around the rough and tough football team, you should be good."

I don't know what to say next, so I keep quiet.

"Oh, and stay away from the bathrooms near the music room, the band kids aren't afraid of PDA." He shivers a little. "Some things you'll never unsee."

"Hmm," I hum, hoping he'll take that as an answer.

We stay mostly quiet as he leads me to Chemistry. "The thing about Chemistry is that it's at the back of the school, so you really have to run to the cafeteria if you want the edible stuff. Mr. W's pretty cool though, he'll let us out early sometimes." Nathan reads over my schedule again. "Do you know him? I saw you two in the office yesterday."

"He's my brother-in-law."

"Oh, wow. I'm surprised they let you into his class." I don't mention it, but I have a feeling Thomas orchestrated that. Nathan knocks on Thomas's open classroom door. "Morning, Mr. Waller."

Thomas is sitting at his desk in the far corner of the room. "Morning, Nathan, still showing Ben around?" he asks, scribbling something down.

"Yeah." Nathan leans over the long counter at the front of the room, balancing one knee on a stool.

"Is he as good of a tour guide as he claims, Ben?" Thomas marks something on one of his papers before spinning his chair to face us, hands propped up on the armrests like some sort of supervillain.

"Yeah." I gaze into this small aquarium situated on the counter at the front of the room, where I watch the biggest tadpoles I've ever seen swim around in the murky water.

"He's not a talkative one," Nathan adds.

"No, Ben isn't." He sighs. "You two better move along, you don't have much longer."

"Right. Guess we'll see ya in a few, Mr. W." Nathan waves, leading me back into the hallway. We walk toward the cafeteria next. I'm seriously doubting I'll ever bother coming here; I never did in Goldsboro. "So, do you have any questions? Concerns? Thoughts or opinions? Complaints? You haven't really said much."

I can't think of any off the top of my head. Of course, my brain is so rattled right now. Last night I passed out around midnight, but woke up about two hours later, unable to fall back asleep. So far this doesn't seem that much different from my old school. But with the way Nathan is looking at me, I feel like I need to ask something. "Are you a senior too?"

His face sort of twists, like the question surprises him, but he just laughs it off with a grin and the shake of his head. "Well, I meant about the school." He tucks his hands into the pockets of his hoodie. "But yeah. I am."

"Oh."

"So, what do you do in your free time? You're in Art 4, so I'm guessing you like to draw?"

"Sometimes."

"Oh, nice, you'll like your teacher. Everyone loves Mrs. Liu. I'll show you your Calc class next." We cut across this walkway outside. From here I can see the parking lot already filling up. "Don't you want to ask me another question?"

"Is that what we're doing?" I ask.

"If you want to. It's only fair, Benjamin . . ." He unfolds my schedule again. "De Backer?" He reads off my last name. *And* he gets it right on the first try. "How about that? A question for a question, answer for an answer?"

"Okay," I say.

"Is that last name German?"

"Belgian. I think." Mom and I actually spent a good amount of time tracing our last name. She was really into that genealogy sort of stuff, so when Hannah and Dad were having one of their huge arguments, she'd take me to the library, and we'd sit and read all the books they had about our family. After a few visits, we ran dry though and just started finding names and making up backstories about them and what they were doing now.

Then one day we sort of just stopped going. Guess it wasn't fun for her anymore.

I stop walking, my heart twisting in my chest.

Nathan gestures to me. "And now it's your turn."

"Huh? Oh, are you from here?"

His mouth folds into a smile. "Nothing more interesting?"

I shrug.

"My family moved here the summer before I started middle school."

"Where from?"

"Nuh-uh." Nathan wiggles a finger back and forth. "I get a question."

I wonder if there are any limits to the kinds of questions he'll ask. "All right."

"What do you like to draw?"

"Oh, um." And suddenly everything I've ever drawn just vanishes from my brain.

Poof! Gone.

"Um, anything really, I guess." I have a few characters I like to draw; landscapes are always fun to paint too, but I hardly get a chance to do that.

"Anything?" Nathan raises an eyebrow like that's supposed to mean something. "Maybe I could take a look at your sketchbook one day?"

"Yeah . . ." I rub my arm. "Maybe."

Definitely not going to happen. Not in a million years.

"Excellent! Now come on." I feel Nathan's hand on my elbow. "Let's go to the art room, I have a feeling you're going to freak!" He leads me outside and we walk along the breezeway to the front of the building. "Technically it's its own building, they added it on a few years ago, and before that, it was where the drama room is now. Mrs. Liu is really cool too."

"Yeah?"

"Definitely, there's no way I should've passed last year. Even my stick figures are hideous. But she passed me anyway. Guess

Mrs. Liu could tell I was trying at least." Nathan stops at this outside door, propped open with a huge can of paint. "Oh, Mrs. Liu," Nathan sings, tapping on the door.

There's a loud crash somewhere near the back of the room. I try to rush to help, but Nathan hangs back, so I figure I should too.

"Oh, crap in a basket!" someone hisses, followed by a long groan and the sound of approaching footsteps. Mrs. Liu is a short Chinese American woman, with her hair tied into a messy knot and a pen tucked behind her ear. The apron she's wearing is stained with paint splatters, and so is the white blouse underneath. At least it looks dried.

"Nathan!" She rushes toward us when she realizes who's here, wrapping Nathan in a hug. "What are you doing here so early?"

"Showing the new guy around." He hugs her back. "Ben, this is Mrs. Liu."

"Nice to meet you." I hold out my hand.

She shakes it so quickly that I'm pretty sure my arm's going to pop right out of the socket. "It is so good to meet you too! How are you liking North Wake so far?"

"It's fine," I say.

"Well, I look forward to having you. Unfortunately, I didn't have enough kids for an Art 4 class this year, so you'll pretty much be by yourself."

"By myself?" I ask.

"At your level, you'll pretty much have free rein, after I get to know you a little better, of course." She beams. "But I'll be teaching a freshman class in here. And—" She motions for Nathan and me to follow her through this small hallway. On the other side there's another classroom. I can't tell if this one is bigger since there aren't any desks, but it feels that way. "You'll be working back here."

"Oh." I take it all in. The walls are covered with paintings, cabinets left wide open, showing off tubes of paint and racks upon racks of canvases and easels. It's all sort of marvelous. We probably had about half of this back in Goldsboro. "Wow."

"Impressed?" I hear Nathan ask me.

"Yeah." I nod slowly, taking it all in. Maybe this won't be so bad after all.

———

First days are weird, especially when you're the new kid. Walking into class isn't this super awkward moment where everyone goes silent and just stares me down. But I do catch a few strange looks, and the people sitting beside me do try to talk to me. But I guess they give up when they realize I'm not as interesting as I seem.

Thankfully none of my teachers make me introduce myself to the class. They just pretend like I've always been here.

When the bell for lunch rings in Chemistry, I hang back in Thomas's classroom, heading in the opposite direction of the cafeteria once the hallways are clear. There's this really nice quad area that sort of resembles an amphitheater at the back of the school. A crowd of kids is already huddled at one end, but no one tells me to get lost when I take a seat at the other side, and for the first time in a long time, I can draw in peace and quiet.

Out here I can breathe.

Not that I don't appreciate everything he's done, but Nathan can be a little . . . suffocating. In a good way. If there really is a good way to suffocate. He just seems so eager to do everything. And Thomas decided to seat me next to him in Chemistry. So every day I'll be getting at least an hour-and-a-half dose of Nathan Allan.

I flip open the brand-new sketchbook, a gift from Mrs. Liu after I said I lost my last one.

It's weird to think this one is totally empty. My previous drawings and doodles and notes all gone. Probably forever. I stare at the first empty page and try to think of what I can draw.

SIX

"I can pay you back, when I get a job, I mean," I whisper to Hannah when the guy at the store goes into the back to get my new phone.

Hannah just rolls her eyes. "Don't worry about it, br—" She stops herself short. "Ben. Can I call you bro? That's not okay, right? I should find something else."

On the message boards, I found many enby people asked their brothers and sisters to call them sib, short for "sibling." I liked the idea myself but had never really played with the notion that someone might actually get to use it for me.

"Sib is good," I say. "Instead of bro or whatever."

"Sib. Got it. Well, sib, you don't have to worry about paying me back, it's fine."

It feels good to have a phone again, even if I can't help but feel slightly guilty. "Hey. I know what you can do to pay me back." Hannah sort of looks at me funny when we get in the car.

Uh-oh.

"Just go to one meeting with Bridgette."

"Bridgette?" I ask. I don't remember any Bridgettes.

"Dr. Taylor. The psychiatrist I told you about?"

"You can have your phone back." I pull the box out of the bag and hand it back to her.

"Ben, please." She pulls the car out onto the street. "Just one meeting."

I slouch down in the seat. "Hannah—"

"Just one. I really think she could help you."

"Why?"

"Because this hasn't exactly been the easiest time for you, and I think that talking it out with someone could help you." She almost spouts all of this in a single breath. I'd be impressed if I wasn't getting so annoyed. "Just one appointment," she says again. "That's all I'm asking."

"Only one?"

"One, I promise. After that, you can decide if you want to keep seeing her."

"Fine," I say, resisting the urge to unbuckle my seat belt and roll out of the car. At least that'd buy me a few weeks in a hospital without having to meet with a therapist. Though Hannah's case would probably get stronger if I did that.

"I'll call her when we get home, okay? Maybe she'll have an opening next week."

"Great."

"I just think it would help, maybe talk out the things that happened at home."

"Yeah." I stare out the window, carefully watching everything we pass by. I want to ask her if she went to some kind of therapy, but in my head that sounds like an insult.

"Did they ever get any better?" Hannah asks. And I can feel that knot in my stomach slowly crawling up my throat.

"They didn't really change," I tell her.

"I'm . . . I'm really sorry . . ." Hannah stares down at the wheel. "For leaving you like that. I just couldn't stand it anymore, and when I found my chance, I took it."

I glance over at her, the guilt on her face obvious. She left just after her graduation. We were supposed to go eat lunch, but Hannah never showed. And when we got home, her room was completely empty. Mom and Dad both tried to call her, but she wouldn't answer her phone.

It took me almost a week to find the note hidden in our bathroom, the one with the name of her college and her cell phone number. Telling me to call her if I needed anything. I think it was supposed to be comforting, but really, it just made me mad. Because she'd left.

She'd left me with them, to fend for myself.

After that, Mom and Dad changed. I sort of became the punching bag for all of Dad's issues. He didn't actually hit me, but overnight, I essentially became an only child. The focus of anything and everything. If I did something wrong, it was blown way out of proportion. It was almost like they'd seen what'd happened with Hannah and were determined to make sure I didn't turn out the same way. Except I don't know how getting more frustrated with me over school and chores was supposed to change that.

"Hey, you okay?" She nudges me.

"Just thinking," I say. "It wasn't your fault."

"I should've . . . I just . . ."

I shrug. "Whatever." I don't want to have this conversation. Not right now.

And if I have the choice, not ever.

———

Sunday is a day of nothings. I sleep in way too late, not recognizing my room when I open my eyes.

"Breathe," I tell myself out loud, and for a second I don't recognize my own voice. My heart pounding in my chest. "Just breathe. This is Hannah's house, you live with her now." I will my hands to unclench from around my sheets, but I can feel the sweat in the small of my back. I don't remember what my dream was about, but Hannah was there, and Mom. "Breathe."

I spend most of the day in my room, sort of in this haze. I eventually try to draw something, *anything*, really, but any time I so much as pick up my pencil, it's like my hand refuses to cooperate. After that, I try to watch TV with Thomas and Hannah, just doodling in the corners of the paper. Nothing too elaborate.

I waste the rest of the day chatting with Mariam for a bit, trying to catch them up with everything that's happened this weekend, before lying down. It's hard to believe that it's almost been a week since that night. It feels so impossibly long ago. My alarm comes way too early Monday morning. For the first time in a while, I've managed to get a full night's sleep and I can't even enjoy it that much.

Then I remember my appointment with Dr. Taylor. Hannah took care of setting it up for me, but there was only one slot open, at noon today, so she is going to pick me up from school early and take me. I sit up with a groan and walk to the bathroom. Try as I might, there's no avoiding my reflection while I wait for the water to warm. I eye the faint stubble that doesn't belong. I still haven't found the time or the energy to shave, even though I hate the way it makes me look. And then I notice the bags under my eyes, the way my hair falls over my forehead, and the scars my acne has left behind.

Such a contrast to the other nonbinary people I've seen online. Their smooth, hairless, acneless faces, their trimmed hair that always seems perfect. These things I could never be. Because no matter how hard I will it, my body isn't how I want to see myself. Not that there's anything wrong with those kinds of enby people, I just . . . it's hard to describe. Bodies are fucking weird, especially when it feels like you don't belong in your own. But it's too late for things like puberty blockers, and surgery isn't something I want.

Hell, even my name isn't very "neutral." It's a boy's name, even if there really isn't such a thing. But changing it is long, and complicated, and I don't even know what I'd change it to. I'm Ben; that's just who I am.

I don't know what I really want, but it isn't this body. It's almost like it knows, with the way it taunts me. It takes everything I have not to climb back into bed, even though I know Hannah won't let me miss this appointment. "What is wrong with me?" I whisper.

I just need to make it through half a day. That's it. Hannah's going to pick me up before lunch and take me to the appointment. But even half a day feels like it will be too much. I breathe in and out. I can do this.

"I don't think I can do this," I whisper to myself.

"So where are you going during lunch?" Nathan leans over the counter, head tilted to the side like a puppy.

We're sitting in Chemistry. Thomas finished the lesson early today, so I decided to get a jump on all the homework I've been given. It's a lot to handle after just a few days, especially since I've apparently missed the deadline on a few things. I also have to play catch-up in a few classes. I'm pretty much good in Art and Calculus, and Thomas promised me he'd help me catch up in Chemistry. But I can already tell I'm going to need a tutor for English. I've never been good at the whole paper-writing thing anyway. Too many rules that are too hard to remember.

"What do you mean?" I rub at my eyes. All this stuff is starting to blend together. Dozens of signature lines and trying to figure out how much everything is going to cost me here. Or, I guess, cost Hannah.

"I mean, we have the same lunch period, but I haven't seen you there once." Nathan sticks up his hand.

"I go somewhere else," I say, not really interested in this conversation.

But clearly he is. "Where?"

"Does it matter?" I sigh, shoving all the papers back into my bag, zipping it up with a little too much satisfaction. It hasn't taken me long to figure out the quad is the "official-unofficial" smoking area. What they smoke varies between them all apparently, but they leave me alone and I leave them alone. It's quickly becoming one of the best relationships I have at this school.

I did the same thing at Wayne, except there wasn't a courtyard or anything like it, so I used the back entrance of the gym. The one no one really thought about. There, I could be alone. I never had to worry about someone finding me or bothering me or asking me what I was working on.

"I'm just wondering. Plus I'm your accountabilibuddy." Nathan cracks a smile.

I just stare at him with a blank look. "My what?"

"I'm supposed to look out for you."

"You were just supposed to show me my classes."

"Are you okay? You seem a little irritable."

"I'm fine," I lie.

"Okay, Mr. Attitude." Nathan chuckles.

"Please don't call me that." I rub my eyes again, like I could just wipe away the tired, burning feeling inside. I don't even know if I'm talking more about the "Mr." part or the "Attitude."

"It's okay, man."

I think I sound angrier than I mean to. He's just asking a question, after all. I guess I'm just stressed out about this appointment.

To Nathan's credit, he doesn't look offended. "You should come to lunch with me sometime, my friends want to meet you."

"I'll think about it." I lean forward, burying my head in my backpack, already actively planning to never think about it. This morning has been a mess, and I'm sure it's not about to get any better. "Doesn't matter today though." The phone on Thomas's desk starts to ring, probably the front office.

"Why?"

"I have a doctor's appointment. I'm leaving after this period."

"Oh, urologist?" he asks with probably the straightest face I've ever seen.

"What? No," I sputter. "And why was that your first guess? Never mind."

"Relax, man." Nathan starts to pack up his own bag. "I'm playing with you."

"Yeah."

"Ben." Thomas hangs up the phone. "They're ready for you in the office."

"Good luck," Nathan whispers when I push my seat under the counter. A few of my new classmates glare at me as I make my way to the door, backpack thrown over my shoulder. Thankfully Thomas avoided any lengthy introductions, which probably means that everyone here is still wondering about this weird-ass kid who's randomly been put in their class.

"Ready to go?" Hannah grabs her purse as I push through the doors of the front office.

"Yeah." I'm not really, but I figure it'll be better to go ahead and get this over with.

"Had a good day so far?"

Hannah's got her car pulled up in front of the building. It's unseasonably warm outside today, but it's the first day I haven't needed three layers, so I don't plan on complaining. "So far."

Hannah spent the last two nights showing me reviews from past patients of Dr. Taylor, assuring me she is one of the best in town, which really only made me more nervous to talk to her. I wonder how much Hannah's told her exactly, if anything at all.

I've been mentally preparing myself to come out all over again, but I've been doing that for a while now. That was one of the things I realized early. If you're queer, your life has the potential to become one long coming-out moment. If I ever want to be called the right pronouns, I'll have to correct people and put myself out there first and who knows what could happen.

"Are you nervous?"

"To have someone poke around my brain for an afternoon?" I buckle my seat belt. "I'm thrilled."

Hannah shoots me this look, that sort of brows-pointed-down "you need to chill out" look. "Okay, sassy britches. I just think it will help, and it's a short meeting. Only forty-five minutes."

"Hmmm." Forty-five minutes too long if you ask me.

"I haven't told her anything." Hannah's car rolls to a stop. "About you being nonbinary. I didn't know what you'd be okay with."

"But she knows Mom and Dad kicked me out?"

"Couldn't avoid that detail. Sorry, sib." She glances around to check for the traffic before she pulls out onto the road.

"It's whatever." I sigh and rest my head on the cool window, not knowing whether to feel relieved or angry that she shared that with a stranger.

The doctor's office is a part of this long row of complexes, the ones that look like an apartment building but are really just filled with offices. In this one alone, there's a place where you can get your teeth cleaned and get a few X-rays done if you want, all while checking to see if you're pregnant. I glare at the way they all seem to tower over Hannah's car.

I really want to ask Hannah if we can reschedule or something. I'll even go back to school if I have to. Just anything to not be here. Do I really need to see this woman? Can I air out all my problems to a complete and total stranger? My eyes fly from the ground back to the buildings, my stomach clenching. There's nothing for me to let out, but I can feel the bile rising.

"Her office is on the third floor." Hannah locks the doors of the car and stuffs her keys into her bag.

I make it as far as the entrance, reading the board of names for the offices. There's an entire block worth of counselors, their titles, their office numbers. I try my best to focus in on Dr. Taylor's name, but it's like my eyesight goes blurry for a split second. I close my eyes and pinch my brow, trying to calm myself.

My hands get that same clammy feeling they did in the Walgreens that night. It's this sudden feeling like I've been punched in the gut, like I can't catch my breath.

"Hannah?"

"What's wrong?"

"I don't know if I can do this."

"Hey, hey, hey. It's okay." Hannah closes the space between us, grabbing my hand, and it takes everything in me not to pull it back. "It's all right. Listen. It's going to be okay. Dr. Taylor is going to help you, all right?"

"What is she going to do?" I try not to breathe too deep. I

feel like I should be crying, but there are no tears, just this pocket of air in my lungs that I can't get out.

"She's just going to talk to you about what you're feeling, what you're going through."

"What am I supposed to tell her?"

"You tell her whatever you want, but it'll help her to know at least what you identify as. That's the first step." I try to nod, but I still feel like I'm going to be sick. This was exactly how it felt before I told my parents.

I can't do this again, can I? I can't come out all over again, not here, not right now.

"I don't know if I can do that."

"Okay." Hannah sighs, brushing the hair from her face. "Try this. You told me once already. Just keep telling me. That should be easy, right?"

"What?"

"Just keep repeating it back to me. It's like that thing where words lose their meaning after a while."

"Do you really think that'll help?" I ask. I mean, I guess it makes sense. In theory, at least.

"If you get used to saying it, it'll get easier. I think that's how this works?"

I take a deep breath and force the words out slowly. "I'm nonbinary."

"Again."

"I'm nonbinary."

"Come on, keep doing it."

"I'm nonbinary. I'm nonbinary. I'm nonbinary." It's silly, standing in the middle of a lobby, repeating back the same words over and over again. But it does feel easier with each time I say it, despite the heavy feeling in my stomach. "I'm nonbinary. I'm nonbinary."

"One more."

"I'm nonbinary."

"Good, you've got this." She presses a hand to the small of my back and leads me to the elevators. "Just picture me if you have to, okay?"

I nod. Just get there. Get in there so there's no turning back.

"And I'll be in the waiting room if you need me. If you want to leave early, if you need me to sit in there with you, anything at all."

"Okay." The elevator doors slide open, and we walk in together.

———

I'm not exactly sure what to expect. Maybe stark white walls, ugly tiled floors, and an inescapable medical smell. But Dr. Taylor's office looks just like what it is. An office. The walls are a light blue and decorated with colorful paintings. The furniture is bright too, and the floor is a warm hardwood.

"Hello! Ben, right?" She smiles and opens the door wide for me.

"Yeah."

"I'm Dr. Taylor, but you can call me Bridgette if you'd like. You can take a seat right on the sofa." Dr. Taylor points to this hideous mustard-yellow couch that sits against the wall. By some miracle, it fits the look of the room though.

"So." Dr. Taylor grabs a small notepad and pen from her desk. "Your sister called to tell me about a few things."

She's older than I thought she'd be. Maybe midforties? She's pretty short too, with brown skin and short, tight curls.

"What did she tell you?"

"That you'd been kicked out of your home." Dr. Taylor takes a seat in the chair across from me, folding her legs over. "And that you might need someone to talk to."

"That's it?" I ask, a little surprised. I know Hannah said she didn't tell Dr. Taylor anything else, but I didn't really believe her. And now I feel bad for thinking my sister might out me like that.

"That's it. I thought it wasn't appropriate to discuss anything further without your knowledge."

"Oh . . ." I'm not sure what to say. "Thanks, I guess."

She nods. "So, can you tell me why your parents made you leave?"

I close my eyes, rubbing my knees. Here we go.

"You don't have to, but it might be a good starting-off point," she says.

"No, it's . . ." I shake my head, picturing Hannah. Just say the words. Two little words, that's it. "I'm . . . I'm nonbinary."

"Oh." I hear the distinct sound of a pen being clicked, and then something being written down. Opening my eyes slowly, I watch her move. She doesn't seem surprised, or horrified, or like she misunderstood me or didn't know what I was talking about. "Did Hannah tell you that I work with a lot of LGBTQIAP+ youth?"

That pit in my stomach is still there, but I can feel my hands relax. "You can say 'queer' around me, it's fine."

She chuckles at that. "Sorry, a few of my clients aren't comfortable with that word. So, you're nonbinary?"

I nod.

"Can I ask what pronouns you use?"

"They and them," I say. It's still weird, for some reason, to be asked that.

"And so what's the connection there, between you being nonbinary and your parents?"

"I came out, or I tried to. They both sort of freaked." I've never felt smaller than in that moment. The way Dad stood over me, his hand raised. I thought he might actually hit me or something, but no. He just pointed at the door.

"Where do you want me to go?"

"I don't know, just get out of this house."

I'd never seen that look in his eyes before.

"Can you tell me how they behaved? As parents."

"Like parents, I guess," I say. "I don't really know." As far as I know, they were mostly normal. But I don't exactly have another set of parents to compare them to.

"What was Hannah's relationship with them like?"

"She got along with Mom, for the most part. But she'd fight a lot with Dad."

"And you? What was your relationship with them like?"

Better than whatever their relationship was with Hannah, but still rocky. And it only got worse as time went on, the fights getting more and more frequent. "Fine, I guess. Things got worse after Hannah left."

"When did Hannah leave?"

I sigh. "The night I called her, that was the first time I'd spoken to her in about ten years." My fingers find the little balls of fuzz on the couch and can't resist picking at them, twisting them together until they get too big. I just leave them sitting there when I'm done.

"I see. Are you comfortable staying with your sister right now?"

"Is there an alternative?"

"Do you want one?"

I shake my head. "Just wondering. This all stays between us, right?"

Dr. Taylor uncrosses her legs and leans forward in her chair, the leather squeaking underneath her. "You're my patient." She points to the door with the end of her pen. "I won't discuss anything that happens inside this room with anyone but you. Not only am I legally required to, but the privacy and safety of my patients is important to me, Ben. We could go over informed consent if you'd like?"

"Informed consent?"

Dr. Taylor walks over to a filing cabinet in the corner of the room, sifting through the rainbow of folders situated there. "It's an important procedure, where I lay out everything I'll be going over with you, the limits of what we'll be discussing, as well as the benefits of treatment, and, more importantly"—she walks back across the room and hands me the stack of paper—"confidentiality."

I take a deep breath through my nose, trying to read through everything the documents entail. Sure, there's the Hippocratic oath and everything, but I don't even know if that's supposed to apply to therapists, or if that's just the surgery sort of doctor. This woman hasn't given me anything to base a level of trust on.

But the papers lay it all out, or at least they seem to. "We can go over each part step by step if you like." Dr. Taylor leans in closer. "But I swear to you that unless I think you are an immediate threat to your own life or someone else's, I'm not going to tell a soul what goes on in here."

"I . . . I'm sorry." This weird sense of shame creeps up my face.

"You don't have to be sorry, Ben. I realize it's scary, I can only imagine what you've been going through these last few days, even months." Dr. Taylor speaks quietly. "But that's what I'm here to do. I want to help you, help understand what you're going through."

"Thank you."

"It's what I'm here for. Do you want to go through the forms?"

"If we've got time?"

"Sure. We can review them while we talk."

It's a lot. There are some things that are simple or self-explanatory, but there's even more that I don't understand. Then Dr. Taylor says, "So are you out to your sister?"

"Oh, um . . ." I flip through the next page and read briefly over what it says, sign my initials where Dr. Taylor tells me it's needed.

"We don't have to talk about it."

I try to breathe. "I mean, I'm out. To her. And to Thomas. I sort of had to be, didn't I?" I try to laugh, but even to my own ears it sounds forced.

"Are you comfortable with that?"

"I have to be, don't I?"

"No. Of course, circumstances were out of your hands. I know in this scenario, telling them why you'd been forced out of your home was the easiest option, and maybe the only one. But that doesn't mean you have to like it."

"They're trying. Hannah and Thomas correct themselves when they use the wrong pronouns."

"That's good. And what about at school? Are you adjusting easily?"

"I mean, it's school. I'm not out, if that's what you're asking."

"Uh-huh." Dr. Taylor clicks her pen and adds that to her notes. "Do you want to talk about that?"

"Nothing to really talk about."

"You think so?"

"Doesn't exactly feel safe."

"That's a fair point." There's this shine in her eyes, and I expect her to fight me on that, but she doesn't.

"But?" I say.

"No 'but.' Have you met anyone at your new school? Any new friends?"

"No."

"Really? That's a shame. No one at all?"

"No," I repeat. "No one." We've reached the last of the forms. I read over it quickly before I sign my name. Dr. Taylor flips through all of them one more time before she gathers them all up.

"Was there anything else you wanted to tell me?"

"Like?"

She shrugs. "Anything you feel that may help me know you better. Or anything specific you've been dealing with?"

"I don't think so." There's Mariam, but that feels like a private thing, something I don't need to share here. Not right now, at least.

"Okay." Dr. Taylor stands up, tossing her notepad on her desk.

"Okay?" My eyes follow her all the way to her desk. "Is that all?"

"For today." She slides open a drawer and grabs a small pamphlet. "I'd like to keep seeing you, Ben, if you want to, that is. But I also have something here." She holds the paper out for me to take.

"What is it?" I flip it over in my hands, reading the header, which is in bright multicolored letters.

"It's a support group for kids on the LGBTQIAP+ spectrum."

I open my mouth to speak, but she sticks up a finger to silence me. "I know, but not all the members use 'queer' to identify with. I'd like you to think about attending. It's mostly young adults and teens. I really think it could help.

"They usually meet every other Friday around six thirty. Just think about it." I eye the pamphlet, reading the contact information and address for the meeting on the back. "Would you be open to seeing me again?"

I consider it for a second. I mean, I don't really feel any better, but am I supposed to after just one meeting? I really just sort of want to go home, crawl into bed, and wait for tomorrow. "I guess."

"You don't have to," she adds.

"I can meet again," I say. That's probably what Hannah wants.

"We'll try for next Thursday, okay? I'm free in the afternoons, and that way you don't have to keep missing school."

I stand up, folding the pamphlet to slip it into my back pocket, knowing I won't be going to this support group thing. If I could hardly face coming out here, how am I supposed to come out to a room full of strangers?

"I'd also like to talk with Hannah briefly, if that's okay." Dr. Taylor eyes me.

"Why?"

"I'm not telling her anything we haven't agreed to. I just want to make sure she understands everything, if she has any questions."

"Oh, okay."

"So you're comfortable with that?"

Not really, but maybe it would be easier for Dr. Taylor to handle this instead of Hannah grilling me in the car ride back home. Dr. Taylor pokes her head out the door and says something, Hannah trailing in right behind her.

"Everything okay?" she asks.

"Just fine," Dr. Taylor says. "I just wanted to talk about a few things regarding Ben's appointments."

"Okay."

"Ben and I will meet on Thursday; every other week should suffice unless Ben tells me they want to change the frequency of the appointments." Dr. Taylor says this about as straightforward as I can imagine someone can. "I'll be communicating with them directly and won't be sharing any information unless Ben signs a release form."

"Oh" is all Hannah says, and I can't look at her right now. I wonder how it feels, having the woman you're paying to treat the sibling you just took in tell you that you don't have a right to know anything that goes on in here.

"I just wanted to let you know that I won't be able to discuss any details about their appointments besides when they will occur."

"No," Hannah says. "I mean, yeah, of course. No, I totally understand." She seems a little jumpy. Maybe from the knife I just stabbed her in the back with. "Was there anything else you needed to talk to me about?"

Dr. Taylor looks my way. "Ben?"

"I'm done."

"All right, I'll see you next Thursday." The last thing Dr. Taylor does is grab a small card from her desk. "Here's the contact information for the office, just call if you need to change the times."

I tuck the card in alongside the brochure.

"Thank you, Dr. Taylor." Hannah and Dr. Taylor shake hands. "You ready to go?"

I nod and eye the clock on the wall. It's only one in the afternoon, but it feels later than that.

"Want to stop and get some lunch?"

My stomach lurches, totally empty, but I shake my head. I don't think I have it in me to keep food down right now.

SEVEN

"Interesting." Mrs. Liu eyes the painting, and I'm trying not to feel self-conscious. A task I'm failing at miserably. "I like the empty space here, and the choice of colors, especially the dark blues. What made you pick that?"

I just picked blue because I like blue. Isn't sky supposed to be bluish anyway? "It felt right," I say instead. I don't think my other answer will win me many points. Mrs. Liu is an interesting teacher, to say the least. Over the last two weeks, she's been circling over me like a hawk while I work, even if it was just a sketch. So far she's had me at the wheel making this hideous clay pot. And before that, she gave me a bag full of wire clothes hangers and told me to make something out of them.

Yesterday, she gave me an easel and a canvas and told me to paint the first thing that came to mind. Mariam had been texting me about cardinals during lunch, and how they're Mariam's favorite bird. So that was the first thing I blurted out.

And I painted a cardinal, just like I'd been told to.

"It's a nice contrast, especially with the red," she tries to joke. At least I think it's supposed to be a joke. "Do you like painting, Ben? You're very good at it."

"Yeah." I actually enjoy it more than drawing. I guess maybe it feels fresher, since I can't do it as much as I want to. I couldn't exactly drag out paint sets at home, and at Wayne, art classes weren't much to write home about.

Not that they were worse, and I learned a lot. Things were just definitely stricter there.

That's when the bell decides to ring. I scramble to get my paint and brushes into the sink. "Oh, take your time, kid." Mrs. Liu pats my shoulder.

"Sorry, wasn't paying attention," I say, my hands already stained with the watery orange.

"It's okay. I wanted to ask you something anyway."

"Yeah?"

"I noticed you're going out to the courtyard during your lunch."

Jesus, I'm ready for everyone to stop being obsessed with where I go for my lunch break. "Oh, yeah, not a cafeteria fan."

"Well, if you ever want to come in here and work . . ." Mrs. Liu pulls a small key out of the pockets on her smock.

"Are you serious?"

"Of course. I've got a good feeling about you, Ben." She slaps the key down on the counter. "But just a warning, I don't give too many chances."

"I'll be careful. I swear."

"You better." She winks at me and goes back to her office. Near-unlimited access to the art room? Most definitely not a bad thing.

It's an uphill climb to Friday, but I get there. Between homework and trying to catch up on all my classes, it's nice to just have a night to myself. Hannah and Thomas both decide they want to go out to dinner; I decline the invitation, figuring they probably want some time to themselves after everything I've put them through.

Plus, this way I can draw without interruption, and I don't really have to worry about walking in on them or intruding on their space. Nights alone at home were rare, and normally I reserved those times for more drawing or marathoning Mariam's videos.

"So, what're we doing tonight?" Mariam's voice echoes through the speakers on my laptop. It's been way too long since we've had a night like this. Just me and them, talking while we both work. It's actually relaxing.

"Nothing special. What're you working on?" My eyes drift from the TV to my computer to my sketchbook. I've been sketching so many ideas for paintings over the last few days.

"Speeches. I've got to get ready for this conference. And I'm looking at dates for the next tour." They show me their notebook. Even just a single page is crammed to the margins with their messy writing. It never fails to amaze me that Mariam can speak in front of hundreds, or in some cases, a thousand people, without a care in the world.

"Sounds like a fun time," I say.

"Yup." They pop their lips. "What about you?"

"Drawing." I show them the sketch pad.

"Nice, when are you going to give me a new header for the channel?" Mariam leans on their hands and bats their eyelashes.

"That would require the right tools, my friend." Some kind of drawing program on the laptop, probably a drawing tablet too. Too much for me, especially since those things cost money.

Mariam just rolls their eyes, the master of the eye roll. "Want to see my latest haul?"

I smile. "Always."

"How about new scarves?" They lean back to show more of the scarf wrapped around their head in the frame of the webcam. It's hard to tell from here, but the material looks glossy, and the bright red really goes well with their lipstick.

"I love it."

Mariam and I have had long conversations about being religious and nonbinary. For Mariam though, their hijab represents comfort, security, a connection to their faith. They could spend hours talking about how it made them feel. In fact, they made a whole series on their channel last year, what being Shia Muslim and being nonbinary meant to them.

For a second, I remember what Mom told me that night. How God doesn't want this. Mariam's the only reason I can't believe that.

"I bought a few more, but this one is my favorite. Oh!" They reach off-camera for something. "And this sweater." Mariam stands up quickly, pushing their desk chair out of the way, and twirls in front of the camera. It's one of those that sort of looks like a cloak, but it's cut so it won't fall off you or anything. The kind I was always sort of jealous of when I saw them in stores, out shopping with Mom.

"Oh my God."

"I know, right?" Mariam twirls again. "I'm never wearing anything else. Thirty percent off too!" They do a little dance. "Not that I'll have much of a chance to wear it at home. The lowest it gets here is like sixty degrees, if we're lucky. But maybe on tour."

"I'm jealous."

"You'll get there one day, Benji. I promise. When you're designing logos and painting masterpieces, no one can tell you what to wear."

"Yeah, right." Technically no one could tell me what to wear now, but I know exactly what would happen if I dared to go out in public dressed like that, or in some of the cool-looking polka-dot dresses I've seen online, or maybe in calf-high boots I know would never fit my feet.

I settle into the couch and go back to my drawing. I've been thinking about portraits for a while now. There's always been something about faces that just feels so interesting to me. I spent the last few days saving photos of various models I found online, their smooth faces and sharp lips, eyebrows perfectly plucked and eyes like they're piercing you.

I heard a car pull into the driveway. Instead of the headlights dimming and the engine cutting off, it just sits there idling.

"Weird," I whisper to myself.

"Huh?" Mariam asks.

"Nothing." I resume drawing. "Hannah and Thomas just got home."

"So how are you liking the new school?" Mariam's in front of the camera now.

"It's fine."

"Any new friends threatening to take my spot?"

"None so far." Nathan kept trying to get me to come to lunch with him, but once Mrs. Liu let me in the art room, any hope of that was crushed. He didn't seem too bothered by my rejections though. It was almost like it was becoming a game to him or something.

I glance back out the window. The car is still there, just sitting in the driveway with the engine running and headlights shining through the curtains.

"Everything okay? You seem a bit spacey tonight."

"Hannah and Thomas are just sitting outside in their car."

Mariam starts laughing to themselves. "Maybe they're making out."

"Gross." I crawl toward the window, pulling back the curtains as slowly as possible. The driveway isn't that long, but it's still too dark to really tell the color or make of a car. Not that I would've known anyway. There are cars, trucks, and SUVs. That's pretty much the extent of my car knowledge.

But my stomach sinks when I realize that this car definitely isn't Hannah and Thomas's large black SUV. That much I can tell, even in the dark. No, this car looks an awful lot like Dad's.

"No."

"Ben?" Mariam's voice scares me. I'd already forgotten they were here.

Panic fills my chest as I pull back the curtains and run to the front door to check the locks. Mom and Dad can probably see my shadow running from one end of the house to the other, but that doesn't really matter right now. I grab my phone and keep my thumb hovered over Hannah's number.

Mariam's voice keeps echoing through the hallways. "Ben? What's going on? Hello? Ben?"

I hover at the top of the stairs, making sure I can just barely see the glow of the lights through the dense curtains, ready to sprint to my room if I need to. But after a minute, the headlights turn off. I run back to the window, brushing past the curtains. It's still there, the engine no longer running.

Then there's a knock at the door.

They're coming. Holy shit. They're coming for me.

"Ben? What happened?"

"I need to call you back!" I shout without meaning to.

"Ben!"

"I think my parents are here," I choke out. I can hear the crack in my voice. I don't wait for their response, I just close the laptop and grab everything. I run back to the guest room, taking the steps so quickly that I almost fall at the top. I make sure to lock the door behind me.

They can't be here. Right? Do they even know where Hannah

lives? Why would they even be here? They didn't want me in their house, so there's no reason for them to be here.

My phone starts to ring in my hand. I've been holding it so tight that I managed to switch it off silent mode. It's Mariam, texting me, and trying to restart the FaceTime call.

No matter how hard I try, I can't seem to calm my breathing, can't take my eyes off the stark white bedroom door. I have to listen closely, for a car coming up the driveway, or the front door opening and shutting, the sound of feet coming up the steps.

Then come those unmistakable sounds. The door swinging open, then closed, quiet chatter that I can't make out. It's Hannah and Thomas. It has to be; it's their voices. They gave me the only spare key they had. They even told me that themselves. And the doors are locked. It has to be Hannah and Thomas. But is that really what they sound like? Is that their muffled voices? Their footsteps?

What if it's not?

One set of feet, two sets, slowly approaching the top of the stairs. "He's probably in his room," someone says. Hannah?

At least, it sounds like Hannah, but I can't be sure. *"Their,"* she says. *"They're* probably in *their* room." It's got to be Hannah; it has to be. But my mind refuses to accept it, no matter how much I want it to.

"Ben?" There's a knock on the door, and the handle jiggles a little. "Ben, the door's locked."

I open my mouth to speak, to say something, *anything.* But nothing comes out.

"Ben, are you okay?"

"No," I force out, like I'm swallowing nails.

"Can you open the door?" The handle keeps wiggling back and forth.

"Ben?" It's Thomas, or at least it sounds like Thomas. "I need you to open the door for me, okay?"

I can't, I'm stuck. Because what if that's Mom and Dad on the other side of that door? Nearly every part of my brain is screaming that it can't be, but there is still that chance, no matter how slim it is.

They both whisper something I can't understand, and then I hear footsteps fading away.

"Ben? Thomas is going to unlock the door, okay?"

I try to say something, but my mouth feels impossibly dry, and I can't control my breathing. It's almost like there's a fifty-pound weight sitting on my chest, and no matter how many times I wipe my face, I can't seem to stop crying. It's worse than it was in Dr. Taylor's office. Or that New Year's Eve night. This feels like I'll never know the end of it.

"We've got one for the bedrooms. Just in case of emergencies."

There's the sound of something on the other side of the door, and the *click* of the lock sliding and the door slowly opening. Thomas steps away and lets Hannah walk in slowly ahead of him.

"Ben?"

"I'm sorry." I tuck my knees to my chest, trying my best to hide my face. I can't even look at them.

"Ben? Can I sit down?" She points to the bed.

I shrug. "'S your room."

"It's *your* room." The bed dips under her weight. I can tell she wants to reach for me, raising her hand before pulling it away again. "Ben, what happened?"

"Mom and Dad." My voice is barely a murmur.

Hannah freezes. "What about them? They didn't come here, did they?" Hearing their names, it's like a switch flips inside her.

I shake my head and tried to clear my throat.

"I don't know if it was them." I wipe my eyes. "There was a car. It pulled into the driveway, and there was someone at the door." Now it feels like I've breathed too much, like the air is going to poison me.

Hannah turns and mouths something to Thomas, but I can't tell what it is. He nods and vanishes down the hallway.

"Ben?" Hannah turns back to me. "Do you want anything to drink?"

I shake my head.

"Want me to call Dr. Taylor? Maybe she can help you through this?"

"No, don't bother her. Please."

"Well, maybe it wasn't them," she offers. "Maybe it was just someone who was lost and turning around? That seems pretty wild, that they'd show up out of the blue, right?" I think she's trying to talk me down, but it isn't helping.

"I'm sorry."

She touches my back gently, almost like she's scared I'll break if someone so much as breathes on me too hard. "I know this isn't easy."

I turn away from her hand. I can't deal with touches right now, not even from her. "I'm sorry, I just . . ."

"No, it's fine. I'm sorry." She clasps her hands together. "Maybe you should try to get some rest, okay? We can talk more in the morning."

I nod slowly, feeling the bed shift as Hannah stands, turning to glance at me one more time before she closes the door behind her. I want to scream, I want to yell, but my voice isn't much more than a whisper. "Please don't leave me."

But it's too late. She's gone.

I hear her say something to Thomas. It sounds like he's still on the phone. But everything just feels so muffled, and I don't even have the energy to eavesdrop. I pull my knees in closer, wanting to do so many things. Pick up my phone and talk to Mariam, or even get Thomas in here to talk to me. A different voice. Anything to fill the room.

Hannah and Thomas don't bother me for the rest of the night, even though I'm silently begging them to. I hear their footsteps creeping back and forth, moving between the rooms, I guess. Around midnight, after my back aches from sitting against the wall for so long, I finally pull off my shirt, throw it onto the floor, and crawl underneath my sheets.

———

In the morning I shuffle into the bathroom, the hot water of the shower calling to me. I don't want to leave; I want to just stand here. Maybe I'd eventually just drown; that's easy enough to do in a bathtub, right?

It's mortifying watching Hannah and Thomas look up from the table in the kitchen, both of their gazes settling on me. I can already see so much of what they're thinking on their faces. It's pity and sadness and fear and I fucking hate it so much.

"Hey, kiddo. How're you doing?" Thomas asks.

"Fine." I'm pretty sure we all know that's a lie.

"Why don't you sit down? I think we need to talk." Hannah pats at the empty space on the table.

"Do we have to?"

"Yes," Thomas says, no room for question in his voice.

I force myself to move forward, no point in running back upstairs and hiding in my room all day. Especially if they have a key.

"I think Dr. Taylor needs to know about what happened last night." Hannah pauses.

"You didn't call already, did you?" I ask.

Hannah shakes her head. "Didn't want to do that without you. I remembered the confidentiality stuff and didn't think you'd be comfortable without me asking you first."

Maybe she just doubted that I'd ever tell Dr. Taylor myself, or maybe she was so scared of what I might do the next time this happened. "You can call," I say.

"Do you want to talk to her yourself?" Thomas asks.

"No." I won't even know where to start.

"Okay." Hannah searches through her contacts for Dr. Taylor's number. I hear it ring for a few seconds, and then the muffled sound of her voice. Is she actually in her office on a Saturday? "Hey, Dr. Taylor. It's Hannah Waller. Ben's sister? I just, um . . . I don't really know where to begin with this."

There's some noise, the sound of someone talking.

"No, yeah. Ben is fine. Well, kind of. They're right here. But last night, there was an incident. I think it might've been a panic attack or something. And we just wanted you to be aware of it."

Dr. Taylor says something else.

"Yes. I understand. Okay." Hannah puts her hand over the phone. "She wants to know if you want to meet earlier than next Thursday?"

I shrug, a non-answer. But Hannah accepts it.

"If you don't mind," Hannah says. "Mhmm. Yes, thank you.

I'll bring them Monday right after school. Thank you, have a nice weekend." Hannah ends the call. "Sorry." She gives me a guilty look.

"It's whatever," I tell her. Maybe I'm actually a little happy she took the lead on this one. I don't know, I think if I'd actually told them what I wanted to do, I might've said no.

"Ben," Thomas cuts in. "Do you want to talk about anything?"

"No, just not today." I try to make the words sound like a firm statement, but I doubt it actually comes out that way. "Please?"

Hannah and Thomas pass a look between them. "Okay," Thomas says. "Do you need us to do anything?"

Even if there is something they can do, I doubt I'd be able to tell them. I've never been so scared like that. It was like I shut down. I couldn't even speak; it was like my brain just refused to form the words.

"No, there's nothing."

EIGHT

Every night that weekend, I dream about my parents. I wake up covered in sweat, the sheets tangled around my legs. I only remember Mom's face, the frigidity of that night. Saturday night I manage to fall back asleep after a while. Sunday is a different story though. No matter how hard I try, my mind refuses to rest. So after an hour of wrestling with my sheets, I know it's no use. I'll be a zombie tomorrow morning at school.

In some combination of my insomnia and curiosity, I go downstairs to the living room and pull out the laptop, googling the causes of insomnia, but that doesn't help. One, because I'm not sure that's what this is, and sometimes self-diagnosis can be dangerous. And two, the results yield anything from asthma to sinus issues to arthritis. None of which I've ever had to deal with. But there are two causes that stick out to me, right near the middle of the page.

Anxiety and depression are two of the key factors contributing to insomnia. Patients will usually experience—

I stop, almost looking up anxiety, but I don't want to open *that* can of worms. I close the tab and grab my headphones, killing time by listening to one of my playlists and taking BuzzFeed quizzes. Eventually I go to Mariam's channel and watch their latest video.

A few hours later, the sun starts to peek up from behind the curtains, bathing the room in a warm glow. Another night lost. I head back upstairs and take a quick shower. Hannah and Thomas are still asleep, or one of them is. I can hear someone moving around in their bedroom.

"Morning, Ben." Thomas marches down the steps about an hour later, buttoning the sleeves of his shirt.

"Morning."

He opens the refrigerator and grabs a bottle of water. "You're up early."

"Couldn't sleep." I swallow the last bit of cereal and drink the leftover milk, which is the best part, honestly.

"Oh, that sucks. I've had those nights." Thomas leans against the counter. "So . . ."

Uh-oh. I'm already bracing for the worst. "So . . ." I repeat.

"Nathan's been asking about you."

I eye Thomas suspiciously. "Asked what about me?"

"He, uh . . ." Thomas laughs, less like he finds this funny, and more like he doesn't want to say the next part of his sentence. "He was wondering what he did to offend you."

My heart drops. "Oh." It's all I can really think to say.

"I told him I didn't think you were mad at him or anything. Just that you were going through some stuff."

I open my mouth to ask a question, but Thomas is already one step ahead of me. "I didn't tell him anything," he assures me. "Kept it vague and mysterious, just how you like it."

I let out a sigh of relief and walk over to the sink to rinse out the bowl. "Thank you."

"He's a good kid, just a little nosy."

I glare at Thomas. "A little?"

That makes him genuinely laugh. "Okay, he's a lot nosy, but he's got a big heart. He likes to make people feel welcome."

"Yeah." I open the dishwasher, stacking the bowl so it fits perfectly. I don't know what to make of Nathan yet, honestly. He seems cool enough, and he's been nothing but nice to me since

I got to Raleigh, almost to a fault. Like he has something inside him that's telling him he can't leave me alone for more than five seconds. "I should be nicer to him, shouldn't I?"

"Maybe," Thomas begins to say. "You should at least give him a chance. It can't be easy, I mean, your life is . . . Well, a lot has happened over the last few weeks, Ben. You need someone you can talk to."

"I thought that's why I was seeing Dr. Taylor."

"Okay, well, it helps to talk to someone your own age who you aren't paying to dissect everything you say."

"I guess." I sigh. I can only rely on Mariam for so much. Between the time difference and them traveling so much to speak with nonbinary and queer groups across the country, having a friend might not be so bad.

Thomas pats my shoulder and gives me one of those awkward smiles. "You want to go ahead and leave? I can get a head start on my grading."

"Okay."

———

There's not really anywhere for me to go so early in the morning. Mrs. Liu won't be in for another hour, and it feels awkward to be in the art room before she is.

I like Thomas and all, but I'm not prepared to spend an extra hour in his classroom with nothing between us but awkward conversation and even more awkward silence. So I head back to the quad. At least now I can be alone, and the place doesn't reek of cigarette smoke and pot yet.

I find a spot to sit down and pull out my sketchbook, but I'd really rather be painting right now. Maybe I could do the sky, the mix of light blues and almost transparent purples. With just the barest hints of orange and green from the sun. It's like now that I can pick up a brush, it's all I want to do.

There's this really cool drip painting I did last week, that I'm really proud of. Mrs. Liu was teaching the Art 1 class about Jackson Pollock, so she had me study and show off the way he did his drip-style paintings. Mrs. Liu actually liked it so much that she put it on the wall of the other student paintings, across from the one of the cardinal.

I pull my phone out of my pocket and search through my reference photos. The one true benefit of getting a new phone is that I can now clog all my extra storage with useless reference photos I'll never get to use.

There's one of a rose I *have* been using though, and I'm really liking how the sketch is coming out. I think I've got the perfect brushes to try and paint it too. The kind that will capture the delicate softness in the petals.

"Now, Benjamin, you know phones aren't allowed at school." I jump, and Nathan plops down next to me. "Sorry, didn't mean to scare you."

"You didn't scare me," I lie. "And school hasn't even started yet," I argue without looking at him.

"Touché. What's that?" He points to the half-finished drawing. I guess it is hard to tell what it's supposed to be when it's just vague lines sketched out.

"A rose."

"Oh, nice." He dramatically rolls over onto the grass next to the concrete steps, lounging out. "Draw me like one of your French girls."

I stare at him.

"*Titanic?*"

"That's a little dated, don't you think?" I say.

Mom loves that movie. I remember begging to stay up and watch it with her so many times when it was on TV. Little did I know that it's almost three hours long, so I'd always fall asleep before we even got to the iceberg scene.

"Whatever." He shrugs me off. "Hey, can I see any more?"

It takes me a few seconds to realize he means the sketchbook. "Oh, um."

"Just one? Come on."

I sigh and start flipping through the pages quickly to find something that's actually finished. There's this idea for a painting I've been playing around with. It's just a sketch, but I'm done with that part of the planning. "Just one," I say, handing it to him.

Nathan's smile grows wider, if that's even possible, as he takes the pad. He handles it with the same care I'd expect him to give a baby.

"It isn't going to break, you know."

"I know," he says, still setting it in his lap carefully. "This is really cool, Ben."

"Thanks." I feel my face get hot, so I turn away from him. Oh God, I'm not blushing, am I? "It's an idea for a painting I have."

"You paint too?"

"A little." I reach for my phone. "I've just got some photos though."

"Can I see one, please?" He hands the sketchbook back to me, leaning closer to get a look at my phone. I hope he doesn't question the background. There's this ice-skating anime Mariam and I both love, and I don't think now's the right time to explain just how gay it can really get.

"Hold on." I flip through the camera roll, trying to find something he might like. "Give me a second?"

"Sure, I'll even turn around." Nathan tucks his knees up near his chest and swivels around on his butt, which can't be comfortable on these concrete steps.

"You didn't have to do all that."

"Now you tell me!" He doesn't sound too offended though. "I gave myself a wedgie doing that."

I could show him the drip painting, but that doesn't seem too impressive. There is this small painting of a skull I did, partially a study in anatomy. It isn't perfect. I messed up on some of the colors and the shading, but overall it isn't terrible. I tap Nathan on the shoulder and he leans back without turning around, grabbing the phone.

Please don't start going through my phone. Please don't start going through my phone.

"Ominous. You aren't, like, secretly some dark lord or anything, right?" He laughs.

"If I was some evil overlord, I'd like to think I'd have better things to do than go to school." I reach for the phone, but Nathan pulls it away at the last second.

"Not done." He eyes it closely, spreading his fingers to zoom in.

"I messed up on the shading at the back, and the eyes are way too dark for where the light is supposed to be coming from."

"Ben, this is pretty awesome."

"Yeah, right."

"No, I mean it. You need to give yourself more credit, dude." He hands my phone back, and I feel that sting.

"Thanks." I slide the phone back into my pocket. "So what are you doing here so early?"

"I could ask you the same thing." He leans back, trying to turn around without getting another wedgie.

"I asked you first."

"Choir practice." He grins.

"No way." I try my best not to laugh. "Really?"

"Ha!" Nathan tosses his head back. "How gullible are you?"

"Shut up." I shove him.

"For real though, I'm here for student council."

"Serious this time?"

"One hundred and ten percent. Our lovely president, Stephanie, has to work after school and wanted to go ahead and start planning Spring Fling stuff. It isn't even for another few weeks, but there's a lot to do." Nathan tries to keep back a yawn but fails miserably, wiping at his eyes.

"Spring Fling?" I ask.

"You know how most schools are obsessed with football and homecoming?"

I nod. I'm all too familiar with Spirit Week, and the pep rallies, and the football game, and dances.

"Well, here at good ol' North Wake High we're more of a baseball crowd, but that season doesn't start until the spring, so we have Spring Fling. Just take everything you'd normally do during homecoming but crammed into March instead of November. There's even a dance."

"What's the theme?"

"A Night Under the Stars!" He accentuates every word by sticking his hand in the air. "It's going to be about as fun as you'd imagine."

"Sounds like it." I haven't been to any dances since middle school, and those were pretty sad excuses to corral students in the gym for an hour and listen to "clean" versions of popular songs.

"My vote was for Godzilla Attack, but that was shelved pretty fast."

"They turned that down?" I pause. "Can't believe it."

"My, my, someone took his smartass pills this morning." Nathan bumps into me with his shoulder. "So spill. What are you doing here?"

"Thomas wanted to come in early to grade some papers. Figured I'd get some peace and quiet while I was here."

"Oh." Nathan glances around. "I can leave if you want me to, then." He makes like he's going to stand up.

"No," I say, before I even know I've opened my mouth. "I mean, you don't have to."

"You sure?"

"Yeah."

"You know," he starts to say, relaxing back into his spot, "I sort of thought you might be mad at me for something. If I did something to make you uncomfortable, I'm really sorry."

"No, it's not you." I sigh, wishing it was as simple as telling him the truth. "I've, um . . . just been going through some personal things."

"Oh." He spreads out his long legs. Really, how is it even possible for someone to have legs that long? "Want to talk about it?"

"Not really."

"Okay. So, what do you want to talk about?"

"Don't know, you got anything on your mind?" I ask.

"Not really? Maybe collapsing in on myself at the idea of dealing with all these school events, and homework, *and* college letters coming in, but that's not exactly great conversation."

"Right," I agree wholeheartedly.

"So we'll sit here in silence?" Nathan pushes himself forward a bit, leaning his head back. "I'm cool with that. The world's too loud sometimes."

"You're the last person I'd expect to say that." I sneak a look at him, grateful that his eyes are closed. He'd make good money as a model, honestly. He has those sharp cheekbones and that smatter of freckles across his nose and cheeks.

Striking. That's the word.

"Underneath this smooth and handsome exterior lies the soul of an isolated poet, Ben." Nathan cracks a smile. He's even got dimples, how is that fair? "Can't you tell?"

"I never would've guessed."

"Damn. Really?" He laughs. "I should work on that image. What do you think? More brooding? Or should I start wearing black turtlenecks?"

"Definitely more turtlenecks." I grab my sketchbook again to work on the rose, not even bothering with the reference photo this time. "Don't forget the black coffee though, and the hipster glasses with fake lenses."

"Blegh, black coffee? Why would you punish yourself like that?"

"Hey, you're the bohemian writer. It's for the aesthetic," I add.

"Noted." He lets out a long, slow sigh. "If I fall asleep, you promise to wake me up?"

"Sure."

"Pinky promise?" He sticks out his hand, pinky finger extended, and for a second, I just stare at it before it occurs to me that he's serious.

I wrap my own finger around his.

"Pinky promise," I say.

"This is where you go during lunch, isn't it?" Nathan asks, his eyes still shut.

"Sometimes," I whisper after what's probably too long a silence. "Or I go to the art room." I'm not quite sure why I tell him the truth. Maybe I owe him that much at least?

"Seems lonely."

"Sometimes the world is too loud," I repeat back to him.

That makes him laugh again. "Touché." He takes another deep breath. "I guess there's no point in asking you to join me for lunch today, huh?"

There's this thud in my chest. Make a friend, Ben. Make a friend. "I'll go."

He opens an eye. "What?"

"I'll go," I say again. "For today at least."

"Are you serious?" He nearly leaps up from his spot.

"Pinky promise," I say.

He grins, and he can't stop giggling as he takes my finger.

"You really want me to go to the cafeteria that bad?"

"It's the sort of experience you only get in high school, my friend." He winks. "Besides, Meleika and Sophie have wanted to meet you for a while now."

"Meleika and Sophie?"

"My friends."

"Oh." I'm not sure why I imagined it would be just the two of us, but maybe with more people there the chances of it getting awkward will be diminished? At least a little.

We sit in silence for a bit before. Nathan starts humming a song I don't recognize, but that dies out quickly. At one point I'm sure he's fallen asleep, because his breathing changes and there's a slight hitch. When the parking lot begins to fill with cars, I nudge him awake, but he doesn't seem groggy or tired or anything.

"Almost that time?" he asks.

"Almost," I say, closing my sketchbook and sliding it into my backpack.

"Did you finish the rose?"

I stand up and brush the gravel off my jeans. "Not yet."

Nathan grabs his own bag, checking something on his phone. "Can I see it when you're done?"

"Yeah," I say without hesitating.

"Hey, do you have any paper?" Then he pauses. "Any that you don't use for drawing? I'd hate to steal the artist's resources."

I grab my bag and dig through the front pocket, looking for the pack of sticky notes I keep there just in case. In case of what? I don't really know.

"And a writing utensil?"

"So needy," I tease, reaching for a pen.

He writes something down and folds the sticky note around the pen, handing it back to me before taking off across the parking lot and shouting back, "See you in Chem."

I unfold the note and stare at the ten-digit number he's written inside, along with the message scrawled messily underneath.

Text me ;)

———

"Can I help?" Nathan leans over the counter in Chemistry to watch me wash the beakers. Today we've been messing around with some chemical reactions. According to Thomas, our next big quiz is going to be a lab.

Toward the middle of the period I pretty much took over. Nathan had nearly poured too much of a solution into one of the beakers, which would not have been good considering I don't think either of us would look very attractive without our eyebrows.

I don't even mind, really. I like chemistry. Even with the numbers and the formulas, it's more interesting than math. Except my gloves are way too big for my hands, so I have to keep pulling them up, and then water gets in the tips of the fingers and the whole thing makes them feel totally pointless, but Thomas said it's unsafe to wash without them, so I guess I'll have to suffer.

"I think I've got it," I say.

"You sure?"

"Yeah, thanks though."

"You still up for lunch?"

I glance out the window of the classroom. Even if I wasn't, there's really nowhere to go. Apparently, Mrs. Liu is out sick today, and I really don't want to spend any more time than I need to around her substitute. And whatever sunlight was hanging around this morning is now hiding behind thick layers of black clouds and rain. So the quad's out too.

"Don't really have a choice, do I?" I tease, rinsing out the last beaker.

"Not unless you plan on making a paper boat out of your sketches, which is not something I recommend you doing, as it would be a huge waste of talent. So yes, you have no choice."

"I could go to the art room."

"There you go, poking holes in my plan. Besides, I hear Mrs. Liu is out today or something."

"So you orchestrated this thunderstorm and made Mrs. Liu sick, just so I'd have to have lunch with you?"

"Nooo." He drags out the O sound. "But if you happen to see an evil-looking weather machine in someone's backyard, I most definitely do not live there."

"No worries, I won't call the FBI or anything. And I already told you yes."

"Just making sure you weren't having second thoughts."

"Funny, I think all I have these days are second thoughts."

Nathan gives me a sort of look, but then he just laughs me off.

"Hope you two are getting real excited about cleaning your station," Thomas says from his desk.

"Sorry, Mr. W!" Nathan grabs a wet rag and starts wiping down our desk, smiling like a goof the entire time.

The moment I step through the cafeteria doors with Nathan I want to turn around and run. Maybe a paper boat isn't such a terrible idea. I can probably make something fairly safe with a few layers. But leaving is impossible, thanks to the crowd of my fellow classmates pushing us farther and farther in.

"Sorry, it's a bit of a jungle in here. Don't fight the crowd, that's how you get trampled." Nathan takes me by the shoulder and leads me to this set of tables that's in an elevated part of the cafeteria. We steer right toward the one at the far end, settled in the corner where two girls are sitting together.

"Ladies." Nathan grabs my shoulders. "This is the mysterious Benjamin De Backer you've heard so much about."

Both the girls look around my age. One of them has dark brown skin, darker than Nathan's, and her hair is done in this mix of black and blue braids. She's currently unpacking her lunch from this polka-dot lunch box that I have to admit I'm sort of in love with.

The other girl is Korean American, thick-frame glasses sitting on the very edge of her nose, wearing a denim jacket decorated in at least a dozen different buttons and enamel pins. They both look up when Nathan starts talking.

"Ben, this is Meleika Lewis." He points to the girl with the braids, and Meleika waves at me.

"You can call me Mel." Meleika smiles.

Then he points to the other girl with all the buttons. "And

this is Sophie Yeun." Nathan claps his hands. "I'm gonna go get in line. You want anything, Ben?"

It's then that I realize I don't have any money on me, and I doubt there's been any magically added to the student account I've yet to touch. "No, thanks, I'm good." I'm used to not eating until I get to Hannah's house anyway.

"Okay, girls, don't tear him apart." Nathan claps me on the back and leaves me with two girls I've known for all of twenty seconds. I take the empty seat in front of me, right across from Meleika, mostly so I'm not standing there like some total creep.

"It's nice to meet you, Ben." Meleika tears open a bag of chips and offers them to me. "Want one?"

"I'm good, thanks though."

"Nathan's told us a lot about you," she says.

"He has?"

Sophie answers first. "He said you ate lunch out on the quad, with the burnouts."

"I do." Then I think about what that implies. "I don't smoke though. It's just quieter out there."

"I'm sure you've at least gotten a contact high, dude. The quad is big, but not *that* big." Sophie laughs, mostly to herself, while I shift uncomfortably in my seat.

"So, Benjamin, why haven't you taken advantage of our cafeteria's fine dining options?" Meleika glances over to the neighboring table, where there are other students sitting with trays filled with something that looks relatively close to pizza. I mean, it's square, and that's probably a pepperoni slice?

I shrug. "Never felt the urge."

"Well, at least now you get to hang out with the two greatest people at this school," Sophie says, beaming.

"I don't see them around." I laugh so they know it's a joke, and they both start chuckling, so I'm taking that as a good sign. I'm actually a little proud of that one.

"He's got jokes," Meleika adds.

Sophie taps her nails on the table. They're painted this really neat turquoise. "I like you, Ben."

"Thanks." I feel like I'm grinning too much. "That's a first." I try to laugh.

"Is the interrogation over?" Nathan sits his tray on the table with the same suspicious-looking pizza as the other table.

"Not even close, but he's passed the first test." Meleika bites into her sandwich.

"Is there going to be a quiz at the end of this?" I ask.

"He's funny, unlike a certain someone." Sophie eyes Nathan.

"My jokes are always fantastic, thank you very much." I can't tell if Nathan's pretending to be offended or if he actually is.

"Oh yeah?" Meleika asks. "Go on, tell Ben the one about the scarecrow."

"Fine." Nathan turns to me. "Why did the scarecrow get an award?"

"Um." I actually try to think of any possible answers, but I've got nothing. "Why?"

"Because he was outstanding in his field!" He throws his hands out, big goofy grin on his face.

All three of us just stare at him, blankly.

"You get it?" he asks. "'Cause you put them in fields?"

"Oh, I get it. It's even funnier when you have to explain it," I say, before I turn to Sophie. "You're right."

"See?"

"Whatever." Nathan rolls his eyes and bites into the pizza. "Y'all just don't appreciate good humor when you hear it."

"Sure . . ." Sophie says under her breath. "So, Ben, do you like it here?"

"It's okay," I say.

Meleika huffs. "You picked a great time to transfer," she adds sarcastically.

"You guys dressing up for Spirit Week?" Sophie asks.

Meleika pulls out her phone. "Yeah. I need the extra credit in Biology."

"Extra credit?" I ask. I saw the list of theme days, but nothing about extra credit.

"Teachers will give you credit if you dress up for the theme days," Nathan says. "Sometimes it's just ten points on something, but some teachers will drop your lowest test or give you a free one hundred if you dress up all five days."

Meleika giggles. "It's probably the only way I'm passing Bio."

"Told you to get a tutor." Sophie sighs, like this is the thousandth time she's said these exact words.

"And I told you I don't have the time. Between planning for this dance, studying, and work, I've got nothing but weekends, and no one ever does weekends." Then Meleika leans against Sophie, using her shoulder as a pillow. "If you loved me, you'd tutor me."

Sophie scoffs. "Yeah, I know next to nothing about biology. Your grades might go down if I tutored you."

"They're going to go down anyway!" Meleika groans.

Nathan pushes his tray away, his food left half-finished. "I'll need one for Algebra, but no one's put up any listings yet."

"People are busy, dude," Sophie says.

"You need a tutor?" I ask, and I'm not sure why. Oh God, I'm not really doing this, am I?

"Yeah, it's kicking my ass." Nathan rubs his forehead like just talking about math has given him a headache.

Yep, I am apparently doing this, because no matter how hard I try, I can't stop my mouth from moving. "Oh, I mean, I could . . ."

"Really?" He raises an eyebrow.

I do sort of owe him for showing me around the school and trying to make me feel welcome. "I don't know how good I am at tutoring, but I can try." Besides, if he's good in English, he might be willing to help me too.

"I don't know if you want to do that," Sophie says. "He's a bit of a lost cause."

Nathan turns back toward her. "Bite me."

"Just saying," she sings.

"We'll meet up this weekend. Okay?" he says.

"Oh, yeah. Sure." I probably nod a bit too enthusiastically, while I try not to think too hard about what I've just volunteered to do.

———

I'm just as nervous about this second session as I was for the first. This time Dr. Taylor actually has *something* to discuss. We're going to have to spend the whole hour talking about my panic attack, no more nice introductions or paperwork. This time it's all about me.

Maybe that's a good thing.

I *want* to know what's wrong with me.

But at the same time, I don't.

"How are you feeling, Ben?" Dr. Taylor asks me when I take a seat on the couch.

I try to make myself comfortable, probably moving around too much in the process. "Fine, I think."

"I was happy when you agreed to see me earlier than planned."

I want to ask her why, but that seems rude.

"Why don't you tell me what happened over the weekend."

I open my mouth, but the words are still hard to find.

"It's okay, Ben, take your time."

"It was a panic attack . . . I think."

"Why don't you start from the beginning for me?" She gets her pen and notepad ready.

I do what she asks. Hannah and Thomas went on a date night, so I was home alone, talking with Mariam. I saw a car in the driveway, and after that the details get a little fuzzy. I remember grabbing the laptop and going to the guest bedroom.

"You can't remember anything else?"

"I do . . . sort of. It's like it's there, but not."

Dr. Taylor nods her head. I wonder what that could mean. "Have you ever experienced anything like this before, Ben?"

Never in my life. "No."

"Would your parents know where Hannah lives?"

"I don't know." It seems impossible, but I'd heard them talk about her once or twice. Nothing more than whispering to make sure I couldn't hear them. I guess it wouldn't be that hard, especially if Mom Facebook-stalked Hannah like I did.

"Do you really think it was them, in the car?"

I shrug. "It looked like the one Dad drives." But I guess I can't prove it was them. "You don't believe me, do you?"

Dr. Taylor actually looks surprised. "Why wouldn't I believe you, Ben?"

"It seems like you don't."

"I'm just trying to get all the information." Dr. Taylor writes something down quickly, and that guilty feeling settles in my stomach. "Did anything else happen?"

"There was a knock at the door."

"You didn't answer, did you? Or see who might be on the other side?"

I shake my head. "I couldn't. I felt like I was stuck."

"Can you tell me a little about your relationship with your parents, Ben?"

"What do you want to know?"

"What kind of people are they?"

Oh boy.

"Um . . . well . . ." I rub the back of my neck.

"In your own words, not how anyone else sees them."

"Dad is . . . difficult." Especially with Hannah. "Mom isn't great either. She never says much, not that she has the chance." It feels weird talking about them like this. Like I'm being disrespectful. It's not like they don't deserve it, but I still don't like the bad taste it leaves in my mouth.

"Can you elaborate a little?"

"How?"

"However you want."

That seems vague. "They're just . . . they're my parents. I don't really know what else to say about them."

"That's okay." Dr. Taylor sighs. "I want to ask you about your coming out. We can skip over that for now if you aren't comfortable, but it's something I'm very interested in talking about with you."

"I . . . okay?"

"You're fine with that?"

"I guess."

"What made you want to come out to your parents?"

"I wanted them to know, I didn't want to hide such a big part of myself from them."

"This might sound a little harsh, but did you think what happened would be a possibility?"

I did actually.

Before I was out, when I was planning the whole thing, I couldn't really see it being all happy and carefree like it was in some of the coming-out videos I'd watched. I'd imagined Mom and Dad might be a little reluctant or confused. And I figured it'd take them a while to get used to the pronouns.

For just a second I considered that they might not like who I am. They didn't necessarily have the greatest opinion of gay people.

"Your parents, have they exhibited any homophobic or transphobic behavior in the past?"

I nod.

Not a lot, but there were comments here and there. Dad used to throw around the F-word, but that'd died down over the last few years. Maybe part of me thought they'd changed.

"So why come out? Why not wait a few years, maybe until you're in college or out of the house?" Her question isn't accusatory. Dr. Taylor isn't telling me it would've been smarter to just wait.

Maybe it would've been.

Actually, it definitely would've been smarter to wait.

"I wanted them to know. I was tired of constantly living this lie in front of them. And I thought . . ." I trail off, not sure where my words are going.

"I thought maybe it'd help them change or something."

I don't really know.

"I see."

"I should've just waited." I sink back in the couch, not realizing how heated I felt. "Then I wouldn't be here."

"Maybe," Dr. Taylor starts to say. "But don't you think you deserve to live openly as yourself?"

I don't say anything. "Do you think what happened was a panic attack?"

Dr. Taylor nods. "Yes. That's what it sounds like to me."

"Okay . . ." I let out a long sigh. "Do you believe me? That it was them?"

"I do, Ben."

"Why would they show up though? After all that?"

"Well, I don't want to give them any credit, but maybe they've realized their mistake."

"Seems a little late for that," I tell her.

Dr. Taylor nods slowly. "That it does."

NINE

Nathan doesn't beg me to go to lunch with him again for the rest of the week, but I do anyway. Sophie and Meleika are nice, and they sort of act like they've known me for years instead of just a few days. But the closer we get to the weekend, the more I worry about tutoring Nathan.

It's not the actual tutoring that worries me. I think it's more that it'll just be the two of us again. It shouldn't scare me. We've been alone before. Or maybe it's because I don't know where he wants to do this. He can't come over to Hannah's house, and the idea of going over to his, where his parents will probably be, is scary.

I have no idea what I am going to do, so I text the only person who might give me a straightforward answer.

Me: *So I need some advice.*

Except Mariam must be busy, because I've been waiting for their reply for a few hours now. I even go down to the kitchen to grab a bag of Doritos, less because I am actually hungry and more because I just want something to do.

I'm about to give up before the laptop makes the *ding!*

Mariam: *What's up, buttercup?*

Me: *it's a boy.*

Mariam: *ohhhhhhhhhhhhhhhhhhhhhh*

Me: *no, not like that!*

Mariam: *Okay start from the beginning.*

Me: *He's the one who showed me around the school.*

Mariam: *Nathan? That guy you were telling me about?*

Me: *Yeah*

I feel bad for venting about Nathan behind his back, especially since he's been nothing but nice to me. But Mariam is always willing to listen to my rants, no matter the subject. One time we spent the entire day arguing back and forth against the need to gender robots in *Star Wars*.

Mariam: *He sounds really nice tbh*

Me: *Sometimes to a fault*

Mariam: *So what's the issue???*

Me: *I offered to tutor him.*

Mariam: *And????*

Me: *I don't really know...*

Me: *He can't come over here, he doesn't even know I live with Hannah.*

Mariam: *And you don't want to go over to his house?*

Me: *It makes me nervous.*

Mariam: *Understandable.*

Mariam: *Well, what if you went out? Got some lunch or coffee or something? Go to a public place.*

Me: *I don't know, this is the first time I've done something like this...*

Mariam: *Your parents didn't let you go out with friends?*

Me: *They would... but no one ever really wanted to hang out around me.*

I was always seen as that "weird" kid. The one who was too quiet and never wanted to hang out with kids on the playground. That reputation sort of followed me through middle school and right up until I left Wayne High.

Mariam: *that sucks, I know the feeling all too well*

Me: *Why am I freaking out so much?*

Mariam: *You've been through a lot, Benji, I mean, the last month has been rough for you, it's okay to be scared or worried.*

Me: *But he's just a boy. And I don't know...*

Me: *He seems too nice to hate what I am*

Mariam: *Trust me hun, boys are scary. I lived with two of them and dated three. And you've seen Twitter, right? A cesspool.*

Okay, that makes me laugh. This is why I always go to Mariam. They can usually make me feel better, no matter how stressed I am about something.

Mariam: *But this Nathan dude seems like a good guy. And not one of those self-proclaimed good guys or whatever who tips his hat with a m'lady.*

Me: *Maybe...*

Mariam: *Do you actually want to hang out with him?*

Me: *Yeah. He's nice.*

Mariam: *I think you owe it to yourself. Making friends is hard but having someone your own age can help. Even if he doesn't know what you're going through exactly, you both know that feeling. I've never met a single teen that has it all together.*

Mariam: *And as much as I love my title as your bestie there's only so much I can do when we're a country apart from each other.*

Me: *How'd you get so smart, Mariam?*

Mariam: *I didn't graduate from Berkeley with a 4.0 for nothing.*

Me: *Thanks.*

I roll over and grab my phone off my nightstand. Nathan stole it at lunch yesterday, so now there's a close-up selfie of the two of us set as my background. In fact, I'm pretty sure my camera roll is now an even 60 percent reference photos, 40 percent Nathan selfies.

We didn't confirm anything about the tutoring yet, and I'm not even sure that he remembers what we agreed to. Oh God, what if he doesn't remember, and I just text him right out of the blue and he has no idea what I'm talking about?

Or what if he doesn't want me to tutor him anymore? I'm not sure which might be worse.

Me: *Still up for tomorrow?*

I hit send before I can delete the message, and go back to watching this YouTube tutorial on brushstrokes and how to control them better. The laptop and my phone go off seconds apart, the little *ding!* letting me know that Nathan's texted back.

Nathan: *Ben?*

I'm a moron. This is the first time we've texted, so he wouldn't have my number, which means that he just got a completely random text from some unknown number.

Nathan: *Bennnnnnnnnn is that youuuuuuuuuuuuu?*

Me: *Sorry, forgot you didn't have my number.*

Nathan: *It's cool. This is Ben De Backer right? Not some weird coincidence where I've somehow caught the attention of two Bens?*

Me: *That seems statistically improbable. But yes, this is De Backer, Ben.*

Nathan: *So what are we up for tomorrow?*

Me: *Tutoring, if you're still interested?*

Nathan: *Oh right! Yeah I need it. Ms. Sever gave us this practice exam to do. Do you just want to come over to my house?*

I read back through Mariam's messages on my laptop before responding. I don't really know how to explain myself to him.

Hey, can we maybe meet somewhere that isn't either of our houses? As if I'm not already enough of a weirdo.

Me: *That sounds fine.*

I hit send before I can delete it.

Nathan: *KK.*

I switch back to messaging Mariam on my laptop, double-checking the name and number just so I don't start talking about Nathan *to* Nathan.

Me: *Sorry. I texted Nathan, he wants to meet at his house...*

Mariam: *You gonna do it?*

Me: *I already said yes.*

Mariam: *Yay!!! I'm so proud of you Benji!!!!*

Mariam: *See what happens when you listen to your elders?*

Me: *Sorry, forgot you're a total grandparent.*

Mariam: *And don't you forget it!*

I don't feel like I should be celebrating right now though. My phone buzzes again and there's a notification at the top of the screen. Another message from Nathan.

Mariam: *Okay, I've got to head out. Busy weekend.*

Me: *Kay, thanks for the help.*

Mariam: *What I'm here for ;)*

I close the laptop and leave it at the end of the bed.

Nathan: *So what're you up to?*

My heart clenches a bit. I thought we were done, but I guess not. Maybe texting will be easier.

Me: *Nothing, lying in bed.*

I don't add that I'm currently digesting more cool-ranch dust than anyone probably should.

Nathan: *So what're you wearing ;)*

I swallow all wrong, and it's almost like I've been swallowing knives instead of a handful of Doritos.

Nathan: *jk jk, kiddinggggg!!!*

He sends this last one a few seconds later. I wonder if he can tell that he almost gave me a heart attack.

Me: *don't do that. Please.*

Nathan: *Okay, I promise. Pinky promise even.*

Me: *Sorry... Pinky promise.*

Nathan: *It's my fault, my fingers are as bad as my mouth lol*

Nathan: *I just realized what that sounded like. Again, my bad.*

I type a quick "lol," even though I don't feel like laughing.

It's not even that what he's saying is gross or anything. I don't hate the idea of kissing someone, or even having sex with them. But there are just things about my body . . . things I'm still not quite over. It's hard to describe.

Nathan: *Still there?*

Me: *Yeah sorry, got distracted.*

Nathan: *It's cool lol, I know the feeling.*

Me: *Yeah. So what are you up to?*

Nathan: *Trying to study, at least a little before next week.*

Me: *I should probably do that too...*

I have a Calc and an English test, plus an essay on Chaucer and a lab to get ready for in Chemistry. All in one week. It's like Thomas, Mrs. Williams, and Mrs. Kurtz got together to see what would lead to the quickest emotional breakdown from me. Joke's on them, because I already know it won't take much.

Nathan: *At least you've really only got 3 classes, I'd kill for Art again.*
Me: *True, I guess.*

Art's no walk in the park, but it's definitely easier compared to some other classes.

Me: *Hey will your parents be there tomorrow?*

Probably the most awkward way to ask that question, but I want to be prepared. For what, I'm not sure.

Nathan: *Nah, they're going to see my cousin at a science fair, apparently it's an all-day kind of thing.*
Me: *Oh*
Nathan: *Why? You want to meet them?*
Me: *Oh no.*

Shit. I might as well just actually put my foot in my mouth. It would be easier than this.

Me: *Sorry, I meant . . .*
Me: *I meant I didn't have to meet them.*
Me: *Not that I didn't want to meet them.*
Me: *I'll shut up now*
Nathan: *lmao I'm dying*

He adds a few emojis. The ones that are laughing so hard they're crying.

Me: *ugh, sorry. I'll go bury myself now*
Nathan: *Oh come on, don't do that.*
Nathan: *Don't deprive me of that face of yours. It's my one joy in that miserable place.*

I clutch my phone, trying hard not to think about what that's supposed to mean. But part of me can't resist wondering *what that's supposed to mean.*

Nathan: *Hey what's your address, I'll pick you up tomorrow.*

And now I'll be in a car, alone with him. Great. I type out the address and hit send.

Nathan: *Okay, you aren't going to believe this shit*

Nathan: *But we're neighbors*

Me: *Really?*

Nathan: *You're at 337 Sycamore? I'm 341.*

I walk over to my window, pushing the curtains back. I can't really see his house, but I think it's the brick one Thomas and I drive past when we're going to school.

Nathan: *Small world.*

Yeah. Small world.

Me: *Cool. I'm going to go pass out. Should we go for noon tomorrow?*

Nathan: *Yeah, do you want me to go pick you up?*

Me: *That's okay, it won't even take three minutes*

Nathan: *I don't mind...*

Me: *You're serious? It's like two houses away.*

Nathan: *Alright, but let it never be said that I'm anything short of a gentleman.*

Me: *Noted. Will you lead the search party if I get lost?*

Nathan: *Are you kidding? I'll hang up flyers of that handsome face all over town!*

I can almost picture his grin.

Me: *Good to know, I'm going to bed now.*

Nathan: *Sleep tight!*

Before I plug my phone in, I scroll back through our conversation. He thinks I'm handsome? No, I don't need to think about that. He was probably just joking or something. I sigh and reach down to the floor for my charger, crawling under the sheets and trying not to feel nervous about how I'm tutoring Nathan Allan tomorrow.

TEN

I've passed by Nathan's house nearly every day since I got to Hannah's. And I never even knew it.

"Nice place," I say to myself, walking slowly up the steps of the front door, wondering if it *really* is too late to try and run home and avoid all of this.

No. I can do this.

I knock on the burgundy door a few times, and there's this loud bark from somewhere in the house, and then the sound of footsteps. Nathan opens the door slowly, leaving it open just enough for me to see one of his eyes and part of his mouth. "Hey!"

"Should I even ask?"

"Okay, just to warn you, my dog, Ryder, is inside. He doesn't bite, but he *loves* company and he will try to hug you."

"It's okay. I like dogs. What kind is he?"

"Ryder, get back!" I can hear Nathan wrestling with Ryder behind the door. "Golden retriever." Nathan holds the door open for me. "Come on, he should be fine."

I follow him into the house, and there isn't even a second before Ryder goes right for me, sniffing at my jeans and leaping up on his hind legs to knock me over with his front paws. Next thing I know I'm on my ass, hitting the hardwood floors, and Ryder's licking at my face.

"Ryder, no!"

"It's okay." I rub him behind the ears. Ryder's got these huge brown eyes that make it impossible to be mad at him. "I like kisses." I immediately realize what I just said, and blood rushes to my cheeks. "From dogs, I mean." Could I be more awkward?

"He's totally shameless. You should know better by now, shouldn't you, boy?" Nathan asks him.

Ryder looks back at Nathan before giving me a mouthful of gross, hot breath right in my face.

"Hey, you want to go outside?" Nathan's voice switches from serious to that fake sort of excited you use for dogs and babies.

Ryder kicks up his legs, bouncing up and down all the way to the back door, waiting impatiently for Nathan to finally slide the glass open. The moment the door is wide enough, Ryder bolts.

"I swear, I love that dog, but he's a total doofball most of the time." Nathan hurries back over to help me up off the floor.

"That's been the case with every golden retriever I know." We walk back over to the door.

"Wouldn't trade him for anything." Nathan whistles, interrupting Ryder's very important task of rolling around in the grass. "Ryder, ball!" Nathan uses his excited voice again.

Ryder's ears perk up. He waits just a split second before starting to run around the yard in a big circle, grabbing something without stopping and bringing it to Nathan.

Nathan grabs the slobber-covered ball and chucks it into the far corner of the yard. Ryder was gone the moment Nathan raised his arm, ready to catch the ball before it even hit the ground.

I sit back and watch them repeat this a few times, Ryder never failing to jump up and catch the ball with his mouth. "He's good at that," I say.

"We've had a lot of practice." He throws the ball lazily one more time, wiping the slobber on his jeans. "You ready to do some book learnin'?" He says this with what I can only describe as the worst southern accent I've ever heard.

"Sure." I follow Nathan back inside and up the stairs, trying not to get nervous at the fact that I am probably being led to his bedroom. I try to distract myself with the photos lining the walls. Young Nathan is cute. I mean, teenage Nathan is cute too, but he doesn't have the pinchable cheeks anymore.

And why am I thinking about that?

Different thoughts. Different thoughts.

His parents look really happy too. It's incredibly obvious that he got his smile from his mom. In fact, he seems to share most of his traits with his mom, at least at a glance. They have the same eyes, same nose, same smile.

"You look like her, like your mom," I say, stopping at a picture of the two of them at what I guess is Easter. The big purple wicker basket and the bright polo shirt Nathan is wearing are sort of giveaways.

"I get that a lot." He grins.

"Is this your dad?" I point to another picture of a much older man and Nathan behind the wheel of a boat.

"Stepdad. Mom married him when I was about twelve."

"Oh." That explains why he doesn't seem to be in any pictures with baby Nathan.

"Yeah." He bounces on his heels. "Come on, my room is just up here." He leads me up the rest of the way and down the hallway to his bedroom.

It's messy. Not quite disastrous, but there are clothes over everything, posters of various bands and rappers I've never heard of hanging on the walls. And there's a shelf in the corner filled to the brim with books. What he hasn't managed to fit on his shelf there or the ones above his desk, he's stacked on his nightstand or on his dresser. Oddly enough, his bed is completely made. "Sorry, should've thought about cleaning up." He kicks off his shoes.

"It's cool," I say, wondering where I can take a seat. The chair at his desk is filled with discarded clothes, and Nathan just plops down on his bed, grabbing his backpack.

"Okay. So, what do you want to do first?" The springs squeak underneath him.

"Algebra's probably easiest."

"Yeah, 'easiest,'" he says, making the quotations with his fingers. "Come on, don't be shy." Nathan pats at the empty space next to him on the bed. "This is where the magic happens."

"Are you more of a rabbit-out-of-a-hat guy, or do you do card tricks?" I ask.

"Oh, funny boy." Nathan reaches for his algebra textbook.

"Yeah, funny." I try to force a laugh, but even I can't believe it. Every "boy" or "him" has been like a stab in the gut. And for some reason, it hurts worse when it comes from him. Even worse than when Mom or Dad called me their "son" or their "boy."

"Okay, so, Mrs. Sever said that the test would cover these two chapters." Nathan shows me the part in his textbook.

"So how much do you need to review?"

"All of it."

"Oh, okay. Wow. Well, let's go ahead and get started."

Nathan isn't totally hopeless, and I'm not sure why he thinks he is. There are a few times where he'll mess up on an equation, or misremember the order of something, but he isn't a lost cause. I try to recall all the ways I've remembered the dozens of formulas over the years, rhymes or songs or acronyms.

"How do you remember all this stuff?" he asks me.

"Don't know." I've always been good at math. "It's sort of easy." I flip through his review packet again. "It says there's a practice test online you can take, and you'll get ten extra points on the quiz."

Nathan grabs his laptop and types in the website. "Math should be illegal."

"It's not that bad."

"Says you." When prompted for his school, he picks "North Wake High School," types in his student ID, and hits the big blue start button underneath. "Shit," he whispers under his breath after reading the first question.

"Look." I grab his notebook and flip to an empty sheet. "Here, just work it out." I watch him copy down the problem, carefully making his way through it. "Remember to move that over," I add.

"There?" He shows me his work.

"Type it in, see if it's right," I say, even though I know he's got it.

The website gives him a little "Good Job!" before it moves on to the next question. "Jesus, how long is this quiz?"

I reach for my bag at the foot of his bed. "You've done one question, stop whining." I open my sketchbook to the newest page. It's only been a few weeks, but I'm already close to needing a new one. The pages are sticking out, notes and sketches pouring from the seams, and I've only got a handful of empty pages left. "Just keep going."

"Fine, Mom." He groans, pulling the laptop closer. "What are you drawing?"

"Not sure yet. I'll let you see when you're finished." I turn so I can hide the sketchbook from view. "Now get to work. Those ten points will come in handy."

"Fine, fine." He starts to work again. "Hey, what about this?" Nathan hands me his notebook, and I check over his work. "The answers aren't adding up."

I read over his equations quickly. "Close, you got the root wrong here." It's not that far up into the problem, so he won't have to redo too much work. "Try that again and it should work out." I hand the notebook back to him.

He lets out a long sigh and erases his work. "This is torture."

"I know, but you're getting there," I say, trying to focus back on my drawing. Except I can't think of anything to draw. My mind has gone totally blank, I can't envision anything; hell, I can't even think where I'm supposed to start. Just a line, and then another line. I huff and lean my head back.

"Stuck?" Nathan asks without looking at me.

"Sort of."

"I get that way sometimes too. When I'm writing."

"Oh yeah? Any tips for getting out of it?"

"I'm not the artist here." He grins. "Maybe draw something around you?"

"Like?"

"That, my Padawan, is all up to you." He points at me with the eraser end of his pencil.

"Have I ever told you how helpful you are?" I ask.

"No."

"Good, because you aren't." It doesn't occur to me how mean that could sound until I've already said it, but Nathan's just laughing away.

"You asked," he half sings. Maybe he's right, except there really isn't anything in this room that I know. Well, there's one thing. But would drawing Nathan be too creepy? He's sitting still enough, and there's enough light.

You know what? Screw it.

It's weird to have a Nathan that isn't moving or talking with his hands. He's in the thick of it, the gears in his head turning. He's even sticking out his tongue a little, and I hate to admit that it's totally adorable.

In fact, I don't think there's one imperfection. Not the bumps on his chin, the small cut on his cheek that I'm guessing is from shaving, the slight circles under his eyes. It all feels on purpose. I don't think Nathan Allan is capable of accidents. He doesn't seem like the type.

I start with his pose, a skeleton. Easy enough, his back against the wall, both knees propped up so he can balance his notebook, because he's where he belongs, in his own environment. I wonder what that feels like.

The hook of his nose to his mouth might be my favorite part, the straight lines suddenly curving right down to his mouth. But then he starts chewing on the end of his pen, and I just have to huff and roll my eyes. I'll get back to that later. It's his smaller details that will be the hardest to capture. The freckles across his nose, the shape of his brow, the way the corners of his eyes slope down just a little.

"Hey." His voice makes me jump. Guess I was in deep. "I don't get this one." He hands me his notebook. God, how long was I out like that?

"You just need to find b." I look over the question. It's complicated. In fact, I'm really not sure it needs to be on an algebra quiz, it looks so advanced.

"I got that, Einstein, but that really isn't helping."

"Einstein was more into physics, though you aren't far off." I scoot closer to him. "Here, rewrite the equation with the log terms on one side."

"Then you rewrite the substitution, right?"

"Yeah. And now you can solve it like you normally would," I say, pointing to the newly formed equation.

"Okay, I think I've got it." He grins, showing off those dimples again. I watch him quickly move through the rest of the problem until he finally comes to the answer, showing it to me for approval.

"Yep. That's it."

"Oh God, man, I could kiss you."

My heart sort of sinks in my chest. "Yeah."

He types in the answer, and I move back to my spot, grabbing my sketchbook before I sit on it.

"Okay, let's see it." Nathan sticks out his hand.

"Huh?"

He turns his laptop so I can see the screen. There's a big "Congratulations" and a "Click Submit for Extra Credit" underneath it. "I finished the quiz, and you said you'd show me what you're drawing when I was done."

"Oh, it's really nothing." I can't show him this. Jesus, what if he thinks I'm some weird stalker?

"Uh-huh. I called on you twice to help me out, and you were so focused on that thing you didn't even hear me. So I really doubt it's nothing."

I didn't even realize. "Oh, shit, I'm sorry."

"It's cool. At least I know I can solve logarithmic equations by myself." He closes his laptop and moves to sit next to me. "Now, show me."

"You're going to think I'm weird." I flip open to the drawing.

"Well, you already sort of are but—" He stops when he sees what I've done. This is exactly what I was afraid of. He hates it, or he's creeped out by it. I wonder if he'll just yell at me or do something worse. I don't think I can handle Nathan hating me.

"I'm really sor—" I start, but he stops me.

"Ben."

"What?"

He takes the sketch pad from my hands, staring closely at the drawing. "You drew me," he says, reaching toward the drawing like he wants to touch it, but at the last moment he stops himself. I guess he thinks he'll mess it up or something.

"It's not that good." My voice isn't much more than a murmur. Right now, my mind is pretty occupied with trying not to grin like an idiot. "It's not even close to done." There are no details in his clothes or his hands. Even the background is nearly blank, simple lines to fill in for the posters and pictures on his wall.

"You've got to give yourself more credit than that." He starts to trace a hand along his nose. "You even got my freckles."

"It's okay." I shrug.

"Have you ever thought about showing off your art?"

"Where would I even do that?"

"I don't know. But people need to see your stuff. It's amazing." He looks back at the sketch pad, staring in silence. And I feel my heart thudding in my chest.

ELEVEN

I'm walking through the empty halls of the school. It's sort of eerie to be here when things are quiet. But Thomas has to stay after school today, some meeting about exams and graduation and spring break. I really can't believe it's March already.

I'd go to the art room, but it feels weird being there after hours. Plus, last time I did that, the janitor walked in on me, and there's really nothing more awkward than just sitting around while someone else is cleaning, all while you try your best not to get in their way.

I wish Nathan was here to help pass the time. I texted him, but he hasn't answered yet. Must be studying or something. His algebra exam was today, and I want to know how he did.

He tried his best to teach me a few tricks about the essay I'm supposed to turn in by the end of the week, but I'm hopeless. Something about getting the words from my brain to the computer. It just isn't working. That and Chaucer is *really* boring.

My mind is a million miles away right now, and I'm not paying attention to where I'm walking, so when a classroom door bursts open, I run right into someone, which makes both of us fall onto our butts. I can't really blame anyone but myself.

"Oh God, I'm so sorry." The papers they were carrying fly everywhere, and it's not until they're all settled that I realize I ran into Meleika.

"Ben?" She's already on her knees, scrambling to pick everything up.

"Sorry, it's my fault." I start grabbing for the flyers, ignoring the new sting coming from my tailbone. A few of them catch my eye. They're all different designs, but it's clear what they're for.

"Spring Fling Dance!"

"It's my bad," Meleika says. "In too much of a hurry." She shuffles the flyers to try and make them even. "I was supposed to have these up last week, but we're still trying to get everything together for the dance."

"Isn't prom in like two months?" I ask. "Why bother with planning another one?"

"It's tradition." Meleika says this with about as much enthusiasm as I'd expect. "What on earth are you doing here this late?"

"Waiting for Thomas."

She raises an eyebrow. "Thomas?"

"Mr. Waller. He's my brother-in-law. And my ride home." I make sure to pick my words carefully. "What are you doing?"

"I've got to hang these posters around campus." We both stand up slowly, but she still has the panicked look. "Listen, I hate to ask you, but can you help me? Stephanie's going to chew my ass if they aren't up by tomorrow morning."

"Yeah, sure. What do I need to do?" I guess anything's better than just walking around campus.

"Here." Meleika hands me this huge roll of tape. "I hold, you tape." She pins one of the flyers against the wall in front of us. I quickly rip the four pieces and tape down each corner. "You're fast, good."

"Trained for seven years to be an expert tape ripper. Glad the classes paid off."

That makes her laugh, and we move farther down the hall, making sure we don't hang the same style of poster as the last one.

"So, are you going to the dance?" Meleika asks, pinning up another poster.

"Wasn't planning on it."

"What? Why not?"

"Dances aren't really my thing." I start ripping more pieces of tape, letting them hang ready on the ends of my fingers.

"There's a game too."

"Sports *and* dances aren't really my thing."

Meleika chuckles, brushing her hair out of her face. Over the weekend, she got rid of the braids and came back to school with huge, long curls. "I don't really blame you, honestly. I wouldn't go unless I had to."

"You have to?"

"Everyone from student council has to show up to all our events, or else we don't get the credit hours."

"That sucks."

"You're telling me! I'm missing my shows to watch some beefcakes knock around balls with a big stick?" Then she stops. "I suppose the baseball butts aren't so bad though."

I keep my mouth shut, but I definitely wouldn't argue with her.

"Meleika?" An all-too-familiar voice echoes down the hallway. Nathan, of course. "And Ben!" He smiles when he sees me. "What are you doing here?"

"He's busy." Meleika gets another poster ready.

"Thomas had to stay after, for some meeting," I say.

"Oh." Nathan's smile drops. "So why are you helping Mel?" he asks.

"'Cause he's a decent human being who helps when asked, unlike you." Meleika takes a piece of tape from my fingers and tapes a flyer to Nathan's forehead.

"I had to help paint set pieces!" Nathan protests, ripping the paper off his face. Apparently, he underestimated the strength of the tape because next thing we know, he's doubled over hissing and rubbing that spot on his forehead. "You try telling Stephanie no!" he says through gritted teeth.

"Whatever." Meleika crosses her arms. "What are you doing here anyway? You're painting, remember?"

"Mr. Madison said you had the spare key to the art room. Mrs. Liu was supposed to get us more paint, but I think it's locked in her room."

Meleika stares at him. "I don't have a key."

"You're joking."

She shakes her head. "Nope."

"But we need the paint, and no one else has a key." Nathan rubs the back of his neck. "Stephanie's going to go nuclear."

"This Stephanie sounds like a piece of work," I add.

"I'm honestly surprised she hasn't demanded we call her Your Highness yet," says Nathan.

"Just go get the key from Mrs. Liu." Meleika holds up another poster, and I tape the corners down.

"They're in the auditorium, and the door's locked." Nathan drags his hands over his face.

Meleika's groans echo through the hallway. "What are we supposed to do, then? We aren't going to have any other time this week to get it done."

"I have a key," I say.

They both just look at me like I've grown an extra head. "Why do you have a key?" Nathan asks.

"Mrs. Liu gave it to me so I could use the art room during lunch."

"Great." Meleika looks at Nathan. "Get the key from Ben and get the paint."

"I mean, sure." I reach for the ring of keys in my backpack. "But I'm going with you."

"Awesome."

"Oh, you are not ditching me!" Meleika stares at me, her mouth hanging open. "Ben!"

"I'll be back, I promise."

"Don't trust me?" Nathan's already got my arm, leading me down the hallway.

"I'm not risking anything." I doubt Mrs. Liu would be angry with me, I mean, it's just Nathan. But you never know, and I don't want to risk losing this privilege.

We run to the art building, double-checking each of the doors. Sure enough, all three are locked. I peer through the small glass windows, and four huge cans of paint sit right there on the counter.

I unlock the door and walk in ahead of Nathan, snagging the two cans of paint, handing the other two to Nathan. "Come on, I need to finish helping Mel."

"Which one is yours?" Nathan asks. It takes me a minute to realize he's talking about the paintings Mrs. Liu's hung up on the wall.

I want to tell him we don't have time, which makes me feel bad, because he's been nothing but supportive of my art, but he's only seen my drawings before. Never my paintings, at least not in real life.

"That one." I point to the drip painting. "And that one." The one of the cardinal is hanging on the other side of the room.

"Oh." Nathan gasps, walking right over to the drip painting. "Hmm . . ."

"What?" I ask. For just the briefest second, I wish I could read minds. I mean, that'd open me up to a whole other slew of problems. But right now, I *really* want to know what Nathan's thinking.

"Just . . . unexpected."

Unexpected?

Nathan still looks awestruck. "And this one?" He crosses the room in just a few steps, staring at the one of the cardinal. Part of me wants to hide it, because I really don't think it compares to the drip-style one.

"Yeah. What do you think?" I'm almost scared to ask. He's liked everything I've done before, but I've never seen him react this way.

"They're great!" he says, but something about the way he says it seems un-Nathan.

"They're fine. It's really no big deal," I say. "I probably should've worked on it some more."

"Yeah." He scoffs. "Right, just don't forget about me when your paintings hang in the Louvre or something."

I laugh a little more loudly than I mean to. "Because that will totally happen."

"Never say never, De Backer." Nathan starts back toward me, his eyes bouncing between both of my paintings.

"Come on. Mel's going to kill both of us."

"Are you going to the game?" Nathan asks.

"It's funny, Mel asked me the same thing."

"And?"

I shrug. "Baseball and dances? Not really my thing."

"You know, prom is in a few months." He adds that out of the blue.

"Oh yeah?" It's a hard thing to ignore. Student council's already ambushing people inside the cafeteria to vote on the theme. "Do y'all ever rest?" I ask.

I'm not saying that two dances in three months seems excessive, but . . .

"Tradition is tradition," Nathan says.

"Is that all student council is good for?" I tease him. "Planning dances?"

"Hey!" He sounds angry but his grin gives him away. "We plan other things. We did a bake sale last October."

"Was there a dance?"

"No," Nathan says, sounding totally unconvincing. "Technically."

"How do you dance at a bake sale?"

"Stephanie managed to find a way. So, are you going?"

"To?" I ask, knowing full well what he means.

"To prom?"

"I don't think so."

"Really?" His smile fades. Is he actually disappointed?

"Dances," I say again.

"Even prom?"

"Even prom," I repeat. "I didn't go last year either."

We walk all the way across campus to the gymnasium, where there are a bunch of my fellow classmates running around, trying their best to follow the orders of the girl standing around in the middle with the megaphone. "I'm guessing that's Stephanie?" I say under my breath.

"Nathan! There you are." She runs toward us before Nathan can answer, eyeing the cans. "Is that the paint?"

"Well, Steph, it's not chocolate pudding."

"Funny," she says, while aggressively not laughing. "Okay, you two go ahead and get to painting the stage pieces, we need those first."

"Oh, I'm not in—" I start to say, but she shushes me with a hand.

"Didn't ask. I name you an honorary student council member, we'll get you credit hours if you need them. Now get to work." Stephanie points to the large wooden panels propped up on the stage. "Now!" she screeches into her megaphone when we don't immediately run onto the stage. Stephanie almost earns herself a can of paint emptied on her precious gym floor for that.

"Sorry, she can be a little . . ." Nathan considers his words carefully. "'Abrasive' is the nicest word that comes to mind."

"Meleika is going to kill me." I climb the short ladder to the stage.

"When she finds out Stephanie dragged you into this, she'll forgive you, no worries."

"Why are you guys waiting until the week of?" I grab the screwdriver from the toolbox on the stage and pop open the paint can, reaching for the wooden stir stick.

"We were more behind than we realized, and now we're scrambling." Nathan eyes the boards in front of us. "At least we won't need these pieces until Friday."

"Are you going to dress up the rest of the week?" I swipe the excess paint on the edge of the can and pour it slowly into a tray.

Today's theme was simple: school pride. Everywhere I looked, there were people dressed in royal blue and gold. Nathan's sweater is less royal than azure, but with the gold trim at the bottom I don't think anyone's going to challenge him on the specific shade.

"Yes, and where is your blue and gold, my friend?" he asks.

"Don't have anything," I say. I probably should've dressed up. I have a feeling I'll need the points in English.

"You don't want to dress up? Tacky Thursday is going to be fun."

"Tacky Thursday?" I eye him.

"You dress up in your tackiest clothes!"

"Of course!" I try to mimic his enthusiasm.

"Where's your school spirit?" Nathan pops the lid off his own can.

"Don't really have any." I roll my brush through the deep blue. "Are we just painting this whole thing?" I ask.

"Yeah, top to bottom, then we paint the gold stars."

"Fun." I let the brush roll onto the wood. "So how did the quiz go?"

He scoffs. "Which one?"

"You had two today?"

"Yup."

"Oh, bless your heart," I say. "How did Algebra go?"

Stephanie shouts something into her megaphone again. Thankfully it's not directed at us, but it's enough to make the two of us jump. Nathan just rolls his eyes and shakes his head.

His smile gives him away. "Passed. At least, I think I did."

"Nice," I say.

"The test was easier than I thought. I triple-checked everything too, and it came out the same almost the whole test!"

"I told you that you could do it."

"Boys! You aren't painting!" Stephanie's voice echoes through the megaphone again.

"Yeah, yeah." Nathan waves her off.

"So stop flirting and paint!" she yells.

I feel my face get hot and I turn forward, focusing on where exactly my brush is going. I've already missed a few spots anyway. "That's great, about your test," I say.

"I owe you, De Backer."

"Oh, you don't . . . really . . ." I stammer.

"Come on, let me treat you. Whatever you want to do, we'll go out this weekend."

"I've already got plans, sorry." Hannah had mentioned going out and doing a little shopping. I wasn't really planning on going with her, but it could be fun.

"Get to thinking, because I owe you. Big-time."

"Okay," I say, and try to get back to the painting, but every few seconds my eyes sort of drift down, and he's there, right in the corner of my vision. I don't want to grin, but I can't help myself. And when he catches me, Nathan looks up, and he's smiling too.

———

"So how has your week been?" is the first thing Dr. Taylor asks me when I sit down in her office. I'd been digging into my hands the entire drive over here. I can still count the eight crescent-shaped marks on both my palms. These sessions have been getting easier, appointment by appointment, but I still feel sick when I remember I have a visit coming up.

"Ben?"

I finally look up, lost in the zigzag pattern of Dr. Taylor's black-and-white blouse. "Yeah? Sorry, it was fine."

"Anything in particular happen?"

"Not really." There were the theme days, and the pep rally, which everyone is forced to go to. "It was Spirit Week at school."

"Oh, those are fun. Does North Wake do the dress-up days?"

"Yeah, but I didn't really do any. Not my kind of thing."

"Understandable. My class used to go all out for those kinds of things." Dr. Taylor chuckles. "I never really understood the appeal myself, but everyone seemed to have fun."

"Hmmm." I really don't know what to say next.

"How are things going with Hannah and Thomas?"

I shrug. "Fine. Can't really complain."

"They're getting better about the pronouns?"

I nod. I can't really remember the last time I had to correct either of them.

"I wanted to ask you"—she crosses her legs—"how you felt when Hannah left?"

I really don't want to answer her. I want to move on to a different question, maybe ignore what she just asked me. I know the answer. I've known it for ten years, but now it just makes me feel guilty. Do I really have a right to be mad at her, to *still* be angry at what she did, after everything?

"I . . ."

"Ben?" Dr. Taylor eyes me.

"I was really mad at her," I say.

"For leaving you?"

I can't help but feel like this will somehow all get back to Hannah. Like there's a bug on my clothes or something and Hannah can hear every word I say from her spot in the waiting room. Just feet away. "That's pretty much what she did, right?"

"Well . . ." Dr. Taylor's head sort of bounces. "Is that what you felt happened?"

"Maybe you should ask Hannah about all this." I don't mean for it to sound rude, but I really don't want to talk about this.

"Ben, I can promise you that I don't discuss anything that goes on in this room with her."

"Sorry." I dig my nails into my palms again, trying to fit them in the same exact places. "I . . . I get why she did it," I say, guilt washing over me. "And I get that she really couldn't take me with her. But it still hurt, you know?"

"Of course." Dr. Taylor jots something down. "Perhaps it is unreasonable for a college student to take on the responsibility of adopting their younger sibling, but that doesn't invalidate the hurt caused. How do you feel about her now?"

"She's trying." I stare down at my hands. "And isn't that what matters?"

"Does that matter to you?"

I nod.

"Can you tell me about a good moment you shared with your parents?" Dr. Taylor says, basically out of nowhere.

"Why?" I ask.

"Well, a lot of our discussions on them have focused on the negative, with reason, of course. But surely you had to have good moments with them, over the years?"

"I mean . . . yeah, kind of." I rub my palms on my knees. Of course we had good moments. There were a lot of them actually. Moments where I could forget just how bad they could be. Where we could laugh at something on TV, or joke around with one another, or spend the day out and about, just enjoying one another's company.

Times where I actually thought they might love me for me.

"Tell me about a good moment you had," she says. "Doesn't have to be anything big or anything. Just a nice thing you remember." Dr. Taylor smiles.

"Well, it isn't really just one specific memory," I say. "But my mom works at a hospital, and during a lot of my summers I'd have to go with her to work. I guess she didn't trust me to be alone with Hannah."

"Afraid of Hannah's influence, I'd imagine."

I manage a chuckle. "Probably. But Mom would let me help out. She mostly did paperwork, so she taught me where things go and how to make sure they were in the right order." I feel a smile creep up on me. "She even let me shred stuff. That was my favorite part."

And then everything sort of stops, and for a split second, I feel numb.

"Ben?" Dr. Taylor looks at me.

"It's nothing."

Except the tug I feel on my heart.

The Friday nights we'd go out to dinner, Dad watching his terrible old Western movies way too loud or forgetting what he was talking about mid-sentence and Mom and I laughing about it. The days Mom and I would work in her garden, coming back inside sunburned. Entire days we'd spend alone, Mom shopping for something and me following her around, cracking jokes. "Sorry," I say, wiping my eyes.

"It's fine." Dr. Taylor pushes over the box of tissues, but I don't take one. I can't be crying, not about this. "Do you want to talk about it?" she asks.

"No."

"It's natural to miss them, Ben. They are your parents, after all."

"Just . . . after what they did." When I thought I could trust them. "I thought . . . I thought being their child would be enough for them."

"I know, I know. But you lived with them for eighteen years, they raised you, and it seemed like they loved you." Then Dr. Taylor leans forward. "Did you love them, Ben?"

I want to tell Dr. Taylor no, and I want to be able to say it with confidence. I don't love them, I didn't. Not after what they did. But they are my parents. I'm supposed to love them, no matter what, right?

"Do you think they miss you?"

I have no idea. "Can they? I mean, they kicked me out."

"Doesn't mean they won't miss you. If that really was them outside Hannah's house that night . . ." Dr. Taylor doesn't finish her statement, but it's the first time she's brought up that night since I told her about it. "Are you feeling well, Ben? Physically?"

"I haven't really been sleeping." This morning I woke up around two thirty, and the night before that it was around three. It's getting harder to keep my eyes open during the day now. I've even thought about faking being sick one day just so I could try to catch up.

"It's getting closer to the end of the school year. Things can get pretty busy."

"Yeah."

"Have you tried any over-the-counter medication?"

"I've taken some NyQuil, but it only works for a few hours." That was the only thing Hannah and Thomas had in their medicine cabinet. Besides, the stuff tastes like ass, and I don't want to make that an everyday thing.

"Not much of an acquired taste?" She chuckles. "Is this the first time you've experienced something like this?"

"Sort of. Last year, when I had the PSATs and final exams right after each other." I rub the back of my head. My hair's gotten longer, longer than Dad would've ever let me grow it. "I usually just watch TV or draw until it's time to wake up."

"Would you like to try medication?" she asks.

"You can do that?"

Dr. Taylor nods.

"I don't know." I hadn't thought about it a lot. I don't love the idea personally; it just doesn't feel right for me.

"Well, if it's this bad, then maybe we should consider it."

"Do you know what's causing it?" I ask.

"I have an idea, yes."

"And?" God, why do I even ask?

She exhales slowly and almost seems reluctant to tell me. "I think you're dealing with depression, but to me, anxiety seems to be the biggest issue."

"Oh."

"And that's perfectly fine. Everyone deals with anxiety, Ben, it's just—"

I finish for her. "Some people don't know how to cope with it?"

"Sometimes it's too much to handle. You're still growing up, still figuring things out, and this is an extra layer of issues. It's common for someone your age to be dealing with this sort of thing. And your situation certainly hasn't helped that."

I don't know what to say next, so I blurt out the first thing that comes to my mind. "It's scary, Dr. Taylor."

"I know, Ben. I know." She sighs. "But the medication might be an outlet worth exploring, don't you think?"

"Do you believe it'll help?" I ask.

"I truly do. With patients dealing with depression and anxiety, medication can be a godsend. We could do a trial run, see how it works for you?"

I nod along to her words. "Okay, we can try it."

TWELVE

I crumple up the paper, tearing it right out of my sketchbook and throwing it into the bin halfway across the room. It misses.

Of course.

"You need to work on your free throws." Mrs. Liu eyes the balls of paper sitting around the trash can.

"I'll get those in a second," I say.

"Stuck?" She walks over to the little workstation I've built myself in the corner of the back room.

"I've got nothing," I say. The ideas are there, floating around, but I can't get them onto the paper, let alone a fucking canvas. And the medication Dr. Taylor has me trying is making me drowsy, which wouldn't be so bad at night, but the last few days it's been hitting me right in the afternoon.

"What are you trying to do?" Mrs. Liu asks.

"At this point, anything."

"Honestly, I think you could quit now, just not do anything. I'd still probably pass you." She chuckles. "Have you tried painting something real?"

"That's what I'm doing."

"Okay, but like, something you know. Take from your life, Ben."

"What do you mean?"

"When I'm stuck, I take a photo off my phone, one that I've taken myself, and just start drawing that. It usually gets my creative flow going. Sometimes art needs an instruction booklet."

"I wish it came with one sometimes," I mutter.

"Hey!" Mrs. Liu shouts at one of the freshmen in the other classroom. "Put that back down. Heathens." She whispers that last part under her breath. "Just try it. Not some photo you got online, but something you *really* know."

Maybe that's not such a bad idea though. I take out my phone and flip through the hundreds of reference photos I've saved. I probably need to delete some of these soon. There's no way I'll need them. But what if I do?

Then I get to this string of Nathan's selfies, then more photos, then Nathan selfies, then photos. It's this weird back-and-forth because every few weeks, the boy has the urge to steal my phone and take a dozen selfies. Most of them are of me and him, me trying to grab my phone. There are a few of him and Meleika, or him and Sophie too, or ones of me taken secretly, with his head barely in the frame while he takes a picture of me.

But most are just of him. I zoom in on the picture and stare at it. He would be a good model.

He doesn't have to know, right? I've already drawn him once before.

I sketch out the shape of his face, the angles of his cheeks and his chin, the shape of his eyes, the way his mouth is curving upward. I sort of have to combine the photos to get the right angle, but I can make it work. I don't even know where to begin with the painting though. I want to do something different.

My eye catches the drip painting on the wall, the controlled messiness of it, all the colors mixing together. I still want Nathan to be a part of this, but I don't want it to be some hyperrealistic re-creation. I could try this monochromatic technique I saw online.

When I think of Nathan, I think of warmth. Of reds, and oranges. But most of all, I think of yellow. That just seems like such a Nathan-y color. Happiness, joy, his optimism, that smile.

I make my sketch purposefully rough, adding to the sharpness of Nathan's face. It doesn't take me longer than a few minutes. This is the outline, the skeleton. Details come later. It takes me a few tries to find the yellow I want to use for the majority of his face, but eventually I do.

And I find a rhythm, painting in broad strokes, switching between different-size brushes to get in the finer details. There's only so much I can shove into the forty-five minutes I have left, but when the bell rings, it feels like that list has only gotten longer.

"Fuck." I look around for Mrs. Liu. I can't stop now.

"Find your muse?" She walks to the back room, holding a stack of pallets decorated with watercolor paints.

"Mmh" is all I can say. I'm too distracted.

"Oh, wow, Ben." I don't know if she means the mess or the painting.

"Sorry, got into it. I'll clean up."

"No, no, no." She puts a hand on my shoulder. "Keep going. I love it."

"Really??"

"It's fantastic. I'll call Thomas, let him know you're working."

"You don't mind me staying?"

"Pssh, I've got assignments to grade anyway, so I'll be here for a while."

"You don't think it's . . . like . . ." I stammer. "Creepy to paint him, do you?"

She cackles. "I don't think Nathan's ego is so fragile. But I'd definitely let him know." Then she pauses. "I do want to ask, why him?"

I shrug. "He stole my phone and took a bunch of selfies." I show her the screen.

"An odd form of payback if I've ever seen one, but hey. You do you, kid." Mrs. Liu pats me on the shoulder. "I did want to talk to you about something."

"Oh?"

"Yeah, every year I do a student art show here at the school. I was wondering if you'd want to participate."

I pause and set my brush down. "Why me?"

Mrs. Liu scoffs. "You're joking, right?" Then she starts looking at the walls. "You're one of my best students."

I look at my paintings, but all I really see is how they don't hold up to the ones around them. I don't know any of Mrs. Liu's other students, besides a few of the freshmen in the other room.

But I do know for certain that they're better artists than me. The portraits and the landscapes, the abstract concepts, the sculptures. I doubt I could ever really pull that stuff off the way they do.

"It won't be until May, but I like to plan early. Just think about it, okay?"

I nod.

"Thanks, I'll let you get back to work."

And I do; I get so lost in it, each stroke of my brushes. I have to make sure the yellows won't blend together in some mess of color, so I move from one end of the canvas to the other, letting things dry a bit before I get to work on the smaller details.

"Ben?" I see Thomas out of the corner of my eye, walking down the short hallway between the rooms.

"Here." I wave without looking at him.

"Almost done?"

"Almost." I glance at my phone. Holy shit. It's past five. "Sorry, didn't realize it was so late."

"No, it's cool. I was just getting next week's test ready." Thomas walks to a spot behind me, seeing the painting in all its yellowish glory. "Oh."

Thomas stops short, and I watch his face.

"That's Nathan." He points to the canvas.

"Yeah." I stare at the nearly finished thing, eyeing the spots I've missed, or where I think I've used the wrong shade. "I'm not done yet, but I can quit for today."

"Hannah wants us home. Apparently she's cooking dinner tonight."

I grab my paints and brushes and start rinsing them off in the sink. Hopefully I'll be able to find something close to the right shade tomorrow. When I look over my shoulder, Thomas is still staring at the painting.

"Is something wrong?" I ask.

"No, just looking," Thomas says with a smile. "I like the yellows. For some reason," he starts to say, but then he pauses. "I don't know, it just screams Nathan."

"That was kind of the idea." I put my brushes on the drying rack and rinse off my hands.

"Ready to go?" Thomas grabs my bag for me.

"Yeah," I say, taking one last look at the painting before I turn the lights off.

———

"Did y'all hear about the party Steph's having on Friday?" Sophie asks. We're back in the cafeteria, which was wild enough before the Spring Fling game, but with only a few days left until spring break, everyone's "give a shit" levels are at an all-time low. Even the teachers don't care, which has led to Mrs. Liu calling me to her room during other classes to "help out with a project."

Which really just ends up being code for letting me finish my painting of Nathan. I still don't know exactly how or when I'm going to tell him about it. I've gone through about a dozen different ways in my head and none of them seem quite right.

"Why on earth would we want to go to a party at Steph's place?" Meleika props her head on her hands.

Nathan sips some bright red sports drink. "The girl's been wound tight the last few weeks, she deserves a break."

"It's technically for spring break," Sophie adds. "But it's not like she needs a reason."

"All she gets is PBR and vodka. Not even the good kind of vodka," Meleika says.

Nathan laughs. "This one is BYOB apparently. Maybe she heard the complaints."

"Great, so the only way we get something good is if we bring it ourselves?" Meleika rolls her eyes. "No, thank you."

"I heard Todd's going," Sophie says.

"Oh, never mind, count me in." Meleika chuckles to herself. "He always brings something good. Like, flat-out-wasted-in-three-sips good stuff."

"Todd's a dick," Nathan says.

"Yeah, but a dick with a dad who doesn't keep an eye on his liquor cabinet," Sophie sings.

Nathan nudges me. "You want to go?"

"Where?"

He's still smiling. "To the party."

"I wasn't invited?"

"You're so cute, Ben." Sophie types something into her phone, and my face gets hot.

"Come on, you didn't dress up for Spirit Week." Meleika counts off. "You didn't go to the game, or the dance after. You should at least come to a party. Unwind a little bit, let yourself get loose."

"You don't really have to be invited, you just show up," Nathan adds.

I tuck my hands under the table. "I don't even know any of these people."

"Well, Todd's a douche-canoe, so count yourself lucky. And you've already had the pleasure of meeting Stephanie." Meleika laughs a little too loudly. "Come on, it'll be fun."

"It's one night," Sophie keeps going.

"Just come with us. We'll hang out for half an hour, and then if you want to, we'll leave?" Nathan tries his best to reassure me.

"I've never been to a party before," I say.

"It's basically a cheap and easy way for us to get drunk and make fun of white people who think they have rhythm." Meleika chuckles.

Nathan rolls his eyes before he adds, "She's right though. It's the sort of secondhand embarrassment you only get from watching people drunkenly grind against one another."

"Remember when Megan and Adam started dancing, and he puked all over her?" Sophie starts laughing so hard that I hardly catch the end of what she's trying to say.

"Oh God, yes." Meleika covers her mouth. "Ben, you *have* to come, at least to see what sort of embarrassing shit goes on."

"Come on." Nathan nudges me. "Half an hour, that's it."

"Fine," I finally say, knowing there's really no way I'm going to get out of this one. I'll have to lie to Hannah, I guess. I doubt she'll want me going to a party where there's a bunch of underage drinking going on.

"Excellent." Meleika rubs her hands together. "We'll corrupt you yet."

THIRTEEN

Part of me sort of hopes Nathan, Sophie, and Meleika will have forgotten about me agreeing to go to the party by Friday, since they've pretty much spent the last week discussing their spring break plans.

Sophie actually sounds like she's going to have the most fun. She and her parents are going to visit her grandparents in Busan, South Korea. Meleika's going up to the mountains with her family, and Nathan isn't really doing anything apparently.

But they definitely don't forget about the party. Clearly, I'm not that lucky. Fortunately it's a half day at school, so I have plenty of time to work myself into a ball of anxiety. And I'm at a total loss when it comes to picking out what to wear.

I mean, the shirt's easy, but all my jeans feel too baggy, my shoes feel too dirty, *and* I don't even know what's appropriate for this kind of party anyway. What would Nathan wear? Probably tight pants and a button-up shirt or something.

Of course, there isn't much he doesn't look good in. He's totally one of those kinds of people. Who could wear the absolute ugliest thing in the world and make it some fashion statement.

I really need to talk to Hannah about new clothes. For now, I'll have to settle with the usual; at least I still have a few shirts that don't have dried paint on them.

"Do you need my debit card?" Hannah asks. I almost blow my cover before I remember I told her I'm hanging out with Nathan tonight. So not a total lie.

"No, we're just going over to his house." I scratch at my nose, bending over to pick up my shoes.

"Okay." Hannah leans against the doorframe. "Where are you really going?"

"What?" There's no way she can tell I'm lying.

"Please, I'm your sister. Now, where are you really going?"

"I told you—"

"Yeah, yeah, yeah. Trust me, I lied enough to Mom and Dad to know." She takes a seat next to me on the bed. "So spill."

"There's a party."

"Alcohol? Don't lie to me."

"Yes." I stare at the floor.

"Oh, Ben."

"I'm sorry. Don't be mad."

Hannah lets out this low laugh, which seems weird for her. "Please, I'm not mad. I'm your sister. I did a lot worse shit when I was your age."

I stop myself from saying *I know.*

"Are you actually going to drink anything?" she asks.

"Don't know. I hadn't really planned on it."

"Is Nathan?"

"I don't think so, he's supposed to drive us."

Hannah looks me over from head to toe. "Oh, hon. I'm not letting you go to a party dressed like that, come on." She grabs my hand and leads me down the hall to her room. "I know you're taller than I am, but my pants should fit you better than whatever those are." She points to my jeans.

"You bought them," I argue.

"Well, if I'd known you'd be going to parties we would've gone shopping sooner. You have to look good tonight!" Hannah leaves me standing at the foot of her bed and opens the sliding doors of her closet. "I remember my first party."

"How do you know this is my first?" I ask.

Then Hannah gives me a look. The raised eyebrow, sideways smile sort. And I can't help but feel insulted. Don't get me wrong, this *is* my first party. But her lack of confidence feels sort of like a slap to the face.

"The shirt's fine, but yeah, the pants need to go." She turns on her heels and digs around in her closet for a few seconds. "Haven't worn these in years." She tosses a pair of dark black jeans onto the bed. "Or these." Another pair on the bed.

When she's done, there are five pairs for me to try on. "I don't know about this, Hannah." She shoves the pile into my hands and pushes me toward the bathroom.

"Come on, can't be any worse than what you've got on."

I would argue, but I have a sinking suspicion she's right. I go for the black pair first, since those seem the nicest and most "party appropriate." I try not to think about the fact that I'm nearly the same size as my sister, or that her old jeans apparently fit me really well, even if I do feel them sliding off my hips a bit. I eye myself in the mirror, focusing on the way they hug my legs. I turn, trying to see how the back fits me.

"Hannah?" I call for her.

She opens the door slowly, her eyes covered. "You're not naked, right?"

"Right."

Her mouth drops open. "Holy shit, Ben, you've got an ass. When did that happen?"

I turn to try and look in the mirror but can't get the angle quite right. Never thought my sister would be telling me I have a nice butt.

"Seriously, man—" Her face goes cold. "Sorry. I'm sorry."

I stare at her. At least she knows she's wrong, right? "It's okay."

"No, it's not. I'm sorry."

I shrug. Now isn't the moment to get angry with her. "Do you think these look good?"

"Yeah, with the shirt too, it's nice. Just make sure your phone fits in. I can't remember if that's the pair with the fake pockets or not." She bends over and picks up the folded stack of her other pairs. "See the wonders a decent pair of pants can do?"

"Thank you."

"No problem. And, Ben, I'm begging you not to drink tonight, okay? The medication is new and I don't want you to take any risks."

"I promise." I wasn't planning on drinking anyway. I'd read over the tiny orange bottle probably a hundred times, googling what different things meant. According to most sources it isn't the end of the world to have a beer with the kind of dosage I'm on, but still, I'd rather not risk it.

Especially if it could make me feel worse than I already do.

"Good, I just want you to be safe."

I nodded. "We will."

"Okay." She pulls me into a hug, which seems like a weird move, and it's awkward with the pile of clothes between us, but I hug her back as best I can. "Now go have fun. And use a condom," she teases.

"That's really gross."

She ruffles a hand through my hair. "Whatever, kid."

I walk back to my room to make sure I have my wallet and my phone. By the time I make it out the front door, Nathan is already waiting for me in the driveway, right there in his shiny car.

"Damn, boy." He rolls down the driver-side window.

I want to shrink. "Do I look okay?"

"Yeah! Kind of hot if I'm not lying. Girls will be all over you tonight." He winks at me, and I resist the part of my brain telling me to run back inside and shut myself in my room for the rest of the night. "Are you ready to go?"

"Yeah." I climb into the passenger seat and try not to imagine the worst.

———

Nathan drives the car down this really long dirt path, hitting nearly every pothole along the way. "You know you're supposed to avoid those, right?" I ask after he hits another one. We've been driving for so long that I think we're both convinced Sophie texted Nathan the wrong address.

"You didn't see any turns or anything, did you?" Nathan asks, ignoring my commentary.

"I don't remember one," I say.

Nathan pulls out his phone just before I see some lights in the distance. "I'm gonna call Mel."

"Wait. Maybe there?"

"Worth a shot." Nathan keeps driving. The path curves before finally opening up. The yard is already filled with cars, lights glowing through the windows of the first floor of the house.

"This looks like the place where a group of teenagers gets murdered," I say, eyeing it through the windshield. Nathan snorts as he pulls into the end of a long row of cars. "Half an hour?" I look at him.

Even from here I can see the crowds gathering on the front porch. People already look drunk off their asses, and it's barely eight thirty.

"Half an hour." Nathan glances at the clock on the dashboard. "Nine o'clock, and if you're having a bad time, we can leave."

"Okay." I nod.

And he grins from ear to ear.

"Nathan!" Meleika shouts from across the yard. She sprints toward us, something vaguely bottle-shaped tucked under her arms. "Y'all made it."

"Yes, my dear." Nathan chuckles. "We were worried too. Thought maybe we missed a turn or something."

"Yeah, this place screams murder house," she replies.

"That's what Ben said." Nathan looks at me over his shoulder, still smiling.

I follow them both closely, climbing the front steps of the house with as much enthusiasm as I can muster, which isn't saying a lot. I can already feel my stomach twisting with the beat of the bass, the floors vibrating so hard I'm shocked the pictures on the walls aren't falling off.

If the porch outside is crowded, then the inside of the house is most definitely filled to capacity. Seriously, I don't think any fire marshal would let this go, even if you paid them. "Do you know if Sophie's here?" Nathan asks, his voice barely registering over the music.

Meleika has to shout. "Should be!"

"Nathan! Mel!" Some humungous white dude waves, pushing through the crowd as he makes a beeline for us.

"God. Todd's already wasted." Meleika turns to me. And then I realize I *do* know Todd. Well, vaguely, anyway. He's in my English class, but I pretty much only ever see the back of his head. "I'm going to go find Sophie, good luck."

"Wait, don't leave." I try to catch her, but Meleika's already gone.

"Hey, Todd." Nathan steps in front of me, probably to hide Meleika running away.

"Hey, Nate." Todd glares right at me. "And who is this?" Either he doesn't pay attention during roll call, or he really is drunk off his ass.

"Ben," Nathan answers for me.

"Hey, wait! I know this guy! We're in Mrs. Williams's class together." He gives me his fist. I guess to bump it, but I just stand there, awkwardly, because my hands refuse to budge. And all I say is "Yeah."

"You drinkin' tonight?" he asks Nathan, unbothered by my rejection.

"Nah, driving."

"What about you?" Todd looks down at me. Jesus. I never realized what a giant this guy is.

"Oh, I don't—" I start to say, but it's useless. Todd can't hear me over the music.

"Hey, Megs!" He waves over to the table in the dining room and points to me. A girl, apparently Megs, hands me a red cup filled with something that looks like pee. "We've got the stronger stuff in the kitchen." Todd smacks my back, nearly making me drop the whole thing.

"So, you're drinking?" Nathan asks.

"I guess?" I stare at my cup, filled with the *very* pee-like liquid. I shouldn't drink it, I know that I shouldn't. I don't want to in the first place, and all the warnings about my medication. But Todd's staring at me, and there's this desire bubbling inside me, almost like I *need* to impress him. And then I see Nathan, and I don't want him to think I can't handle this stuff.

I sip whatever is in my cup, and it takes everything in me not to spit it out. "Blegh, what is that?"

"No good?" Nathan tries, and fails, to hide his laughter.

"No!" I shout.

Nathan's still trying his best not to giggle. "It's beer. Try it again, first sip's always terrible."

I take another, but it's still just as bad.

"Maybe you're not a beer man!" Todd bellows and takes my cup, leaving it on some table. "You want to get drunk?"

"Not really."

"Come on." Guess he still can't hear me, or is just choosing not to. Either way his grip on my shoulder is *way* too tight. Todd leads me around the house, weaving through the tight crowds until we finally find what he's looking for.

The kitchen is less crowded than the rest of the party, maybe since the music isn't as loud. There's a couple making out in the corner, though with the way they're all over each other, it seems like they're more into voyeurism than anything else. Everyone else is huddled around the island counter, chatting back and forth. I recognize Stephanie, and a few people from the cafeteria and Calculus, but that's it.

"Everyone, this is Ben!" Todd announces us, and they all cheer for me, raising their cups. Or in a few cases, bottles. But the second they're done cheering, they go back to their conversations, like I wasn't even here to begin with.

"Be gentle," Nathan says. There's something off about his expression, like he's worried.

"Ah, party virgin, eh?" Todd asks.

"I guess." He says "virgin" like it's a bad thing.

Todd leads me over to the area of the counter covered in at

least three dozen different bottles, all of them left open. What sort of animals are my classmates?

"Well, can't have that, we need to break you in. What's your poison?" he asks.

Break me in? "I'm fine, I promise. I don't—"

Todd doesn't let me finish though. "Come on, I can tell you're a man of more refined taste. Here, try this." Todd hands me a small shot glass with a pink liquid that's a few shades away from Pepto.

"What is it?" I ask, swirling it around in the small glass.

"Strawberry tequila," Todd says.

Someone from the counter crowd shouts, "Todd, I think that might be a bit too strong!"

"Just try it." Todd smacks my back again. He really needs to find other ways of displaying affection. "Here, I'll do one with you." Todd pours his own shot.

All my research told me that mixing one beer with a low dosage of my meds wouldn't be a big deal, but I know for a fact tequila is stronger than beer. A *lot* stronger. But everyone's staring at me now, expecting me to take the shot. I don't need to do this, why should I care what these people think about me? But there's that shame again, this desire to impress these people. I down the shot and holy shit, it burns, and whatever sweet taste is implied by "strawberry" definitely isn't there. But it makes Todd and the rest of the crowd cheer, so I guess I did something right?

"You want another?" Todd asks, already holding two more.

"I don't think so." But another one is already in my hand.

"Come on, one more." Todd slips his arm around my shoulder, and I don't ever think I've been more uncomfortable with someone my own age so quickly.

"Seriously, I'm good." I guess that's enough for Todd to drop the subject. Or maybe he just forgets.

"I like this one, Nathan. He's good people." Todd gets in close, and I swear I could get drunk off his breath alone. Jesus, the dude needs a mint, like, yesterday.

"Thank you?" I half say, half ask.

Nathan jumps up on a clear spot of the counter. "You okay?"

"I guess?"

My head already feels fuzzy, and there's this weird warmth in my stomach. Just after one shot? Do people really pay to feel this way?

"So, Benny boy, you having a good time?" Todd's grip around my neck tightens, his words slurring. He doesn't wait for my answer before he's yelling to everyone else. "This here is Benny's first party, everyone!"

There are a few fake cheers, actually they sound more like pity cheers.

"You look like you're having a good time." Todd looks back at me. "But I don't think you've ever looked this good," Todd belts out again, and I get another face full of liquor breath. "Got to show off the goods for the ladies, right? I know the feeling." Then he slaps my ass. I need to get out of here. Has it been a half hour yet?

"Sorry, he's wasted," Stephanie apologizes for him. She sounds nicer when she isn't screeching at me through a megaphone.

"You know it!" Todd shouts at no one in particular.

"I feel like I haven't seen you around school, Ben," this one guy says. He must be one of Todd's friends. They have the same look, tall guys with short brown hair and weirdly strong jaws. He also might be the least drunk of the group. Not counting me and Nathan.

"I moved here back in January," I say.

"Yeah . . . you're in my Calc class," a girl says, and she seems vaguely familiar, but I have no idea if we are actually in the same class or not. "He's really smart."

"Oh, thanks." My face is getting hotter.

"Seriously, I think he's got the highest grade in the class," she adds.

"Oh, geez, Em." Todd starts to laugh. "Go ahead and blow him already, we'll give you two some privacy."

"While we're at it, we'll give you and your left hand some alone time too." Em rolls her eyes, and the room fills with "oooos." Todd seems unbothered though. He just plucks another drink off the counter and wraps his arm around my shoulder.

"Come on, Benny boy here's very attractive." Todd winks at me and then looks at Em. "And you're newly single."

"Hey, um . . ." I tap on Todd's bicep, hoping he'll let go. But I'm pretty sure his grip only tightens. "Todd, I can't—"

Breathe. I can't breathe.

"Leave him alone, Todd," someone says.

"Oh, please. Ben, wouldn't you love to take the lovely Emily Rodgers on a date next weekend?"

"I . . ." I stammer. "Can't . . ." It actually feels impossible to breathe. And I don't know if it's because of Todd's grip, his words, the pairs of eyes staring at me now, the alcohol, or some combination of them all.

"Please don't tell me you're into the fellas, Ben. I like you and all, and I'm cool with the homos, but I don't think—"

I need to leave, right now.

"Hey, Ben, you want to go dance?" Nathan leaps off the counter, and before I can answer, his arm is around mine. I don't care, because this finally gets Todd off me. Nathan pulls me in close, leading me out of the kitchen and back down the hallway.

"Nathan, wait." But he keeps dragging me along. "Nathan." I yank back but he still won't let go. "Stop!" God, he's got a strong grip. At least we've stopped moving. "I don't want to dance," I finally say, worried he won't hear me.

"Oh." He grins. "I wasn't serious. You just looked like you wanted to leave back there."

I slouch against the wall. "Oh. Well, thank you."

"Sorry. If I'd known Todd was that wasted, I wouldn't have let him drag you along. When he's drunk his boundaries totally disappear."

"Yeah, I can tell," I say, rubbing at my neck. I'm sure the skin there is red by now.

"Do you want to go?"

"Has it been half an hour?"

Nathan pulls out his phone. "You know you don't really have to stay, right? We've still got ten more minutes, but we can leave if you want to. I don't want you to be uncomfortable."

"Can we just find Sophie or Mel?" I rub my elbows. Most people have migrated into the living room, where the music is the loudest, but the hallway and dining room are still pretty crowded too.

"Yeah, sure." Nathan glances around. "They're probably dancing." He takes my hand. If I let go, then chances are high I'll get lost in this place.

We push through the crowds in the living room. Apparently, this is the designated dance area. But neither Meleika nor Sophie seem to be here. Nathan's right though, there is something about watching other white people who think what they're doing can legally be called dancing.

After that, we head toward the dining room, and still nothing, but then I spot them hanging around the stairs. Meleika's right above Sophie, both draped over the railing, both looking bored out of their minds.

"You two look like you've had a rough night." Sophie leans forward, resting her head on her arms.

"And it's not even nine." Meleika chuckles, taking a sip of her drink. "Lightweights."

"We had a run-in with Todd," Nathan says, before shooting a look at Meleika. "Would've been shorter if *someone* hadn't left us there."

Meleika laughs again, and then asks me: "Douche of the year or douche of the year?"

I try to laugh, but that sour taste in my mouth has moved to my stomach. There's something about the crowd that's putting me on edge, the way everyone's pressed together. And is it getting hotter in here?

I glance over at Nathan, watching him watch the dancing, his head bobbing along to the beat. He says something to Sophie, but the music drowns it out. Everyone's having so much fun, and he looks like he's missing it, like he'd rather be out there dancing with someone, actually having a good time.

And I've ruined it all.

"I just, um . . . I'm going to wait by the car. You go have fun," I tell him.

"Ben. You okay?" Meleika asks. She and Sophie are watching me carefully.

"It's fine. I just . . . I shouldn't have come, I'm sorry. I'll just be outside, Nathan, whenever you're ready." I finally catch Nathan's attention.

"Ben!" I can see the annoyance in his face, that slight push of his lips. I shouldn't have come here. He just wanted to have a good time with his friends and I'm going to make him leave early.

"Sorry, sorry." I push through the dancing and the tight crowds, muttering apologies as I go along. I hope I can find my way back outside.

"Ben, wait." Nathan grabs my hand again, but I pull it back.

"Listen, go have a good time, okay? I'll just wait by the car."

"Ben!" he says again, more desperate than I've ever heard him sound. I charge back down the hallway, pushing past the crowds.

"Hey!" someone yells.

"Sorry, sorry," I say, trying to get to the door. God, it's fucking burning up in here. The hallways feel like they're closing in on me. I just need to get outside. Just get outside, and it will all be fine.

"Ben!" Nathan shouts, sounding miles away this time.

My hands finally find a door handle and I push through, almost collapsing into the cool night air. I catch myself against the railing; more people stare at me as I pass by them. I still can't tell if I'm at the front of the house, or at the back, but I don't care.

I'm not inside anymore; that's what's important.

"You gonna be sick, man?" someone asks me. "If you've gotta barf, at least do it in the bushes."

"I'm not a man," I whisper under my breath, rounding the corner. This side of the porch is deserted, thankfully. I retch, hanging myself over the railing. There's nothing in my stomach but that disgusting tequila, but it threatens to come up anyway. It wasn't even that much, was it? But that's not it.

No, this feels like something else, like that night I saw their car. Fuck.

Not now.

Dr. Taylor confirmed it was a panic attack and tried to teach me ways of coping. Get to a quiet spot if I can, close my eyes, try to breathe. I try my best to remember Dr. Taylor's advice, but everything's so crowded and foggy.

Just breathe.

"Just breathe," I say out loud. "Breathe." I take in the night air through my nose and hold it for ten seconds before exhaling through my mouth. "Come on, Ben, don't freak out, please. Not now," I tell myself.

"Ben, are you okay?" It's Nathan.

"Just, please." I don't even know what I'm trying to ask him. I run a hand through my hair, my palms sweaty. Christ, I probably look like death.

"Ben?" He puts his hand to my back, and I swear, I almost get sick right there.

"Please don't touch me right now, okay?" It comes out like more of a growl than I want it to.

Nathan pulls his hand back, going to the empty spot on the railing beside me. "I'm sorry," I say. "I just . . ." Just can't get a complete thought from my brain to my mouth.

"Was it the stuff you drank? Do you need some water?"

I shake my head way too fast. "Wasn't the drinks." My chest heaves for a second. I'm fighting a losing battle here.

"Are you sure? Can you move?"

"Just give me a minute, please?"

"Sure, yeah." He backs away.

Fucking breathe, just breathe. I close my eyes, pressing my hands to my forehead. Don't cry, don't cry. I feel that familiar heat behind my eyes, and that ache in my jaw.

I finally manage to spit out something. "I'm sorry."

"It's okay, just take your time."

"Can we go?"

"Yeah, of course." He reaches for me again but stops short. "Can I touch you?"

I nod. "Sorry, I just—"

"No, it's all right. Come on."

The hand on my back doesn't make me want to gag anymore. In fact, I'm certain that Nathan is doing most of the work as he walks me back to his car, even going so far as to open the door for me.

"Thanks," I say, hoping he won't try to buckle my seat belt for me. I can only stand so much humiliation in one night.

He climbs into the driver's seat, totally silent, the car roaring to life as he turns the ignition and slides it into reverse.

"Mel and Sophie?" I ask.

"They're staying a little longer. I told them I'd get you home." He braces his hand against the back of my headrest so he can see behind us.

"Oh." Goddammit. I fucked up. Big-time. Nathan speeds down the dirt road wordlessly, not even the radio to fill the void between us. One of us has to talk, someone has to say *something*, and I know it won't be me.

I'm not that brave right now.

I sneak glances at him out of the corner of my eye. He doesn't look mad, but then again, he's Mr. Positive, so I'm not even sure he has it in him to be more than mildly frustrated.

"If you take a picture, it'll last longer." He still smiles, never taking his eyes off the road.

"Sorry." I shut my eyes, only opening them again to watch the dark trees we drive past.

"I mean, I know I'm handsome and all, but seriously, if you'd rather have a picture, that's cool too."

I pick at the jeans covering my knees, the tight fabric that feels more suffocating now than anything else. "I'm sorry."

"You apologize a lot," he says matter-of-factly.

"I'm . . ." I deny my automatic reaction.

"Ben, man, are you okay? I mean, I know you can't be after all that, but like, I'm worried, dude."

"Don't be," I say. I feel so close to that edge, and it hurts that Nathan is the one pushing me closer.

"Why? I'm your friend. I have a right to be worried, don't you think?"

"No one said you had to be."

Nathan scoffs, and he doesn't sound very happy. "That's a thing friends tend to do."

He was the one who wanted to be my friend. I keep picking at the spot, thinking that maybe I can scratch my way to my skin, and just keep going. No. I force the thoughts from my head and sit on my hands instead.

"Do you want me to take you home?"

"Yes, please" is my first answer, but then I think about Hannah, and her reaction. I'm guessing one look at me would tell her all she needed to know, and the second she sees me like this she'll rush me over to a hospital or call Dr. Taylor. "Actually, no."

"No?" Nathan glances over for a split second, before focusing back on the road again.

"No. My sister's there."

"Why would she care?"

"I just can't go there right now." There might be too many questions. Like why I live with my sister and her husband, or why there aren't any pictures of my parents on the walls. And then that familiar guilt settles in my stomach.

I should tell him.

"Okay, where do you want to go?"

"I . . . I don't know."

"My parents aren't home, won't be until later. We can go to my house."

Any other day, this thought would've terrified me. But instead I nod, knowing that right now, Nathan Allan's house is the only place for me.

FOURTEEN

"Can I show you something?" Nathan asks.

We're in his backyard, tossing the ball for Ryder again. He keeps switching between the two of us, taking the ball back to Nathan, then bringing it to me.

It's simple. Easy. Just what I need right now.

"Sure." I throw the ball again.

Nathan doesn't wait for Ryder to catch up. He goes back inside through the glass doors, leaving them wide open for me to follow. We head up to his room again. It's cleaner this time. Most of the clothes have been picked up, but there are still piles of books lying everywhere, like he doesn't know what to do with all of them.

I expect him to crawl on his bed, but he doesn't. No, instead he walks over to his window, opening it just wide enough for him to duck through.

"Out the window?" I ask.

"Yeah." He grins back at me before vanishing into the night. "Told you I had something to show you."

"And it's on the roof?"

"Technically." His voice echoes back into the bedroom. "The roof has the best view."

I poke my head outside, unsure of how I'm really supposed to do this. I try my best to copy how he moved, putting one foot out first and then bracing myself to get the other. But these pants are so tight that I'm scared I've ripped the crotch for a second. And when I'm finally outside I twist something wrong, and my foot ends up hanging on the windowpane. Fuck, this is how it ends, right? Face-first, thirty feet into Nathan's backyard. What a way to go.

"Whoa there, cowboy." Nathan catches me by the hand, pulling me in close. "Please don't fall off my roof. That would be very complicated to explain to my parents."

"Not like I planned on it." My heart has to catch up with everything around me, and then I realize *just* how close we are to each other. "Okay, I think I've seen enough." I close my eyes. "Can we go back inside now?"

"Not even close." He steadies me. "You good?"

I try to get used to standing at an angle while also ignoring certain death below me. "Maybe it's the alcohol?"

"Come on, you had one shot like an hour ago. You aren't drunk." I feel his hands vanish before one of them settles on my own, his long fingers wrapping around like they belong. I glance down and then back up at him.

"What are you—"

"This way." He leads me around to this spot between two of the windows that poke through the roof. Thankfully this part is pretty flat, so it's nothing to navigate, even in the dark. Nathan sits down like he's done this hundreds of times before, and I don't doubt that he has. He spreads his legs out and rests his head against the part where the steeper angle of the roof meets.

"Come on." He pats the empty space beside him.

I do what he says, careful to watch where I step. I doubt Nathan can make it up in time to save me again. "Is this what you wanted to show me?"

"You showed me your quiet place."

"My quiet place?" I rest the same way he does, my back against the roof, but I tuck my legs in instead.

"The quad."

"Oh, that's not really . . ." I mean, I guess it is, even if I'm not always alone while I'm there.

"This is mine," he continues. "When everything gets too loud or gets to be too much, this is where I go." He lifts his head and stares toward the sky. The light pollution from the skyscrapers nearby hides most of the stars, but the ones that manage to poke through are so bright that you don't really mind.

"It's nice," I say, adjusting so a shingle will stop stabbing me in the back.

"Mom nearly had a heart attack when she saw me up here the first time."

"You have to admit that the quad is a lot safer."

"Can't argue." He folds his arms and tucks them behind his head. "I'm sorry for tonight."

"It's whatever, not your fault."

"I thought it would be fun."

I shrug.

"You want to talk about it?"

Not really, but what else is there to discuss? "My doctor says they're panic attacks. I . . ." Here it comes, the truth. I try to think up a lie. Some childhood trauma that causes them, but I really don't want to lie to Nathan, not about this, at least. "My parents kicked me out of my house . . ."

It feels like the night I came out to Mom and Dad. When the truth was on my tongue for days, weeks even, just waiting to come out until I was worrying myself sick over it. And I knew I had to say it. Because it was all supposed to be fine.

We sit there. I know I shouldn't have told him, but I guess part of me is tired of lying to him. At least about this. It feels like time stops moving, like now I'm frozen in this spot forever, never able to escape. I silently beg Nathan to say something, anything at all. Just break this silence, please.

"Oh," he finally says after what feels like a century. "That really fucking sucks."

"Yeah." Of everything I expected, that wasn't really on the list.

"That's terrible." I watch his throat bob, the rise and fall of his chest.

I take a deep breath. "I live with my sister now. She's married to Thomas, Mr. Waller. He helped me get into Wake."

"What happened?"

"I did something I shouldn't have, made a big mistake." And paid the price for it.

"Big enough to get forced out of your house?"

"Apparently."

"Do you still love them?" Nathan asks. "Your parents?"

The question actually takes me off guard. "I . . . I don't know," I tell him.

I don't. I really don't. I wish the answer was easy, but it isn't. How can you not love your parents? Even after everything they did, I have a problem saying it out loud. Maybe I don't love them; maybe they don't deserve that love anymore.

I think I might.

And I think I might hate them too.

One thing I do know is that I miss them. I don't know why, but I do.

I hate that I do.

Nathan does this little nod and lets out this really slow breath.

I can hear him move, watch his hand slip from behind his

head, and move down quickly until it settles across mine, and our fingers mix together again. I don't even fight it, because for once, another person touching me like this doesn't make me sick to my stomach. "No one should have to go through that," he adds, like it's an afterthought, but really, just the idea of him being here is enough right now.

"Can we talk about something else?" I ask. "Please."

"Anything else?"

I just nod.

"I've got this English paper I need to start on."

"Aren't we supposed to be on break?"

That makes him laugh. "Be glad you never had Cooper. Might as well get a head start on it though."

"What's it on?"

"*The Crucible.*"

"Witches, stoning, and drowning. Fun times."

"Mr. Cooper's letting us pick our own topics, and I got nothing. At least it's not due until after break."

"Such a procrastinator," I tease.

"It'd be easier if there was more gay subtext."

I let out something between a scoff and a snort. "I'm almost afraid to ask."

"In tenth grade we read this book about a gang of boys, and two of them were obviously in love, but my teacher turned down my idea for an essay on their relationship."

"Always stifling creativity." Two boys, huh? Well, at least he's comfortable with queer guys.

"Can't spell 'subtext' without 'butt sex.'" He's laughing so hard that he can barely get the words out, and that makes me laugh. And after a few seconds we're both struggling to catch our breath, all the while, our hands never leaving each other's.

"Do you know anything about astronomy?" he asks when we've both gone totally quiet.

"Not a lot. Why? Oh, tell me you're a total astronomy nerd, please."

"Let's see." Nathan points toward the sky and begins to draw an invisible outline. "You see that there? That's Orion. And if you follow the belt there, it leads you right to Leo." I try my best to follow his pattern, but with all the light pollution, it's nearly impossible.

"And that's Sirius." He outlines something else I can't make out.

"How can you even tell?" I ask.

"I have a secret method."

"And that is?"

He leans in closer and whispers, "I'm making it all up."

"You ass." I want to shove him, but that would require the hand that his is currently occupying, and there's no chance I'm giving this up. Not right now.

"I don't even think I could find that North Star thing everyone's been talking about," Nathan adds as we settle back down. "Dad tried to teach me, but at this point I'm totally convinced it's a conspiracy."

"Yeah, they told me that in second grade. Keep the North Star a total secret from one Nathan Allan. Hush-hush stuff, you know?" I can't keep myself from giggling.

"Good, mystery solved. That means I can finally put it behind me." He lets out a long sigh, and then he looks at me.

Silence surrounds us again, but it definitely isn't the bad kind. I don't know how to describe it, but it feels comfortable. Like we don't have to say anything right now.

We're enough for each other. At least in this moment.

"Thanks." I run my thumb over the skin of his hand. I can

almost feel his heart beat now; it's thudding in his chest. Is he actually nervous? That seems so un-Nathan. "Thank you for this," I say. "For sharing this with me."

His mouth spreads into that smile. "No problem."

———

I wake up early the next morning, because of course I do. I can't even sleep in for spring break. Staying asleep has been getting easier, but Dr. Taylor told me it could take a few weeks for us to see if the medication is working, so maybe I've just tricked myself into thinking the problem is going away.

But last night, it didn't feel like the anxiety was what was keeping me awake. Nathan and I sat out on his roof for what felt like decades, until his phone started ringing, his mom letting him know that they were on the way home.

He offered to introduce me, but I turned him down. I don't know, something about meeting his parents, the way they'd probably look at me as this total stranger who's been home alone with their son for who knows how long. I've also been to their house twice now without their knowledge, so I know it's going to have to happen soon. Maybe one day I'll work up the courage.

It's still pretty cool outside, even if it's almost April, so I throw on a hoodie and sweatpants and sit out in the enclosed area of Hannah and Thomas's porch, the screen windows letting in just enough cool air.

My fingers trace my palm, the exact place Nathan held my hand. That moment on the roof, it's like he knew. What exactly he knew, I have no clue. I don't even know what it means, if it's even supposed to mean something. Was he just being there for me? Am I more than a friend? Does he think of me that way now, or is he just really good at being himself? Or am I totally looking way too deep into this?

I have a feeling that last one is probably the right answer.

But I also know that I really liked it, and that it might not be such a bad thing if it happened again.

No, it'd get too complicated with Nathan. If I can't even be out to him, how can I expect him to be my boyfriend? There's too much going on right now, too much to work through. Besides, we're graduating in two months, and he's probably going off to school, and I'm staying here to live with Hannah until I eventually find a full-time job and try to save up enough money for my own apartment. Never leaving this state, or hell, never even leaving Raleigh.

But I can dream, right?

I draw back my hand when I hear the door slide open.

"You're up early," Hannah says, taking the seat across from me.

"Couldn't sleep." I run my fingers along my empty palm again. There's a dog barking in the distance. I wonder if it's Ryder.

"So how was your night?" she asks, cup of coffee in hand.

"Fine." I scratch the back of my head. I can't tell her the truth, but that's an easy enough lie.

"You got in late. Didn't party too hard, right?"

"I had one drink, and something that tasted really gross."

"Yeah, you get used to it."

I debated all night whether I should tell her about the panic attack, but in the end, I know it'll just cause more worry. That's something to tell Dr. Taylor, not Hannah. "I don't think the party life is for me," I try to joke.

Hannah lets out this tired little chuckle, staring ahead at the line of trees that cut off her backyard from the noise of the city nearby.

I wish I could say she hasn't changed in the ten years we've been apart. Still a little pushy without really meaning to be, still headstrong. She is those things, but other than that, there isn't really much I know about her. The age difference meant we weren't really a part of each other's lives. I mean, what teenager wants to hang around their kid sibling? She had her own life, her own friends, her own hobbies. She spent weekends out of the house, and nights locked away in her room.

It dawns on me that as much as she's saved my life, I don't really know my own sister.

"So what are your plans for today?" she eventually asks.

"Nothing." I shrug. I guess I have a whole week to look forward to. A week without the art room, my portrait of Nathan left alone. A week without Sophie or Meleika. "What about you?"

"Thomas is finally catching up on sleep. But I need to go to the grocery store. Want to come with? It's right next to a shopping center. Maybe we can find you some new clothes while we're out."

"We could do that," I say. Maybe this is the chance we've both been waiting for. We're older, and without Mom and Dad around, it might be easier. Besides, I'd rather not have to raid her closet the next time I want to go out. Not that I'm too eager for another party, but you never know when you might need semi-decent-looking clothes.

"You want breakfast? I'm starving," she says after a solid minute of neither of us contributing to the conversation.

"Not hungry."

"Okay." She stands up and walks back inside. I wait until I hear the click of the door before I pull out my phone. I've gone nearly a week without talking to Mariam. Not totally ignoring, but it's been mostly one-sided conversations. I just really haven't felt like talking much at the moment.

Me: *Morning!*

I text them on the off chance they're up. It only takes a few seconds for them to reply. They must be working on something to be awake as early as they are.

Mariam: *heyo! how we doing?*

Me: *Fine, you're up early...*

Mariam: *meetings, planning, editing, articles to write.*

Mariam: *I'm runnin' on fumes, Benji*

Me: *Yikes...*

Mariam: *What about you? Anything new???*

Me: *Not really, school's kicking my ass, dealing with some more stuff.*

Not a great excuse, but hopefully they will understand my radio silence.

Mariam: *Noice! I'm always up for some existential crises.*

Me: *Always a fun time.*

Mariam: *So what's on the agenda for us today?*

Me: *Hannah wants to go out, get some groceries, look at some clothes.*

Mariam: *Nice, nice!*

I rub my face while I consider the pros and cons of telling Mariam about last night, my hand scratching the stubbly hair that's just poking up on my jaw. I yank my hand away and try to forget about it, but I know I won't feel better until I actually shave it off, which I probably won't be able to do until tonight.

A few of the message boards I've read said things like facial hair growth contributes to body or gender dysmorphia. So that was a fun thing to learn. I don't exactly remember when I discovered the whole thing made me uncomfortable. It was just one of those gradual things, like my hair, or my nose.

Mariam: *gasp! I almost forgot! You haven't met the new girl!*

Me: *New girl?*

Mariam sends me a selfie of them with a girl at a coffee shop or restaurant or somewhere. They're both really cute, Mariam as always, their dark purple lipstick matching their hijab. This girl is kissing Mariam's cheek, her hair dyed a similar purple, eye shadow dark. She looks vaguely witchy, and I love it.

Me: *She's so cute!!!*

Mariam: *omg she's so amazing. Her name is Shauna. like we've been out every day this week. We went to the movies last night and she held my hand the entire time and it was PERFECT! Like I think I died and I'm in heaven right now honestly.*

Me: *Sounds nice*

I stare at their messages while I try to imagine Mariam walking down the street, getting to hold hands with their new girlfriend. I don't know much about Mariam's parents, but they've never had any problem with them being nonbinary or pansexual, so Mariam never really had to worry about hiding their sexuality or their identify from their parents.

I hope they know how lucky they are. Of course, they'd also had more than their fair share of problems. When their family lived in Bahrain, things weren't perfect. Mariam's family is Shia, not Sunni, which made things difficult for them.

But after they moved to the United States, things only got worse. Too many times Mariam has told me about people yanking on their or their mother's hijab out in public or walking in front of them while they prayed. And California isn't some 24/7 queer-pride parade. Mariam told me one time that they never go anywhere without two cans of pepper spray, so I don't really have a right to call them lucky, I guess.

Plus, there's the whole YouTube side of things. Those comment sections can get downright hideous.

Mariam: *You okay???*

I stare at their message, thinking about how I could tell them.

Me: *I think I really like this boy...*

But before I press send, Hannah slides open the glass doors and pokes her head outside. "Hey, I'm gonna shower and head out. You want to come with me or stay here?"

I glance at my phone, holding down the backspace button, and watch the message vanish before I look back at her. The dog that might be Ryder is still barking. "Yeah, I'll go get ready."

FIFTEEN

"This one looks good." Hannah grabs a shirt off the rack and holds it out in front of me. "And it goes with your eyes," she adds.

"Yeah, maybe." I take it, adding to the pile I'm trying to balance on my arms. So far, she's handed me a few button-up shirts, three pairs of jeans, and a cardigan. It's going to get too warm for sweaters soon enough, but it's still pretty cute. Cheap too.

"You want to go ahead and try them on?"

"Sure." I glance around for the dressing rooms, one clearly marked "male" and the other "female."

"Sorry, sib," Hannah says, realizing this for the first time.

"It's whatever." I march toward the "male" side and pick one of the empty rooms. I hate trying on clothes. Besides there rarely being gender-neutral changing rooms, I get all hot and sweaty, and changing out of stuff six or seven times tends to get really old really quick.

I stare at the ones Hannah's picked out. There's one we grabbed that I'm actually excited for, this short-sleeve collared shirt, bright floral print set against black. I've always loved these kinds of shirts.

The rest are fairly basic colors. Burgundy, olive green, and purple. It's not that I don't appreciate what Hannah is doing for me, but the second we stepped in, she took charge, heading right over to the "men's" section without giving it a second thought.

I mean, I should expect these kinds of things by now. Every retailer pretty much does the same thing. Men's, women's, and children's sections; even the ones with the neutral changing rooms can't escape the way things are gendered.

And this is just the stuff that fits me best, I guess, with my body type and everything, but still. Sometimes when I was out with Mom, I'd follow her over to the "women's" side of the store, staring at all the options. The really cool baggy sweaters, the tank tops, and the thin, flowy dresses. It was hard not to be jealous, but I knew no matter where I went, I'd never be able to really go out dressed how I wanted to.

Boys aren't supposed to wear dresses. Even if I'm not a boy, even if clothing shouldn't be gendered. Whenever anyone looks at me, that's all they'll see. I sigh, finishing buttoning the shirt and rolling up the sleeves because it's already getting hot in here, the too-bright lights hanging over the naked ceilings. I turn around in the mirror, watching the tag on my arm fly back and forth. It looks nice enough. Maybe I could save this for more special occasions. Not that I have many.

But the more I stare at my body, the more I hate it. It's the same feelings I had before I realized I'm nonbinary. Things just aren't where they're supposed to be, and I feel like I'm larger and smaller than myself at the same time. Like nothing adds up.

"You okay in there?" Hannah asks.

"Yeah." I unlock the door and walk out.

She's waiting on a bench just outside and has the biggest smile on her face when she sees me. "Damn, kid. You look good!"

I can't resist a smile. "You think?"

"Yeah."

I don't want to try on the other ones, but Hannah makes me. "What's the point of buying them if they won't fit you?"

I don't make a fuss about it, but when we're done and she walks over to the other section of the store, I feel the pang in my gut. There are these really cool-looking sweaters, the "two sizes too big" kind that come down to your thighs and swallow your hands. And they're thin but chunky, so they wouldn't get too hot.

"You should get that one," I say.

"Cute." Hannah grabs one, eyeing it before putting it back on the rack. "I don't think it's me though."

I sort of wish she'd see what I'm saying, but she's never really been the best at that. Maybe I could hide it under my clothes, so Hannah won't notice. But there's really no way to sneak it past her, especially if she's footing the bill for all of this.

"What do you think?" She pulls out this bright white dress with red polka dots. I'd never be able to pull off something like that, but I sort of like the idea of being able to wear it. Maybe how it would feel brushing past my legs.

"Looks good," I say.

"You look like you're thinking," she says.

"Huh?"

"Like your brain's busy." She chuckles. "Thomas says I have a look like that too. Maybe it runs in the family."

"Maybe."

She nudges me a little. "So, what're you thinking?"

"Mrs. Liu's doing an art show at school," I say, the excuse coming easy. It's not a total deflection; I have been thinking a lot about the show. I just don't think Hannah would really understand how I'm feeling about everything else.

"Oh, did she ask you to submit one of your paintings?"

"Yeah."

"Are you going to do it?"

I shrug. "Not sure yet."

Hannah scoffs. "Come on, your stuff is amazing. Why wouldn't you?"

"I don't know. Guess I'm just nervous." I don't know why.

It's just a student show. But there's still this bundle of nerves I feel when I think about showing my stuff off to that many people.

I'm just overthinking it; I know I am. Hell, it is just a *student* show; I doubt there will be a lot of people there. But still.

"I'm sure it'll be fine, Benji. You should submit something." Hannah eyes the dress again before putting it back on the rack, and all I want to do is reach out and grab it. She moves closer to the stacked piles of jeans next. "So, are you excited to be out of school? Must be nice to be able to relax for a few days."

"Yeah."

She grabs a pair of black jeans at the bottom of the pile, checks the size, and then shows them to me for approval. I nod, and she throws them in my arms.

"Yeah, maybe."

"You like Dr. Taylor, right?" The question takes me off guard.

"She's fine." Seems like an odd question since I've been going to Dr. Taylor for almost three months now. "Why?"

"Just wondering. I was talking with a friend, the one that referred me. She said that it can sometimes be hard to find a psychiatrist you can stick with, especially on the first try. Dr. Taylor was their fourth option."

"I didn't know you could switch like that."

Hannah eyes me. "Do you want to?"

"No, no. She's great." Besides, I don't think I can handle a new doctor. Start over, come out all over again, talk about Mom and Dad, and Hannah, and things I've already let out into the world. Even if that world only consists of two people.

"What about the medication?" she asks.

I shrug. "I think it's working; I'm not really sure though."

"Have you given any more thought to that support group?"

I freeze. "How do you know about that?"

"There was the pamphlet in your dresser. I promise I wasn't snooping, just putting away some clothes and . . . well . . ."

"Oh. Not really." Please tell me she wasn't going through my things. That she was just putting away socks or shirts that she'd washed, and just opened the drawer by mistake.

"Can I ask a question?" She throws down the other pair of jeans she was eyeing.

"I thought that's what you were doing?" I try to laugh, but I can feel my face heating up.

"Oh, ha-ha." She cackles sarcastically. "But seriously, like, why don't you want to go? Don't you think it'd help?"

"I don't know."

"Have you looked up their website or anything?"

"No." I look around, we're pretty much alone in this section of the store. "I just don't want to come out to a bunch of strangers." That's part of it, but it's also a local group, and I don't think I could handle walking in there and seeing someone from school.

"What about trying it just once? The pamphlet said you don't have to be out or anything. You don't have to talk about why you're there."

"I just really don't want to go." Even if I don't do the whole coming-out thing again, I'll have a room full of people staring at me, wondering why I'm there. And do I really have the right to sit in on their private meetings if I'm not going to share anything?

"I just think it might help."

"Well, I don't think it will. Can we please drop it?"

"Okay," she says defensively, and my heart sinks. She sounds so much like Dad right now. "Do you think you'll ever come out to anyone else?"

"What do you mean?"

"I mean you're only out to who? Me, Thomas, Dr. Taylor. Mom and Dad. Do you think you'll ever come out to anyone else?"

"Why does that matter?" I don't want to get angry, but I also don't appreciate how she's asking all this. Why is this so important to her?

"It was just a question," she argues.

"Well, that's up to me to decide, okay?"

"Ben." She groans. "Listen, I'm sorry, I didn't mean it . . . That wasn't cool of me."

I sigh. Great. "It's fine." I hang my head down and pretend to look at some sweaters.

"No, it's not." She grabs the clothes in my arms. "You want to get out of here?"

Like no tomorrow. "Only if you're ready."

"Yeah, sure. Mind if we still stop by the grocery store?"

"That's fine." I follow Hannah to the checkout line.

"So, when do I get to meet this Nathan kid?"

"What?" Dear God, let these conversations end, please.

"He picked you up last night, right?"

"We're just friends."

"Well, I didn't suggest otherwise." Hannah gives me a sly smile. Dammit. "But if you say so."

"I do say so," I protest, even though part of me wants to ask her what I can do about Nathan. Either how to get rid of whatever these feelings are, or how I can actually get him to maybe, possibly, like me? Because the thought of this is terrifying.

Nope.

I need to distract myself, because I *cannot* do this right now. I stare at the junk that decorates the shelves along the checkout line. Water bottles, ChapStick, "As Seen on TV" stuff, and other things no one really needs or wants until they realize they don't have it.

My eyes settle on the rack of nail polish, all in these sweet-looking pastel colors. I can't help but think about Sophie and Meleika's nails, always flawless. And the hundreds of designs I've seen online, the countless tutorials I've watched.

It's something I've always wanted to do. Another thing to add to the "I'll Never Be Able to Go Out Like That in Public" list. I wonder what Hannah would say if I just picked up a bottle and bought it. She'd probably be more interested in where I got the money to buy it in the first place.

Would she try to fight me on it? Or tell me to take it off before school starts back up? Like I don't already know that. But at least if I did them tonight that would get me a few days, right? I can't wear the clothes I want to wear, or that I think look good, but shouldn't I at least be able to paint my goddamned fingernails?

"Oh, those are cute," Hannah says. She must have caught me looking.

"Huh?" I shake myself out of my trance. "Oh yeah, they're cool."

"You want to try it out?" Hannah asks.

"Huh?"

"You were staring at them for like five minutes. Want to pick out a color?"

"I, um . . ."

Then she giggles. "Go ahead, they're only like five bucks."

Was I that obvious? "No, I . . ." I lose my train of thought looking at all of them again.

"Listen, if you don't pick one, I will, and I'll tie you down while I paint your nails." The woman in front of us glances over her shoulder. I give her what is probably my most awkward smile until she turns back around. "Go on, pick a color."

I grab the light pink and twist the bottle around in my hand. It looks cheap, definitely not the higher-end brand that most people would go for, but I like this one the most.

"Really? Pink? The blue would match your eyes better."

I'm grinning despite myself. "I like pink."

"You do you, little sib. I'll have to teach you a thing or two about picking colors."

Hannah doesn't skip a beat when we get home. She hands me the bags, fishing out the nail polish, and goes straight for the small hallway bathroom to grab a towel, leaving Thomas to get everything else out of the car.

"What are we doing?" He walks around sort of lost and half-asleep.

"I'm painting Ben's nails," she says, then she points at me. "Living room, five minutes."

"Um, okay." I climb up the stairs and drop my bags on my bed. In the living room, Hannah's already waiting for me, of course, sitting on the floor in front of the coffee table. She's grabbed a few extra things, like a long emery board, a tall bottle of something clear, and two smaller bottles that I'm guessing are the base and top coats.

"Sit." She points to the other side of the coffee table. "And give me your hands."

I kneel on the carpet and stick my hands out. "What are you going to do?"

"Dearest sibling, I'm going to file down these claws of yours." She motions to my fingers, which seems like an exaggeration, but I don't argue. They aren't *that* long though. "And then I'll help you paint them."

"It can't be that hard."

Hannah scoffs. "Okay, I'll just sit back and watch. I'm sure that'll go well." She takes my right hand first. "Spread your fingers."

"Okay."

Hannah just rolls her eyes and goes to work. "So, what do you want to talk about? Cute boys? Are you into guys?"

Well. That was fun while it lasted. "I swear to God, Hannah."

"I'm just kidding." Then she waits a beat, maybe deciding whether or not the nail on my index finger is now even. "But also sort of serious. What are you into anyway? Are you into anyone?"

"Yeah, I like people."

"People? Like what kind of people?"

"People people."

"Like boys, girls, other nonbinary people?"

"That gets a little complicated."

"Really?" She blows away a bit of the dust, which doesn't seem very sanitary? I mean, that's my fingernail essentially being filed into dust. Gross.

"I mean, I'm not like the head of the nonbinary committee or anything."

Hannah huffs. "Well, I know that."

"We're not a committee anyway. More of a cult." I laugh at my own joke.

"Is that where you go every night?"

"You got me."

We both laugh, and I feel myself smiling, but then Hannah opens her mouth again. "But, like, for real, it can't be that complicated. Can it?" She blows again, eyeing her handiwork before she decides to start on my other hand.

"It . . . Yeah, it kind of is."

"Why?"

I can't tell her how many times I've had this conversation with myself, trying to work it all out in my head only to never really come to a conclusion.

"Because, okay, so." I take a deep breath. "For a while I thought I was gay." I would see other guys, and I was really attracted to most of them. But it still felt like I was missing something. Something about myself.

Like who you're attracted to and who you are as a person are two totally different things. It's hard to explain not being confident in your own body. It just *feels* wrong, but only you seem to really know how and why it feels that way.

"But that still didn't feel like the answer," I continue. Because it wasn't. And it wasn't until I'd found Mariam's videos that I really felt like I'd found someone who understood what was happening.

"So what about the sexuality thing?" Hannah asks.

"In all honesty, I'm still working through that." Because I'm still attracted to the more masculine-presenting people, but nonbinaryness isn't something you can tell outright, so the boy at the coffee shop who I think is cute could actually be nonbinary.

But I'm still attracted to him. And besides, I don't exactly have a gender, and being gay implies being interested in the same gender.

Like I said. It's complicated.

"So, you're not gay anymore?"

"That's the million-dollar question." I think of myself as bisexual. I'm interested in guys and more masculine-presenting people. But then there are people who argue that bisexuality is only two genders, and that those two genders have to be men and women. I've heard that argument too many times now, so I've learned to just keep it to myself. "For simplicity, I just say that I'm queer, that I have a type." And definitely a lot easier than explaining that I identify as bisexual. And less gatekeeping involved too.

"And what type would that be?"

"Hot people?" I offer, knowing what she's trying to get at.

"Can't believe you're so shallow," she teases.

"Shut up."

"You ever think that 'straight' and 'gay' are gonna be obsolete one day?"

I try to stifle a laugh. "The goal of every queer person is the extermination of the cis, straight, allosexual people."

"So *that's* the gay agenda?" Hannah laughs. "But no, seriously, with all this stuff sort of evolving—sexualities and identities, the binary stuff being challenged more and more— don't you feel like the labels are kind of pointless?"

"Not really. Labels can help people find common ground, can help them connect, with themselves and other people."

"You know a lot about this stuff."

"The internet." And Mariam.

"Don't believe everything you read. But for real, you're a smart kid, Benji." She gives me a quiet smile. "Okay, done. Now since you believe yourself to be a true master of the art"—she slides the glass bottle across the wooden table—"you can try first. All by yourself."

"You trust me?" I twist the cap off and remove the excess polish before I get to work.

"Put your money where your mouth is." Hannah's grinning.

"So can I ask you something? Sort of personal."

"Shoot. I've done enough prying for one day."

"What happened after you left home?" I ask. The left hand is easy, and surprisingly relaxing. I don't know exactly how much I should be putting on each finger, but Hannah hasn't stopped me yet, so I guess it's enough.

"I applied for a few scholarships that I never told Mom and Dad about. One of them was for State, not a full ride, but enough for me to get on my feet. I moved into the dorms, worked my ass off to save enough for the rest of my tuition. I did the basic thing and got a business degree, but it comes in handy."

"Is that where you met Thomas?" I move from finger to finger slowly.

"We didn't start dating until about two years after we graduated, but we actually met sophomore year, which is sort of awkward because we were both dating different people."

"Really?"

"Did I hear my name?" Thomas peers from around the corner, still in his pajamas. Can't blame the poor guy.

"Just telling Benji how we met."

"Oh, did you tell them about the lobster—"

Hannah reaches onto the couch, grabs one of the pillows, and chucks it at Thomas as hard as she can. "Thomas David Waller!" Hannah shouts. Thomas ducks behind the wall just in time, his giggles echoing through the halls.

I'm laughing so hard, I have to put the brush down. "What on earth was that about?"

She huffs, straightening her shirt. "We don't talk about lobster in this house."

"Okay," I say, still laughing. "So, you started dating after college?" I almost can't get my question out.

"Yup. He ended up moving back home. We kept in touch, and then one day he tells me that he's moving back down here to teach, so we hung out more and more and, well." She shrugs her shoulders. "It just sort of happened."

"Uh-huh." I eye my hand.

"Okay, now I *have* to see you try the right one." She leans forward eagerly, on her elbows, and I realize my mistake the second I pick up the brush. This is so awkward, and is this how I held it the last time? It feels so unnatural. I try for my thumbnail first, since that's the biggest, but I somehow manage to fuck it up almost instantly.

"Fine, here." I wipe the coat away before it dries and hand the brush to Hannah.

"Told you," she half sings. I should've just given it to her in the first place. She's so methodical in how she does it, her hands so much steadier than I could've ever dreamed. It only takes her seconds to coat the nails. "Okay. Paint time. Your other hand should be dry enough." She uncaps the actual nail polish and gets to work.

"Do you think college was worth it?" I ask.

"Eh." She shrugs. "Lot of debt, but I like my job."

I dawns on me that I don't even know what my own sister does for work. Four months of living here and I have absolutely no clue what she spends her day doing. "What do you even do?"

That makes her chuckle. "I'm a Realtor. Lots of paperwork, but it's more fun than you'd imagine." She starts on another finger. "Why are you asking about college?"

"Just been thinking about it," I say. "I don't know if it's really for me."

"I know that feeling. Freshman year I sort of had to wonder if it was all worth it. But I knew I couldn't go back to that house."

Not even for me, apparently.

I don't want to think that, but the thought rears its head like an ugly pimple. I have to actually stop myself from saying something I know I'll regret, and I can feel myself tense up. At first, I don't think Hannah notices, but then she pulls the brush away. "You okay, sib?"

"Yeah." I nod. "Just thinking."

I think she believes me, because she dips the brush in the polish again and goes back to work.

"I'm going to take a year off. After graduation," I say, trying hard to get far away from anything to do with home. I'd been thinking about it for a while now, wondering what Hannah might think. She might be like Mom and Dad, demanding I get some kind of higher education. But the more I thought about the idea of four more years of school, the more I hated it. "Maybe I can think about it then?"

"That's probably a good idea. Gap years can be good. Did you apply for anything yet?"

"A few." But whatever I'm sent, acceptances or rejections, will be sent to Mom and Dad's address.

"Whenever you're ready. Thomas and I can help you with loans and paying for stuff." She keeps her eyes on my hand, her tongue peeking out slightly through her mouth.

"You don't have to do that. I mean the whole paying thing."

"It's fine."

"I'll . . . I'll pay you back when I can. Somehow. For all of this."

"You don't have to do that." She finally looks up. "Just consider it payback for all the birthdays and Christmases I missed."

There we go again. I feel the guilt rising up like bile. "Hannah."

"Nuh-uh." She sticks the brush in front of my face. "No arguing, you just worry about graduating right now, okay?"

"I—"

"Benjamin De Backer." She eyes me. "Don't make me send you to your room."

"Okay, okay," I say. "Sorry."

"You just don't need to worry right now, okay? Things are fine. Thomas and I both make plenty, and we also have our savings. You aren't a burden or anything. I want you to know that. Okay?"

I nod and wipe my hands on my knees, but then I stop. I don't know if that'll somehow mess up the paint or something like that. I just *really* don't want to keep talking about it.

Hannah sets to work on the last nail, not really paying attention to me. "And we are done!" She makes a final stroke with the brush and admires her handiwork. "Not too bad, if I say so myself."

I stare at the color, my fingers shaking a little. "Thank you."

"No problem." Then she stops. "Are you going to leave it on for school?"

Part of me just wants to say fuck it, but high schools are rarely the most progressive places on earth, and the ridicule would probably be endless. "No."

"Okay, when you're ready to take it off use this." She hands me polish remover. "Just get some cotton balls and it should come off no problem."

"Thank you."

"Don't worry about it, kiddo." She ruffles my hair and grabs the towel. I just sit there for a while, staring at my hands. "Now let's do the top coat. I don't want all my work to go to waste."

———

"So, do you think you know what triggered it?" Dr. Taylor asks in her usual pose: legs crossed, head propped up with her hand, notepad on her lap.

"I don't really know, there was a lot of noise and people. And this guy, Todd, he was drunk and talking to me and he had me in a headlock for a bit."

"Do you normally have a problem with people touching you, Ben?"

"Not all the time, but there are some days I just can't stand it." I can remember a few times where family members I hadn't seen in ten years pulled me into hugs, or when total strangers tried to shake my hand. Even with Mom and Dad, there were days they'd hug me, or sit close to me on the couch, and I'd feel ill. "Even with people I'm close with."

"Hmmm." Dr. Taylor hums and straightens her glasses.

"It feels worse during the panic attacks."

"Touch aversion can be common in people who deal with panic attacks, or people dealing with anxiety. In fact, there are some people who are just born or develop that way, like asexual or aromantic people."

"Oh," I say. I'd never really thought of myself as ace or aro. I mean, sex isn't really something I have a strong desire for, but it's something I might be open to. And I've had sort-of-romantic feelings for people before. I suppose I'm also *currently* having those romantic feelings.

"Can you remember any other cases where someone touching you like that made you have a panic attack?"

"Not really. I've sort of been thinking something though. Like maybe it wasn't the touching. He just had his arms around me and he wouldn't let go. And there were so many people."

"This was at a party, right?" She writes something down.

I nod.

"Did you have anything to drink?"

"No," I lie, because I'm not exactly sure what she will and won't report to the police, or if she'll even do something like that.

"I'm not going to tattle on you, Ben," she says like she's read my mind, which would probably be a lot easier than all of this back-and-forth. "Lord knows I was eighteen once too."

"I was given a shot, and a sip of beer. I didn't really want them, but everyone was staring at me and I felt like I had to do them."

"I'm guessing you read the warnings about mixing alcohol with your medication?"

I nod, not meeting Dr. Taylor's gaze, as if that'd help me avoid the shame I'm feeling right now. "I'm sorry."

"You're young, Ben, and I understand the desire to fit in with those around you. But alcohol does tend to inhibit your thinking. You made a mistake, just try to be more careful in the future."

"I will." I'd already realized that drinking wasn't for me anyway.

"Do you think your current dosage is doing enough?"

"If I'm being totally honest, no. It doesn't feel like much has changed up here." I point to my head.

"Well, the medication isn't a permanent fix, Ben, as much as we'd like it to be. It's there to help balance you out, but it doesn't get rid of the anxiety."

"I know, I'm just worried I'm taking it for nothing."

Dr. Taylor writes something down. "We'll try a temporary increase in the dosage, see how that works. Sound good?"

I nod. "Yeah."

"The panic attack, do you think it might have been a sensory overload sort of thing?"

"I'm not really sure," I say. Isn't she supposed be the one with all the answers? "Maybe."

"And do you recall what brought you out of this situation?"

"My friend was there, Nathan."

"They brought you through it?"

"Not exactly, but I got outside and he followed me. I guess just having him there helped?"

"So joint effort?" She smiles. "That's something."

"I guess."

"Are you comfortable around Nathan?"

"Yeah, most of the time, at least."

"Most of the time?"

"Sometimes I get really nervous around him."

"Any particular reason why?"

"None that I can think of." Except maybe it's because I like him? And maybe I like the thought of holding his hand, of being close to him. And maybe I want to go further than that. And maybe I'm terrified of what will happen if we do.

"I'm happy to hear you've got someone you can trust," she says, then her eyes move down to my hands. I doubt it's the first time she's noticed my nails, but she hasn't said anything before now. "That's a beautiful color." She nods. "Did you do those yourself?"

"Oh." I stare down at them, resisting the urge to hide them.

I fought with myself a bit before deciding to go out in public with the paint still on. Not that a visit to Dr. Taylor's office is really "public," but it's outside the house. "Hannah did them for me."

"How are you two?" Dr. Taylor asks.

"Fine, I guess." I rub my hands together, trying to feel less self-conscious about the paint.

"You're doing okay? Better? Arguing?" She goes on after I don't answer.

"We're *okay*." I stress the "okay." "Why do you ask?"

"I was curious," she states.

"About?"

"I was mostly curious if you resented Hannah at all?"

I hate that my answer comes out so easily. "A little, I think."

"Do you think she knows that?"

"Well, it's not like I'm eager to tell my own sister how bitter I am." I rub my eyes, the stinging feeling coming back slowly. "I just . . . She got so much, you know?"

Dr. Taylor nods.

"She got to get out, go to school, get a job she loves, find someone who loves her."

"And you were left with your parents?"

"Yeah." I slouch back on the couch, not meeting Dr. Taylor's eyes. "It just . . . It felt like when she left, she just forgot about me. You know?"

"I do."

"I get that she couldn't call, and that it was impossible for her to come back home."

"Well, that doesn't make your feelings any less valid, Ben. You were hurt by what she did, you can't control that. And in that situation, neither could she." Dr. Taylor leaves her notepad on the coffee table and leans forward. "Have you talked to her about this?"

"No." I shake my head. "How could I even do that? After all she's done for me?"

"Does it feel like she's trying to make it up to you?"

"Maybe. I don't really know."

"Perhaps talking with her would be a good thing? Help you get everything out in the open."

"You think so?" I ask.

"I do, and you never know until you try, right?"

I think Dr. Taylor thinks her words will make me feel better, but they don't. There's still this weird feeling in my gut. I don't think Hannah would be mad at me for feeling this way. But I don't know; it feels like if I told her all this . . .

Then things would never be the same.

SIXTEEN

"Ready to go back to school?" is the first thing Mariam says when I accept their FaceTime call.

"Not on your life," I say.

"Come on, only two more months."

"Two and a half," I correct.

They laugh. "So, me and Shauna went out again."

"Shauna?" I rack my brain, trying to remember who that is.

"The girl, the one I'm quite fond of kissing and holding hands with now? Purple hair, sort of looks like she'll turn you into a frog if you wrong her."

Jesus, how could I forget? "Right, sorry."

"You okay?" They lean into the camera. "You seem spacey tonight."

"Just thinking about a lot of things."

"Talk to your enby mama!" They chuckle. "Dr. Haidari is in the building."

"It's a guy."

"Again? Look at you." They cheer. "Different guy or same guy?"

"Same one." I open my mouth before I realize what I'm doing. "Mariam, how do you get someone to like you?"

They let out a little squeal and I have to put them on mute before Hannah or Thomas think something is wrong. "Sorry, I've just been waiting for this day for forever." They pretend to wipe away a tear.

"Love the vote of confidence," I add.

"How does he act around you?"

"The same way he acts around everyone else, pretty much."

"Is it that confusing sort of friendly where you don't know if he really is just being friendly, or if he's flirting with you?"

"Basically." I sigh. "I don't even know if he's queer. Or how the whole nonbinary thing would even work."

"Cross your heart and hope he's bi?" Mariam even makes the little "x" over their chest.

I can't help but laugh.

"What do you like about him?"

"That's kind of the thing. I don't know if I like him, or if I *like* like him."

"Have you ever had a crush before, Ben?"

"Not really? I mean there are people on TV that I find attractive, but no one I've really been attracted *to*, if that makes any sense," I say.

"Not even Chris Evans?" they ask.

"He's too beautiful, that doesn't count."

"True. How do you feel around Nathan?"

It's such a strange feeling, honestly, and I've never really felt that way around anyone before. "He makes me nervous, but not really in a bad way?" It sounds strange when I say it out loud, but that's exactly how it feels.

"Like your stomach gets all weird and you feel like you're going to be sick, but it never happens?"

"Gross, but accurate," I say, because it is. It's the truth.

"Yeah, you're crushing, my friend. Hard-core too."

"Oh." Is it weird that I had to have my best friend confirm this for me? It feels weird. But at least I know for certain now. I have a crush on Nathan Allan.

"Has he said anything about his sexuality or anything?"

"Nope."

"He doesn't know you're nonbinary, does he?"

"I'm not out to him. I don't think I can be."

"Oh, Benji." They sound heartbroken.

"It's fine, I'm getting used to it."

"You shouldn't have to. Has he said anything that makes you think it'd be a bad thing to come out?" they ask.

"Not that I can really think of."

"You just don't want to?"

"I'm worried. He doesn't seem like the kind of person who would out me or hate me. But what if he is?"

I could never imagine Nathan being that kind of person. But once I say those words, there is no taking them back. Now there's no other school for me to transfer to, nowhere left for me to run. I'd be spending the next few months as a pariah.

"Oh, Ben . . . Maybe if you got him talking? Like, bring up something about sexuality or identity?"

"Because that's totally natural and wouldn't be suspicious in the least."

"I wish I knew what to tell you. I'm sorry."

"Maybe I'll get over him," I say. What's the point in pining so much? It won't help me. Won't help him. He deserves something less complicated, more grounded. "He's probably going off to school anyway." And I'll be here.

"High school relationships hardly last after graduation anyway, if that helps."

"It's whatever," I say as my phone starts to buzz on my nightstand. Speak of the devil and he shall text you. Maybe I just talked about him too much, and his Nathan-sense went off or something.

Nathan: *Hey are you busy this weekend?*

"That's him," I say to Mariam.

We haven't really talked much since that night on the roof. Apparently, his parents sprung a trip to visit his grandmother in Maggie Valley at the last minute. Other than that, it's been a handful of texts here and there, but never a conversation lasting more than a few minutes.

Me: *Not really, I don't think so at least. Why?*

Me: *Are you back?*

"What's he saying?" Mariam asks.

"He's talking about this weekend."

"Ohhh, I'll leave you two alone. I'm about to pass out anyway."

I blow a kiss to the camera. "Good night."

Mariam blows a kiss too. "You too, lover kid." I close the laptop, leaving it right where it sits.

Nathan: *Yeah got back this morning, wanted to see if you want to hang out or something?*

Me: *Oh um sure.*

Nathan: *There's this cool thing happening in town on Saturday, want to check it out?*

Me: *What is it?*

Nathan: *It's a surprise ;)*

Nathan: *If you say yes of course.*

Me: *Okay...*

Nathan: *Awesome*

Nathan: *I can pick you up around 5? It doesn't start until 6:30 but we'll want to get there early.*

Me: *That's fine.*

Nathan: *Trying to make sure we get there with enough time. These things can get a little wild.*

Me: *okay... so how was your grandma's?*

I lean back on my bed and grab my sketch pad, needing something to clear my head. I flip past the pages of sketches. Right near the end, there's the one of Nathan. The one of him on his bed, still mostly unfinished. And that just makes me think of his portrait back at school.

If I agree to this art show, will Mrs. Liu want that one? She seemed to really like it. I don't know how I feel about my classmates seeing it. It just feels too personal.

Nathan: *It was cool, a little boring though. She doesn't have wi-fi and the service down there sucks. Basically the only time I could text you was when we went to the Walmart.*

Oh. So he wasn't ignoring me.

Me: *That sucks, I'm pretty much lost without wi-fi*

Nathan: *Same!!!!!!!!*

Nathan: *So, I'll see you tomorrow?*

Me: *Sure*

Nathan: *Awesome, good night Benjamin*

Me: *Good night, Nathaniel*

———

The more I think about what I'm going to wear tonight, the more worried I get. Nathan still won't tell me exactly what we're doing, just that it's something in Pullen Park. He's also forbidden me from looking at the park's website for a list of events. I'm not really clear on how he expects to enforce that last one, but I keep to my promise.

Why am I even this nervous? I shouldn't be.

It's not like this is a date. We're just friends. Friends hanging out with each other and not doing anything else. I stare down at my hands, my nails naked now.

"Hey, do you need any money tonight?" Hannah knocks on my door while I stare at myself in the mirror. I've changed shirts three times now, finally deciding on one of the button-ups she bought me. Not the floral one. I still think that seems like it's meant for a more special occasion. Maybe the art show if I decide to do it.

"I don't really know."

"Okay, here's forty just in case." She hands me two folded twenty-dollar bills. "Unless this is *another* party that you're lying to me about."

I consider turning it down for half a second, but if whatever Nathan is taking me to tonight requires some sort of entry fee, I'll be shit out of luck without it. "Thank you." I take the cash and slide it into my wallet. "And it's not a party, I promise."

"No problem. What time is he coming over?"

I check my phone. "About five minutes ago." Shit, I'm already late. I run to Hannah and Thomas's bathroom to steal some of Thomas's cologne, because apparently, I'm going all out tonight. I even stop in front of the mirror to try and put *some* effort into my hair, but there's really no fixing this mess. Maybe I should ask Hannah to cut it, but I sort of like it this way. Before I leave the bathroom, I take my second dose of Xanax for the day and make sure to jot down the date and time in the little notebook Dr. Taylor gave me.

After triple-checking I've got everything—phone, keys, and wallet—I wave good-bye to Hannah and Thomas. They're watching some reality show and eating takeout in the living room. "Stay safe, kid." Thomas waves to me.

"No promises," I yell from the door. "I'll be home later."

"Midnight at the latest, please!" Hannah calls back.

Nathan's just pulling into the driveway when I close the door behind me. "Sorry I'm late, Mom wouldn't let me leave without walking the dog," he says after I buckle my seat belt.

"It's fine. So still no hints about where we're going?"

"Ah-ah." He wiggles his finger. "It's a surprise, but I'll tell you it involves one of the greatest movies of all time."

"That still sounds vaguely malicious." I watch him put the car in reverse and back out of the driveway. "Park and a movie, huh?"

Nathan glances over to me, grinning like always.

Pullen Park is huge. Like *huge*, huge. I never really made it a habit of going to parks, even as a kid. This one time I saw a needle on a jungle gym, went and told Mom, and we never went to that park, or any park, ever again. Can't say I blame her after she explained what could've happened if I'd picked it up.

"So, what are we doing here?"

We've just been walking around now. Apparently, there are no parking spots close to whatever this event is, so we had to park on the opposite side. Which means a lot of walking.

"Ever heard of a little movie called *Star Wars*?"

"No. Tell me more!" I give him some side-eye and he just starts shaking his head. "That doesn't explain why we're in a park. Or why you're carrying around a basket."

"It's a showing. The city does this about twice a month, they set up this stage and project a movie on the screen for everyone to watch."

"Oh, so why are we here so early?"

"To get the good seats." He pats at the basket in his arms, and I swear it's the most stereotypically wicker thing I've ever seen. "These things are always wild. If you don't get here early, you'll be stuck in the front section. Not fun."

"So we get to sit here for an hour and wait?"

"They play music," Nathan protests. "Besides." He swings the basket toward me. "I've got a picnic."

"A pic-a-nic?" I try to snatch it away, but he pulls back at the very last second.

"But my *Titanic* joke was dated, huh?" We finally reach this huge gate that leads right to the concert arena, which isn't much more than a hill with a stage. There are concrete sections near the front for chairs, but the majority of the arena is grass.

"Wow," I say.

"It's just like a theater. You want to go for the middle section." Nathan points to where the crowd is beginning to linger. There might be around thirty people already. "See, most people want to go to the front or to the very back, but then you don't get that crisp sound."

"'Crisp sound'?" I try not to giggle. "How much can I pay you to never say 'crisp' again?"

"*Very* funny." His mouth spreads into that big grin. "This is a good spot." Nathan reaches into the basket and pulls out this absolutely huge blanket, letting the slight breeze unfold it for him before settling it down.

"Here. Take a seat, my prince."

"Prince?" I feel myself get smaller. He doesn't know, he can't know. Just stop making a big deal out of it.

He grabs the basket and gets down on his knees. "What's wrong with being a prince?"

"Nothing." I try to shake that weird feeling. "Nothing. So what do we have?"

"I bought a few sandwiches. But I wasn't sure what you like." Nathan opens the basket and starts to lay everything out. "There's ham and cheese, turkey with lettuce and bacon. And in case you're vegetarian, there's a veggie one. No cheese either, so it's vegan too!"

I eye the choices, grabbing the ham and cheese.

"Classic, nice." Nathan picks the turkey.

"What do we do while we wait?"

"We eat, we talk, do a little one-on-one bonding." The music starts to echo over the loudspeakers at the back of the arena.

"Sounds fun." I unwrap the sandwich and take a bite. "So . . ." I swallow.

"So . . ." he says, rocking back and forth a little.

"What do you want to talk about?" I ask.

He bites into his sandwich again. "Well, as much as I'd love to sit here and have an awkward back-and-forth with you, I think we need to have a serious discussion."

"What?" My mind races with at least a thousand possibilities. Did he figure it out somehow? Or maybe the night at Stephanie's really did scare him, and he wants to know exactly what's wrong with me. Maybe he doesn't want to be friends anymore? No, that's silly. Why would he invite me out like this, make us a dinner, if he wanted to stop being my friend?

Nathan grins from ear to ear. "I think we should get to know each other a little better."

"Oh. Um . . . Okay?"

"Come on, I've known you for almost three months now and I barely know the first thing about you." He starts counting off.

"You like to draw, last name is De Backer, you live with your sister, you're a little weird, but I like that about you."

"Am not," I argue.

"Dude, come on." He picks up the veggie sandwich. "I didn't even know if you're vegetarian or not."

"Whatever," I huff. "So, what do you want to know?"

He leans back on the blanket, folding his arms under his head. "Hold on, have to think of a good one." He thinks for a moment. "Okay, so what's your favorite color?"

"I like green, and pur—"

"Ah-ah. I said *favorite*. Not the ones you just like."

"You're going to laugh at me." I put my sandwich on the blanket, my appetite suddenly forgotten.

"I promise I won't laugh. Pinky promise." He sticks out his pinky.

I take his finger. "Pink. I like pink."

"Pink is a perfectly acceptable color. Why would I laugh?"

I shrug. Because pink is "girly," because for some reason even colors have been assigned gender. Because I'm supposed to be a boy, and boys aren't supposed to like pink.

"Is there a particular shade of pink that you're fond of?"

"I thought it was my turn?"

That makes him laugh. And I notice for the first time how breathy it is, the way his chest moves, and how his mouth somehow gets bigger, even though that seems impossible. "Touché, De Backer. So what's your question for me?"

"You said you moved when you were young." There is *something* I want to ask him, but it seems like too much.

"True, but not exactly a question."

"Do you like it here?"

"It's nice. I've made a lot of new friends, but sometimes I miss my old ones. Didn't really have a choice." He tries to laugh it off. "Mom got a better job offer, and we couldn't pass it up."

"Oh, that sucks." He seems so subdued in an instant.

"What about you? Do you like it here?"

I pick at the grass absentmindedly. "It's nice," I say, really not knowing what else there is to say. "The whole city thing is taking some getting used to. Goldsboro's a small city. The kind where everyone pretty much knows everyone, and you're somehow related if you look far enough up a family tree."

"Ugh," Nathan scoffs. "I hate the country."

"It's quiet," I add.

"Sometimes a little noise isn't such a bad thing." Nathan sits up to fold up his sandwich and leaves it beside mine. "Your turn."

"All right." I rock back and forth, trying to think of what I can ask. "And I can't pass?"

"Nope!"

"Okay. You like to read, what's your favorite book?"

Nathan leans back and lets out a low, long groan. "How could you make me choose?"

"Stop avoiding, Allan." I grin. "I've answered your tough ones."

"But this is about books!" Nathan scoots in closer. "Out of all the ones I've read, you expect me to pick just one favorite?"

I roll my eyes. "Okay, whiny baby, I'll amend it. What is your favorite kind of book?"

"Much more manageable," he says. "Still tough, but I think I could answer it."

"Are you planning on doing that anytime soon?" I ask.

"Smartass." Nathan lets out this low laugh. "I like the kind

I can lose myself in, the ones that let me get away for a hundred pages at a time."

"Huh." I stare at him for a few seconds.

"Acceptable for you?" He's still grinning.

I nod. "For now. Your turn."

Nathan takes a deep breath, I watch the slow rise and fall of his chest. "Okay, waffles or pancakes?"

"Seriously?" I eye him.

"Answer the question, De Backer."

"Waffles."

"The right answer. Clearly the superior breakfast treat."

"Is that a deal breaker?" I ask.

"You mean choosing between some soggy, cakey mess, and a delicious treat? No, not at all."

"What about French toast, or crepes?"

"Well, they're perfectly fine substitutes, but the waffle has everything. It's crisp—"

I stop him. "There's that word again."

Nathan rolls his eyes and just keeps going. "It's the perfect shape, with little syrup holders, and you can have so many flavors too."

"Wow, a real Waffle Master." I'm trying not to laugh.

"It's a serious matter, Mr. De Backer." He's still laughing. "Okay, now you."

I don't think it's actually my turn, but if he insists. "Do you want to write one day?"

"Maybe? I don't care for fiction, writing it anyway. I like writing papers and things like that, the research. It's fun."

"Really?"

"I just like it. I always learn something new when I have to write a paper" is all he says about that. "What do you like to do? I mean besides draw."

I turn on my side so I can lie down beside him. "That's pretty much it."

"You don't have any other hobbies?"

"Not really." I stop myself. "Dad and I didn't do much together." I think this might be the first time I've properly discussed my parents with Nathan. "Mom likes to cook, and I'd help her sometimes."

I wait for him to ask about Mom and Dad, but he doesn't. Nathan just keeps looking forward. "Your turn," he says quietly.

"Do you have any secrets?"

He doesn't answer right away, which scares me. Clearly this isn't the easiest question, but it's out there before I realize it. "That sounds ominous," he finally says. "I can promise you I'm not an axe murderer or anything." Nathan turns over on his side, using his arm as a pillow.

"I didn't mean like that. Like nothing bad."

"So what *do* you mean?"

"Just like . . . Is there a secret you have, that shouldn't be a big deal? That you should be able to tell people, but you just can't? Like, it isn't even a bad thing, but it feels like people will think it is."

I expect him to laugh in my face, call me some sort of freak. Or prod and poke at me until I tell him the truth. "Yeah, I know exactly what you mean." His words surprise me. He speaks slowly, his brown eyes staring right into mine. "And it's terrifying."

"Sorry." I try to laugh. "Didn't mean to get so deep."

"No, it's cool. Just a little unexpected." He takes in a heavy breath, his chest rising and falling. "I put my milk in my cereal first."

It's so random I can't help but laugh at him. "What?"

"When I make cereal, I put the milk in first. It's just always tasted better that way."

"How can it taste different?"

He shrugs. "Just does."

"Is that your big, deep dark secret?"

"Not even close, but I can't totally give away all my mystery. I do have to save *some* things." He winks, and the temperature around me definitely rises.

I try to think about something I can share, but nothing as random as putting milk in a bowl before cereal comes to mind. "I put my socks and shoes on one at a time."

"What does that even mean?"

"I do that thing where I put on one sock, then the shoe. Then the other sock, and the other shoe. One at a time."

"Why?"

"Why do you put milk first?" I ask again.

"You got me there, De Backer." He lets out this long sigh and smiles.

Watching a movie in a park is a totally different experience. For one thing, people sneak in drinks. No one gets wasted, but it makes the crowd rowdier. And there's applause at famous lines, and when the Death Star blows up. There's some sniffling at Leia's hologram message, and people full-on bawling at the award ceremony, which probably has more to do with the alcohol than anything else.

But I'll happily admit that it is a lot more fun with other

people. Definitely a lot more fun with Nathan. At a point about halfway through, I catch him mouthing along to the lines, staring wide-eyed at the screen.

"Leia was always my favorite," he says when he catches me looking. "I cried for two weeks when Carrie Fisher died."

"I was always more partial to Luke." He wasn't my "gay-wakening," as Mariam so graciously put it, but he was close. In fact, *Star Wars* is entirely unfair when it comes to attractive leads. Mark Hamill, Carrie Fisher, *and* Harrison Ford? Totally and completely uncalled for.

We stay around for the credits, waiting and watching for everyone else to pack up their things and head out. Nathan balls up the blanket and tosses it into the empty basket, discarding our half-eaten sandwiches in the trash can by the entrance.

"Did you want to grab dinner or something?" he asks. "I know the sandwiches weren't much."

My appetite is long gone, the bread weighing heavily on my stomach even though I only ate about half of it. "If you want to. I'm not that hungry."

"Nah, we'll go some other time."

I check my phone. "It's only eight thirty. Seems early to head back home."

"Up for a little stroll?"

"Sure."

"Come on." We walk back to the car and Nathan leaves the basket in the back seat.

"So where to?"

"Want to see the lake?"

"There's a lake?"

"Well, it's more of a glorified pond, but they put these string lights over the bridge and it's really pretty at night."

"Sounds nice."

"The pond it is."

I'm not sure exactly how far away this pond is, but I definitely don't see any bridges or ponds around me. At least it's nice out, and maybe this is just what I need.

"So, did you like the movie?" he asks as we start down the trail.

"I don't know, the twenty other times I've seen it were great, but this last time . . . The magic's gone, you know?"

"Okay, Mr. Sarcasm, that's enough." He bumps into me with his shoulder.

I swallow the lump in my throat. "It was great, thank you."

"Next month is *Empire*. We can go if you want."

"That'd be nice," I say.

I follow Nathan closely. At least it isn't too crowded anymore. I guess most people were ready to go home after the movie.

"Hey." Nathan stops short, so I nearly run into him. "You okay?"

"What? Yeah," I say quickly, trying to remember where I am. "Sure."

"You seemed a little spacey there. I said your name like five times."

"Oh, sorry. Got lost in my own head, I guess."

"I know the feeling. What were you thinking about?" he asks me.

"Oh, um. Nothing," I tell him.

"Really?"

I nod.

"Want to know what I was thinking about?"

I feel this tiny flare of panic, like he's going to pick now to drop some bomb on me. I have to tell myself to stop it. He isn't going to do that, especially now. It's not going to happen.

But I don't quite believe myself.

"Sure."

"I was thinking about Ryder," Nathan says. "Specifically this one time when we went to this specialty pet store downtown and bought him these chocolate things that were supposed to be safe for him to eat."

"What happened?"

"The little punk wouldn't eat them. I spent twenty dollars on treats just for him, and he turns his nose up at me."

I snort. "What a jerk."

"I told him that too. He just gave me those big eyes, and I couldn't stay mad at him."

"How old is he?" I ask.

"Nine. Mom got him for me when we first moved here, thought it might help the transition to a new place."

"That's cool. I've always wanted a cat." Mom and Dad were strictly no mammalian or reptilian pets. They did let me have a fish when I was ten though. A little goldfish that I named Goldie. Because I was definitely creative with my name choices.

"It's just up here." He points, and I can just barely make out the lights along the railing. "Come on!" He grabs my hand, and we race down the trail and toward the bridge. Not slowing down until we're a yard or two away.

I wait for him to give me back my hand, but he doesn't. It's nice. As nice as that night on the roof. Even better now, because it's getting colder and he's so impossibly warm. I try not to think about how this is what it would be like. If we could be together, if we could hold hands and walk around town without having to hide ourselves.

No. I push the thoughts away. I can't. That'll only make all of this worse.

"You should see this place on the Fourth of July. They have fireworks over the water and everything." It's dark, the streetlights along the walkway and the string lights on the railing only doing so much.

I let Nathan lead us right to the edge, and he finally lets go of my hand.

I don't have the courage to tell him to take it back.

He wasn't wrong, it's pretty. It's small, but it's enough, with this little beachy area on the other side of the water, and a dock filled with those plastic paddleboats people love to rent for some reason.

"The water creeps me out," I say, peering over the wood railing, staring at the way the water moves as the fish swim.

"You're scared of a pond?"

I shrug. "Just never been a fan of water. One time my parents took me to the beach, and I cut myself on a shell. That wasn't fun." I still have the pale white scar along the bottom of my foot. That was also my first time in an emergency room. Apparently, it had cut so deep that it wouldn't clot, and Mom got scared.

"Yikes."

"Another time I was going swimming, and a bunch of fish kept going by me and it creeped me out. So, I started crying." Dad told me to "man up," but I just spent the rest of the day under the umbrella, the sand sticking to my legs like some tight second skin.

Nathan starts laughing uncontrollably, trying to hide his face in his hands. "You've been traumatized by the ocean, oh my God."

"I was five, leave me alone." I shove him. "Besides, you've seen half the things those marine biologists find down there. The ocean's creepy as hell."

Nathan does this thing between a scoff and a laugh. "Can't argue with you."

I lean against the railing alongside him. "I hate the beach too."

"Why?"

"I hate sand. It's coarse, and it gets everywhere." I wonder if he'll catch on.

Nathan groans so loud the people jogging at the other end of the park turn to look at us. "Please tell me you didn't just quote the worst movie of the saga."

"Thought you might like that."

"I hate you," he says with a smile.

We both laugh until we can't anymore, until the night air is filled with nothing but the sounds of the water. It's hard to know that just beyond those walls we walked past is an entire city of people. This place is too quiet for that.

"Tonight was fun," I say.

"Yeah?"

"Yeah. Thanks for inviting me. I know . . . I know I haven't been the easiest person to get along with."

"It's okay." He waits a beat. "Easy people are boring."

Maybe now is my moment. The moment I tell him the truth, or the moment that I reach over and kiss him. Something. I feel like I owe him that much at least. I weigh it all in my head, but the answer is obvious.

"Hey, Ben."

"Yeah?" I look up at him. And that makes the decision for me. I can't tell him; I can't ruin this. And I don't even want to think about how he'll think of me after. I don't want a world where Nathan Allan hates me, even if the chances of that happening are so very, very slim. I just can't.

"Tonight was the first time you've talked about your parents." He waits. "Like *really* talked about them."

"Huh." I guess he's right. "Sorry."

"No, it's cool, I just noticed." He takes in a breath and lets it out slowly. "I can't imagine what that feels like, to just be left behind like that. Especially by people who are supposed to love you."

"I think they did love me," I say. "And maybe they still do. I know a part of me still does. I just . . . I really thought it'd be okay."

"This is the secret, isn't it? The big one?"

I nod. Because I owe him that.

"Do you really think you'd ever speak to them again? After they did that."

"Now who's asking the heavy questions?"

"Oh." Nathan's eyes widen. "Sorry . . . I didn't even . . ." he stammers. "Don't answer that."

"No, it's . . . fine," I say. Truthfully, that's another question I don't know the answer to. I'd like to be able to give Nathan a firm no. They left me, punished me for just trying to be myself. They don't deserve to ever see me again. I've imagined a dozen scenarios. Going back to their house and telling them off. Sometimes I'm with Hannah, or Thomas. Other times I'm alone.

But they're my parents, and I can't imagine never seeing them again. I don't really want to think how our last real conversation was them yelling and shouting for me to get out of their home. Our home.

"I don't know," I finally say.

"Hey." He takes my hand. "They don't deserve you. You're ten times the person they are, combined, even."

"Thanks," I say.

"Whatever happens"—his grip tightens a little—"I wish you all the best, Benjamin De Backer." He says it with a smile. "You deserve it."

———

I get home later than I mean to. All the lights downstairs are off, and the garage is closed, so I have to go in through the back door. Nathan's waiting for me to pop out the front door and let him know I'm safe inside. I climb the stairs, let Hannah and Thomas know that I'm home, and crawl under the sheets of my bed.

Except I can't sleep.

For at least an hour and a half, I toss and turn, closing my eyes and trying to will my body to rest. The thing is, I don't think this is my anxiety. This feels different, like my mind is too busy to shut down like it's supposed to. Which maybe means this *is* anxiety, but it doesn't feel like it normally does. It's working overtime, and it's thinking too much about what Nathan said.

About Mom and Dad.

I pull off my sheets and head back downstairs, careful not to be too loud. Not that there's really anything wrong with what I'm doing.

If Thomas or Hannah wake up I'll just say I was getting a glass of water, or trying to get in touch with Mariam, or something. I grab the laptop from its space on the coffee table, and log in to Facebook, something I haven't done in months. I never even wanted the damn thing, but Mom wanted to be able to tag me in things, and all my classmates who hadn't yet discovered Twitter or Tumblr talked about Facebook like it was the "new" thing. Seriously, we were always so behind in Goldsboro, even on social media.

The first thing I see is my own profile. A weirdly angled selfie I probably thought looked good a year ago when I took it. Then I see the little red icons in the corner. A few notifications, photos I've been tagged in for some reason. But my eyes go right to the message icon, the little red button hanging over it.

There's just one.

And it's from Mom.

I freeze, staring at the little preview Facebook gives me.

Brenda De Backer has sent you a message: Ben... I don't know what to even say to you—

And it just cuts off, waiting for me to actually open it to read the rest. But I can't.

My stomach clenches up, and I'm stuck here, staring at her name, the miniaturized version of her profile picture. One of her and me at the beach. I would almost believe it was some kind of insult, but it's been that way forever now. I look so different. My hair's shorter; I'm smiling. That picture has to be at least two years old now. Back when I was just starting to question everything, when I thought that maybe I was gay, and that would be all I had to hide.

It's almost like someone else is controlling my hand, and I sit helpless as the cursor moves over to her name. Mom's profile comes up, the last statuses she's posted. Nothing too major. Mom was never huge on Facebook, but there are some new photos. Some of her and Dad at the house, out in the yard, at dinners. And after some scrolling, I get to the pictures with me.

"Day out with my baby boy!" one says.

I actually miss them.

The cursor hovers over Mom's message again, and this time,

I open it. It's dated over three months ago. And there's nothing before it except one telling her my phone had died at school and that I wanted to stay late for a little extra tutoring.

Ben... I don't know what to even say to you. Your father and I... we've realized what we've done, and we're hoping we can make it right with you. I'm not sure what else I can say besides we're sorry, and that we were just confused about what was happening. We know you're staying with Hannah, and we're hoping you won't tell her about this message. Maybe we could meet one day, in the city or something, and just talk? Please, Ben? You're our child, and while we may not understand this part of you, your father and I would like to try and make amends.

I hate the way things were left, and I don't think I could ever forgive myself if the last times I spoke to both my children were fights. Please, Ben, just consider it?

I read the message again, and then a third time, this numb feeling washing over me as I try to take in the words all over again. But they eventually lose their meaning, and I click on the little box to type my reply.

The words never come though, and after another half an hour, I log out of my account and close the laptop.

SEVENTEEN

I can't get Mom's message out of my head for the rest of my break. I even download the Facebook app on my phone so I can keep reading it, which probably isn't healthy, but I can't help myself. I just keep rereading it and rereading it, over and over, wondering what changed.

Since it took me so long to find the message, I also decided to check my email accounts. There's my actual, personal email that doesn't get anything other than Michaels coupons. I doubt Mom even knows that address. Then my old email for Wayne, which I guess Mom does know because the exact same message is sitting there too.

The message that would've been sent almost a month after I left.

After they *made* me leave.

I try to fill most of the nights with some kind of noise. When Mariam can't FaceTime or text, I go down to the living room with Hannah and Thomas. I actually think about telling Hannah, but that would probably end with disaster. Part of me wants to talk to Nathan too, but really, I feel like the only person with the right answer would be Dr. Taylor.

Maybe she can talk me through this.

Except we don't have an appointment until next Thursday. I guess I could ask for an earlier time, but I feel like that might make Hannah suspicious. She'd definitely know something was wrong then. Besides, there's so much to do at school now.

It's definitely getting closer to . . . well, everything. So far, I've gotten forms about tutoring for final exams, and even a few people wanting me to tutor them in Calculus; a flyer for senior night; information on prom and graduation tickets. It's almost hard to swallow. Just a few short weeks, and this will all be over.

———

"Hey, I've got something for you." Nathan digs around in his backpack during homeroom.

"What is it?" I eye the monstrosity in Nathan's hands. It's wrapped mostly in masking tape, but I can see the cartoon faces of BB-8 and Oscar Isaac poking through in a few places.

"It's a present," he says slowly. "You open it."

I take the bundle and stare at it.

"You know, you're pretty bad at this whole opening thing." He pulls his chair closer. "Go ahead, I want to see your face."

I try my best to unwrap it carefully, but with the tape the wrapping paper just sort of rips off in clumps. And underneath it all is a brand-new sketchbook. Hardcover, spiral bound, no doodles on the front, or notes or extra pieces of paper poking through the edges.

"I . . ."

"Thought you might need a new one, your other one was looking a little messy."

"Thank you." I look up at him, and he's smiling like a total goof.

"My pleasure. I meant to give it to you the night we saw the movie, but it totally slipped my mind."

"It's perfect." The bell rings, and all our classmates rush out.

We look at each other for just a beat too long. "Well, I guess I'll see you in Chem."

It's a decent distraction from Mom and Dad, at least for a little while. But there's still this gnawing at me. Maybe I should meet with them, just to hear what they have to say. Realistically, I don't think I could ever go back to their house, but just because they messed up once doesn't mean we can't fix what's left between us.

Right?

Hannah won't be too pleased, but maybe she'll understand, and maybe this will be her shot too. It won't be perfect, but maybe we'll get to be a happy family one day.

———

"How was the rest of your break, Ben?" Dr. Taylor asks me when we're both seated in her office. The door closed, that wall between me and Hannah up.

"Good." I feel myself relax on the ugly yellow couch. Things are definitely getting easier with Dr. Taylor. I don't mind the appointments nowadays, and I think they're actually helping me. "I didn't do much, I hung out with my friend Nathan a little," I say. "How was yours?"

"Oh, well." Dr. Taylor chuckles. "Unfortunately, I don't get much of a break, but my daughter was excited. I took a few days off and we went down to South Carolina to see my parents."

"That sounds nice," I say. I think this is actually the first time I've heard Dr. Taylor mention family. There's something sort of neat about it, imagining this whole life she has that I don't even know about.

"Is there anything specific you wanted to start the session with, Ben?" she asks.

"Actually, yeah. I really wanted to talk about something that happened."

"Okay." She clicks her pen, always at the ready. "Go ahead."

"I found a message from my mother, on Facebook. It's a few

months old at this point, but the other night I was talking with my friend. He knows I was kicked out, and it got me thinking about what they'd been doing since I left."

Dr. Taylor hangs on to my every word. I mean, she always does that, but there's something different in her expression now.

"My mom apologized, she wanted to see if I would meet with her and Dad so we could talk." I pull out my phone and bring up the message, letting Dr. Taylor read over it quickly.

"I see, and how did it feel, seeing that?"

"It was . . . weird. I felt sort of numb."

"Do you think she really means it?" Dr. Taylor gives my phone back. "The apology?"

"I don't really know, I guess it's hard to tell over the message. Besides, it's so old, who knows if they feel the same way now."

"Have you thought about telling Hannah?"

"Oh God, no, that wouldn't be pretty," I say a little more loudly than I probably should.

Dr. Taylor actually chuckles a bit, which makes me feel better. "So, do you want to meet with them?"

"That was what I wanted to ask you. If you thought it was a good idea."

"Well." She lets out a slow breath. "That can be a tricky question. On the one hand, you want to hear them out, don't you?"

I nod.

"And on the other," she continues, "was their behavior really something you could see forgiving?"

"I'm not sure." I don't want to think back to that night, but I can't help it. So cold, so alone, scared out of my freaking mind. And all because of them. "I want to think they've changed, but I don't want to open myself up like that again."

"It's a scary thought." Dr. Taylor sighs. "Honestly, I'm not comfortable suggesting you go. You've made a lot of progress, Ben, and seeing them again could potentially undo months of work on your part."

I sigh. I figured she'd say that. And it does make sense. Hell, the night they showed up at Hannah's should be enough to convince me to just ignore the message. Delete my Facebook so they can't contact me again.

But they know where Hannah lives. They *know* where I am. So if I just delete my Facebook, there's still the chance they'll just show up on her doorstep one day. And them showing up unannounced won't be pretty.

"At the end of the day, it's your call, Ben. I can't stop you."

"Hannah would go ballistic if she ever found out," I say.

"And that's her battle to fight, not yours. Maybe I'm wrong. Perhaps this could be a healing thing? Maybe it will bring all four of you together."

"You think?"

"I don't know for certain. I can't promise you'll meet with them and everything will have magically changed, and they'll be as accepting and loving as you'd dream they'd be."

"Right." I feel my stomach lurch. "I think I want to try."

Dr. Taylor nods her head slightly. "Can I offer some advice?"

"Isn't that why you're here?" I try to laugh.

"True." Dr. Taylor shows off her bright smile. "If this is something you decide to do, maybe you should have a friend with you. This boy from school maybe?"

"I don't know if I can do that. I'm not out to him yet."

"Understandable, but perhaps just having him close by would inspire some confidence?"

"Maybe." I can't imagine asking Nathan to be a part of this. But the idea of him being there, even if he just stands outside while we talk or something, it does make me feel better. That would take a lot of explaining on my part though, and I don't know if I can do that to him.

"Ben?" Dr. Taylor peers over the frames of her glasses.

"Sorry," I say, rubbing my hands on my knees. "I think I'm going to do it. I want to talk to them, to hear their side of things."

Dr. Taylor's mouth is nearly a straight line. "Just be cautious, okay?"

"I will."

The second I get home, I head up to my room, making sure the door's closed. That probably seems a little too suspicious, but let Hannah and Thomas think what they want. I open Facebook on my phone and go right to my messages, rereading the one from Mom again. I've lost count of how many times I've read this thing over the last week. Parts of it are burned into my memory, other parts I forget are there until my eyes glaze over them again. I click on the box to type my reply, but the words still won't come. I've tried and tried to figure out how I'd reply, but I still don't know what I should say.

A text from Mariam pulls me away from the app, their message flashing along the top of the screen.

Mariam: *Hey random question...*
Mariam: *You live in NC right?*
Me: *Yeah...*
Mariam: *Awesome!*

I almost ask them what's going on, but they respond a few seconds later.

Mariam: *What city?*

Me: *Raleigh*

Mariam: *Excellent!*

Me: *Why?*

Mariam: *Reasons...*

Me: *You plan on revealing those any time soon?*

Mariam: *I'm finalizing my tour schedule*

I swear I can know Mariam for the rest of my life, and I don't think I'll ever get used to them saying "tour schedule." Or the fact that they're basically paid to give speeches and discuss being queer, and what it means to them. Then I realize what they're trying to get at.

Me: *Wait... does that mean what I think it does?*

Mariam: *That I'm going to Harry Potter World after I talk at the University of Florida? Hell yeah!*

Me: *Mariam...*

Mariam: *What! I get really excited about Harry Potter*

Me: *Are you coming to Raleigh?*

Mariam: *Maybeeeeeeee ;)*

Mariam: *There's this support group there, they wanted me to come and speak.*

The support group. The brochure is still stuffed away in my dresser, under piles of useless paper I've gotten from school.

Mariam: *They partnered with one of the colleges there, NC State?*

Me: *Yeah*

Mariam: *A mouthful.*

Mariam: *They want me to do a little seminar for the group since the university talk is just for students.*

Me: *Oh cool*

Mariam: *My friend, you are not nearly as excited as you should be.*

Mariam: *We're finally going to get to meet! Like in person, like I'm gonna be standing there and you're gonna be standing there and it's going to be magical!!!!*

Me: *No, it's cool. I'm excited*

Mariam: *Really not coming across the chat, friendo*

Me: *It's um... It's weird.*

Mariam: *What up?*

For a split second, I think about telling Mariam, but I really just feel like they'd try to talk me out of it.

Me: *Nothing. What's the name of the group you're speaking for?*

Mariam: *Safe Space Project*

Me: *That's the support group my therapist wanted me to go to.*

Mariam: *Oh, did you ever go?*

Me: *No*

Dr. Taylor and Hannah have both stopped bringing it up, thankfully, but I find myself thinking about it every few days. Maybe it wouldn't be so bad to start going in the summer, when I wouldn't have to deal with anyone at school if they saw me at the meeting, so perhaps that would make things easier? Maybe by then I can work up the courage to actually come out.

Mariam: *I understand, it can be scary*

Mariam: *Either way we're hanging out, seminar or not*

Me: *You know it*

Mariam: *Oh, so guess what happened to me today with Shauna...*

Everything sort of feels like it's crowding around me all at once. Like I have to make a fucking list of everything that's going on. Mrs. Liu keeps asking about the art show. It's definitely happening, she has the support of her other students, who want to start meeting after school to plan everything.

But I still can't give her an answer, and I don't know what's really stopping me. I just hate this pressure, and her constant reminders aren't helping.

There's also Mom and Dad.

I feel like every time Hannah looks at me, she knows. She doesn't, but I feel so damn guilty. And I still don't have a proper response to Mom's message. I keep typing things out, but nothing seems right. What do you say to the people who raised you after they no longer want you?

Then there's the actual meeting. The idea of being alone with them, it's terrifying. I can't ask Hannah to come with me for obvious reasons. And I don't want to force Thomas to lie to her and go with me. It seems like too big a thing to ask Dr. Taylor.

So that just leaves Nathan.

And somehow, asking him seems scarier than anything else.

"Ben?" Meleika nudges me with her shoulder.

"Huh? Oh, sorry."

"I asked if you were going to be part of that art show Mrs. Liu's planning?"

"Oh, I don't know." Then I think about it. "How do you even know about it?"

"She's already advertising for it." Meleika reaches into her backpack. "She wanted the student council to hang up flyers."

"Why wouldn't you enter it?" Nathan asks. "That's like Ina Garten not entering a cooking contest."

"Ina Garten?" I look at him. In fact, all three of us give him a strange look.

"My dad likes the Food Network, but that wasn't the point here," Nathan argues. "You should do it."

"Maybe."

"Well, if you decide to do it," Sophie starts to say, "make sure we get tickets. I've got the perfect outfit."

Meleika eyes her. "You have the perfect outfit for a student art show?"

"Totally!" Sophie says. "Now sit still, I've got to finish these nails."

"And with that, I'm going to get some water." Nathan taps his knuckles against the table. "Anyone want anything?"

"I'm good," I say. Sophie and Meleika are too busy focusing on Meleika's nails. Sophie's got this new black polish that almost seems blue when you look at it just the right way. It's so stunning I'm legit considering asking her to do mine. Then it hits me. "Actually, yeah. I'll go with you."

Nathan looks a little surprised, but it lasts maybe a split second. "All righty, then."

I follow him to the vending machine out in the hallway in front of the cafeteria. I guess the line is way too long to wait in just to buy a bottle of water.

"So . . ." I say, staring at the huge logo.

"So . . ." Nathan eyes the big blue vending machine.

"So." I tuck my hands into my pockets and shuffle my feet around. "I wanted to ask you a favor. A big favor."

"Okay." The corners of his mouth perk up a little. "No chance I could ask you to do this in riddle form?"

"Yeah, no." I sigh. "It's a bit of a weird request."

"It's not that hard to make questions riddles," Nathan says.

"Not what I meant." I shake my head. "I just need your help."

"Hide a body, no, wait. You need to get revenge on someone? I've got the perfect way to ruin someone's gas tank."

"No, it's not that. Just let me talk, please." Though the gas tank trick might come in handy later. "My mom sent me a message online, she and my dad really want to talk to me."

Nathan's smile vanishes in an instant. "About how they kicked you out?" He pulls a dollar out of his wallet and feeds it into the vending machine.

"That might come up, yeah." I get in closer. "And I'd just feel better about having someone there."

"And your sister isn't an option?"

I shake my head. "I don't need you to sit in on it or anything, but just like, knowing you're there might help me."

"Do I have that effect?" Nathan's still not smiling, and I'm getting sort of worried.

I really need there to be a cap on how many times cheeks can blush per day. "Kind of. It'd really help to have a friend there."

"And you really think this is a good idea?" he asks.

"No," I say. "But I feel like I have to hear them out, listen to what they have to say."

"Ben—"

"Just . . . please, just this one thing. Please?"

Nathan lets out a long sigh. "When are you meeting?"

"Friday night." I pull out my phone and stare at the message I sent. Eventually I'd found the right words, which is to say that after all my worrying, I simply told them a time and place we could meet. I'd thought for days about adding something else, about asking for some kind of an explanation, or maybe going off on Mom.

But none of that seemed right. I wanted to hear them first, face-to-face.

"Robin's." I tell him. "That Italian place downtown."

"Oh, I've been there." Nathan takes his bottle of water out of the little dispenser at the bottom. "Don't get the eggplant Parmesan. It's terrible."

"Noted," I say. "Thank you."

"No problem."

"They'll be there around seven, is that okay?"

Nathan smiles. "It's a date!"

EIGHTEEN

Yeah, I'm fucked.

I should most definitely not have agreed to do this, but it's too late now. Short of just grabbing Nathan and running back out into the parking lot.

But Mom and Dad know where Hannah lives, probably.

I catch Nathan's eye from across the restaurant. He looks pretty comfortable for a guy who's basically here alone. He catches me looking and pulls out his phone, then my phone buzzes.

Nathan: *I still think I should've worn the hat and sunglasses.*

I roll my eyes.

Me: *They don't know what you look like.*
Nathan: *Still!*
Me: *This isn't a sting operation or anything.*

"Well, hello."

I jump in my seat and nearly let my phone clatter to the floor before I grab it at the last second. It's my parents, standing there, smiles on their faces as they look down at me.

"Hi," I say, unsure if I should stand up or not.

I stay seated, and the two of them follow after a few beats of awkward silence. My phone vibrates again, but I ignore it. Probably just Nathan.

"You've let your hair get too long" is the first thing Dad says.

"I like it this way," I say, touching the ends. It's not quite to my shoulders yet, but Sophie says I'm like a walking stalk of broccoli.

Meleika said cauliflower, because of how pale I am.

"It gets all matted and tangled though." Mom reaches across the table, but I lean back, avoiding her perfectly manicured nails.

"Let's get to the point," I say. "You two wanted to talk, right? Isn't that why we're here?"

"Well, not if you're going to have an attitude," Dad mutters in that kind of way so he knows I'll hear it.

"I don't have an attitude." I cross my arms. "What did you two want to discuss?"

"How are you doing?" Mom asks.

"Fine."

"How is your sister?"

"She's fine." Not that either of them actually care. "She and Thomas have been really good to me."

I see a bit of pain flash over both of their faces, that little bit of guilt, as if they forgot they'd kicked me out. I hate that I feel a little proud of the moment, that it's *my* turn to hurt them.

"And school?" Dad asks. "You're keeping your grades up, right? Your exams must be coming up soon."

"Yeah, but I'm passing all my classes." I sink back into my chair, guilt creeping up my spine.

"That's great!" Mom smiles a bit too widely, then she reaches into her purse. "You know we got a few replies back, from schools." She slides the thick bundle of envelopes over to me. Some of them are open, some aren't. "You got into State, but UNC said no."

"Huh." I flip through them, staring at the names of the schools and the envelopes decorated with their colors. "That's fine. I'm not going to college anyway."

"What do you mean?" Dad asks. "Of course you're going to school."

"I don't want to." I slide the letters back to Mom.

"Is it because of Hannah? *We* can afford to send you to school, you don't have to rely on your sister anymore," Dad says, almost like he's proud of himself.

"Actually, Hannah and I have already had that talk, and she told me it wouldn't be any trouble. I just don't want to go."

"Ben—" Mom starts to say, but Dad puts a hand on her arm and that stops her.

"We'll discuss that later," he says.

"What did you want to talk about?" I ask again. "Stop avoiding the question."

"Well." Mom presses her hands together. "We wanted to talk with you more about this whole 'being nonbinary' thing."

It's awfully strange hearing my mother actually say the word "nonbinary" aloud. It doesn't really belong, like it's the kind of word you'd never expect someone like her to know. "Okay." I lean forward a little. Maybe this won't be as bad as I thought.

"We, um . . . We're just confused." Mom tries to relax. "So, we tried to find things online, and that didn't really help us."

"And?" I look at the two of them.

"Honey." Mom sighs. "We tried, we really did. We're still trying to wrap our heads around it."

"It's not exactly theoretical physics," I say. "I don't identify as male or female, I fall outside the gender binary. I use they/them pronouns." I keep my voice low so Nathan won't hear me. I doubt he could anyway, all the way across the restaurant, but you never know.

"Well, son, you have to admit that it's all very strange," Dad says. I can't tell if the "son" is deliberate or not.

"I'm not your 'son,'" I say. "And what's so strange about it? This is just who I am. Why can't you two understand that?"

"Are you sure you aren't just confused?" Dad asks. "Maybe you're just gay or something and this has just been a difficult time for you?"

Dad makes "gay" sound like an insult.

"Being gay and being nonbinary are two different things!" I should know; I spent enough time having to tell myself that.

Mom looks taken aback for a second.

And Dad looks furious. Always the dramatic one. "Benjamin De Backer, don't you take that tone with us, we're your parents."

"Well, how am I supposed to sound? You two are sitting here insulting me."

Dad pinches the bridge of his nose and waves his hand around. "Okay, let's start over."

"Tell me one thing, what was the goal here? Why did you two want to talk after what happened?"

"We wanted to apologize," Mom says.

"Well, you're doing a bang-up job," I say.

Dad rolls his eyes. "We want you to come home."

I freeze. "What?"

"We want you to come back home," Mom repeats, and it's obvious she seems happier about it than Dad does. "Obviously it'd be hard with school ending, and we're willing to wait until you graduate. Maybe make the transition a little easier."

That makes me laugh, but they both stare at me.

"I don't think it's very funny," Dad adds.

I breathe in and out slowly. I never pictured my parents as queerphobic assholes. But maybe that's my fault for assuming the best of them.

"We miss you. We want to be a family again." Mom looks at me, those eyes.

I think about their words, repeating them to myself over and over again in my head. They want me back? They want to be a family again?

"Ben, you have to understand how hard this has been on the both of us." Mom looks like she actually might cry.

"What?" One step forward, a hundred steps back. "You kick me out of the house, and it's been hard on the both of *you*?" I make sure I'm talking loud enough so that the people at the next table over are staring. "Do you know how you two sound right now?"

"Benjamin." Dad looks around; he must realize what I'm trying to do. "Lower your voice."

"Listen." Mom sticks up a hand. "We're still learning here. We made mistakes and we want to work to correct them. We've changed, we started seeing a counselor, and we're working through some things. It *was* a difficult time. For *all* of us."

"You two hurt me," I spit. "Do you . . . Do you even realize the shit you put me through? Not just kicking me out, but the months of therapy I've had to go through to get past everything?" It's slowly dawning on me that Dr. Taylor was right, and that I really should've listened to her.

"Honey." Mom puts her hand on top of mine, and I don't think about pulling away before it's too late. Her skin on mine, the warmth of it, it's too familiar and too strange at the same time. I try to suppress the rise in my stomach. "We're so, so sorry for everything, and we just want to make it up to you."

"You'll come home after you graduate," Dad says, and I notice it's more of a command than a request. "We'll take you to the therapist we've been seeing, maybe he can help you work through some of the things you've been dealing with. And help you with this nonbinary business."

I'm going to be sick. "I've been seeing Dr. Taylor, I like her."

"Okay, well . . ." Mom glances toward Dad. "Maybe we could see her? Together."

I stare down at her hand, still on top of mine. "I have some things to think about," I say.

"Of course, just do it quickly." Dad eyes the menus at the end of the table, stacked neatly on top of one another. "Did you want to order something?"

"No." I stand up quickly and push my chair under. "I'll message you when I'm ready to talk."

"Ben, honey." Mom makes like she's going to stand up.

I stop her. "Just let me think, for a few days. Okay?"

She looks back at Dad, and I can tell he isn't pleased. This isn't how he wanted this meeting to go.

I'm betting they both wanted the perfect reunion where I'd run into their arms and hug them and agree to go back home with them, leaving behind what short life I've built here. Hannah, Thomas, Meleika, Sophie, Dr. Taylor.

Nathan.

I look his way and nod. He's already up and waiting at the door for me. I guess Mom notices, so she turns in her seat. "Is that a friend of yours?"

"No," I lie.

"Were you that scared, son?" Dad asks, almost like a joke. Except I'm not laughing.

"I'll see you two later." I keep myself from running toward Nathan and out to his car.

"Well, hold on." Mom grabs her purse and starts following me. "I'd like to meet this boy."

Fuck, fuck, fuck, fuck.

But it's already too late. Mom manages to get ahead of me, stopping Nathan right at the door. "Hello there!" She sticks out a hand. "I'm Brenda De Backer, Ben's mother."

Nathan grins, eyes bright as he shakes her hand. "I'm Nathan."

"Are you a friend of Ben's?"

Nathan looks to me for approval, but what else can we really do? Pretend my mother's shaking hands with a person I don't know? I'm not going to lie, that would be kind of funny, but there's really no use. I give Nathan a little nod.

"Yeah, we go to North Wake together. He asked me for a ride."

Mom gives me a look. "Well, isn't that nice? We were just meeting to talk about some things."

"Are you ready to go, Nathan?" I ask. I need to get the hell out of here.

"Yeah." Nathan digs around in his pocket. "I'm sorry, Mrs. De Backer, but we're meeting some friends downtown, and we're already pretty late," he lies.

Bless Nathan Allan.

"Oh, well." Mom's still all smiles. "We'll talk soon, Ben." I nod, and Mom looks back at Nathan. "It was so nice to meet you. I'm glad Ben's found friends."

"Nice to meet you too, ma'am." Nathan holds the door open for me, and we race toward his car, not looking back.

———

"Roof?" Nathan asks. We've been sitting in his driveway for a while now, no music, no talking. He turned the car off at first, but after a few seconds of just sitting there, he rolled down the windows to let in the cool night air.

Eventually I glance over at him. "Sure."

Ryder gives me a hug, and I rub him behind the ears, but I don't have much in me now. It's like I'm running on empty. I feel exhausted, even though all we did was talk.

Nathan opens the window and helps me out this time, taking my hand and pulling me through the gap. At least this time, with better-fitting pants, I don't almost fall to my death.

It's actually breezy for April, but the sun is shining, so it's more than enough to keep warm.

"So," Nathan says, making his way to our normal spot. "She seemed nice, your mom."

"Hmm." I sit down next to him. I'd be shocked, but that's the normal reaction when it comes to Mom and Dad. They put on that mask for strangers or family friends. Slipping in a backhanded comment about me here or there.

"What did they say to you?" he asks.

"They wanted me to come home." Even to me, my voice sounds empty.

"Wow." Nathan runs a hand along the top of his hair. "That's . . ."

"Yeah."

"Fucked up." Nathan pulls his knees in close.

I look down at his hand, settled so close to mine, and I can't resist. My own hand settles around his. That warmth, it's so much different from Mom's. I want this kind. I feel like I need it. To ground me if nothing else. I feel the dry skin of his palm; and, still looking forward, Nathan wraps his fingers around mine. The rest of the skin I trace with my thumb is smooth, and for a half a second, I wonder if this is how he feels all over.

"Thank you, for going with me. I know it wasn't really fair . . ."

"I didn't mind," he says.

"I don't want you to have to be my protector. That's not fair to you."

He does that thing, that laugh that sort of sounds like a scoff. "You worry a lot."

"And you're a quick liar," I say.

"When I saw that look on your face . . . When your mom realized you were with me." He stops, like he's trying to think of just the right words. "I knew that feeling."

"Really?"

He nods. "That helplessness, right?"

"Thank you. I . . ." I start to say. It feels like a perfect moment. My second chance. I flubbed the night of the movie, but maybe now's the time. Except I'm too much of a coward. "There's something I need to show you."

"Oh yeah?"

"It's a painting," I say, reaching into my pocket to grab my phone. "It's, um . . . Well, it's a bit weird."

"You know you are really terrible at giving people bad news?" he says.

"Yeah. I mean, it's not bad or anything." I pull up the photo of the painting. "At least, I don't think it is. But it's your call to make. It's a painting of you."

Nathan pauses, glancing between me and the phone still in my hand. "You painted me?" he asks.

I nod.

"Please tell me you didn't find a way to paint me nude."

"What?" I sputter. "No!"

"Okay, because you're great, Ben, but that may or may not be a deal breaker."

"How would that *not* be a deal breaker?"

"Depends on how you capture my curves and finesse." He winks at me.

I turn off my phone and slide it back into my pocket. "Okay, never mind. Let the suspense kill you."

"No, wait." He reaches for my hand again. "Come on, I was just teasing."

I point a finger at him. "No jokes, okay?"

"I promise." He sticks out his hand again. "Pinky promise."

I grab my phone again, and the picture of the painting is the first thing that comes up. I brace myself and hand it over to him. He doesn't react at first, then slowly but surely, his mouth spreads into that all-too-familiar grin that I think I've fallen in love with.

I never want him to stop smiling.

"Ben . . ." he starts, but his voice fades off again.

"It sort of happened, and I know it seems creepy or whatever, so if you want to hate me you can, but yeah. I just used a few of the selfies you took on my phone." I'm talking so fast that it jumbles together, and I don't think he really understands me. "I had to change some things, pull from other pictures."

"Ben." He grabs my arm, and that shuts me up. "I love it."

"Really?"

"I'm so yellow." He laughs. "It might be my favorite."

"You're just saying that because it's your portrait."

"I mean you have to admit I make a good model." He won't stop staring at the picture. "I can't wait to see the real thing. Is it going to be in the show?"

"I still don't know if I'm doing it."

"Oh, come on, Ben. You *have* to."

"It's just . . . I don't know."

"Are you scared people won't like your work?" he asks.

"A little, I guess." It just feels like I'm opening myself back up. I've never really felt that urge to share my art with people, at least people I'm not close with. It's always been this private deal, something with myself and a select few.

"Ben." I feel his hand again, right on top of mine. "I really think you should do it."

"Easy for you to say." The warmth of his skin spreads along mine. I swear, this dude's like an electric blanket or something. "I want to do it," I say.

"So you should."

"I'm just scared."

Nathan chuckles. "That's probably a normal response. To be honest, if you totally expected everyone to love everything you make, you'd probably be some super pretentious art douche."

"I'll have to borrow your turtlenecks and hipster glasses."

"Pssh. Like I'd ever give those up. You can have my coffee though." He starts to laugh again. "Can't believe I'm gonna be in an art show." He finally hands my phone back to me.

"*Might* be," I correct. "Sorry for not asking permission or anything."

"Well, this is me giving my blessing for you to put it in the show." He runs a hand along the top of his hair. "It's fantastic. Thank you, Ben."

"You're welcome." I'm trying not to blush, but I can feel my face going hot despite the chill of the air.

At first, I don't even hear the car pulling into the driveway, but Nathan perks up, and there's the distinct sound of car doors closing. "My parents are home."

"Oh." I glance around, as if they'd somehow magically appear on the roof.

"Do you want to meet them?"

I shrug. "I guess I don't really have a choice, do I?"

Nathan stands up and peers over the edge of the roof into the backyard. "That's a hefty drop, so . . . I'm thinking no." Nathan offers me his hand again and helps me stand up. "They're cool, I swear."

"Okay."

This isn't really how I was planning on meeting Nathan's parents. I'd imagined about a dozen different awkward encounters where I'd either call them by the wrong name, or not say my own right, or call them Mom and Dad by accident.

We walk back across the roof to his room. I almost fall again when I try to step through. At least this time the chances of falling tragically to my death are minimal. But Nathan catches me in his arms.

He's really warm, and for a split second I can smell his sort of terrible cologne and his deodorant. I think that's lime. It probably shouldn't make for a good combination, but right now, it smells so good.

Oh, shit.

"Thank you." I try to smile off everything and pull myself as far as I can.

"No problem." He lets go of me slowly, his hands lingering just a little too long. No, wait. Stop, I'm being creepy again. "Hey, what if you stayed for dinner?"

"Um, sure. I don't think Hannah would mind."

"Nathan?" a voice shouts from below. "You home?"

"Yeah, be down in a second!" Nathan yells back, then he looks at me, holding out his hand. "Ready to go?"

I take it, slowly, and let him lead me out of the bedroom and down the stairs.

NINETEEN

"So you're Ben." Nathan's mother takes my hand, shaking it quickly. "I'm Joyce, and this is my husband, Robert. It's nice to finally meet you. Nathan speaks very highly." She winks, and I don't know what that's supposed to imply, but I don't question it.

"He does?" I ask.

"Oh, here and there," she says.

While he packs groceries into the refrigerator, Nathan's dad says, "And every night at dinner, and before he goes to bed, and at breakfast."

I turn to Nathan, who's currently seated at the counter with his face buried in his hands, and God he's so cute right now.

"I do not talk about him 24/7!" he argues.

"He's right." Mr. Allan folds up the leftover plastic bags and slips them into a small container under the sink. "He has to sleep sometime."

"Oh, hardy har har." Nathan rolls his eyes. Then he mouths *Sorry*. But I'm too busy laughing.

"So, Ben, did you want to join us for dinner?" Mrs. Allan asks.

"Um, sure," I say. "If y'all don't mind, that is."

"Of course not!" Mrs. Allan leans against the counter. "We were just going to do pizza, if that's okay with you? I'm too beat to cook tonight, work was a nightmare."

I shrug. "I'm good with whatever."

"Any dietary things I should know about? No meat, no cheese?"

"No, really, I'm good."

"So, what have you boys been up to?" Mr. Allan asks. It doesn't really sound accusatory, but there's still that worry. Like what if they think we were fooling around upstairs or something?

"Just hanging out. I took him up to the roof."

I'm actually kind of surprised Nathan doesn't cover, like say we were studying or something. Nope. We were on the roof, meaning we had to be in his room before we were there. Totally alone, without any parental supervision.

"Oh, lord." Mrs. Allan chuckles. "You mean you weren't completely terrified?" she asks me.

"No." I almost say *wasn't my first time*, but I feel like that would be counterproductive. "I was at first, but it's not so bad."

"I do wish he'd quit doing that," Mrs. Allan mutters. "Scares me half to death knowing he's up there."

"It's not that dangerous," Nathan says. "And I'm careful."

"I know, I know." Mrs. Allan ruffles the top of his head and kisses Nathan's temple. "But you've still got me worried."

"Do you want me to order?" Mr. Allan asks his wife, his phone already in his hand.

"Yes, honey. Just get a large cheese and a large pepperoni."

"Got it. Huh? Oh, yes. I'd like to place an order . . ." Mr. Allan says into the phone before he starts walking down the hallway, his voice trailing off with him.

"So, how long have you been at Wake, Ben?" Mrs. Allan asks. I guess that means that Nathan hasn't told them anything. Not that I thought he would; it's just . . . nice to know he kept that secret.

"A few months now. I moved here in January."

"Are you enjoying it?"

I shrug. "It's nice. Different."

"I was so nervous about Nathan going to a new school when we came here. It's got to feel strange having to start all over. New friends, new classes, new teachers."

"Yeah." I lean back against the counter, eyeing Nathan.

"Do your parents like it here?"

"I live with my sister." For some reason it feels impossible to lie to Mrs. Allan.

She doesn't ask for details, like it's not this super strange thing to her. But maybe it isn't, plenty of people live with their siblings, I guess. "Does your sister like it?"

"Yeah, but she's lived here for a while." I can see her trying to connect the dots in her head. Whether or not she comes to the right conclusion, I'm not sure. Seems doubtful.

"I'm glad you and Nathan are friends. It's tough to go through high school alone."

"Okay, okay." Nathan stands up. "Enough of the interrogation."

"I was just asking questions," Mrs. Allan protests.

"And Ben's had a very busy day, so we're going to go watch TV."

"It was very nice to meet you, Mrs. Allan," I say, before Nathan grabs my hand.

"You too, Ben." Then she has to shout because we're already halfway down the hall. "We'll call you down when dinner gets here!"

"Thanks, Mom!" Nathan shouts, and he takes me right back to his room. "I'm going to use the bathroom real quick, okay?"

"Okay." I watch him vanish back down the hallway, and it dawns on me that I'm in Nathan Allan's room all by myself.

My eyes catch all the titles lining his flooded shelves. I really just want to spend the better part of a day organizing all of these for him. There are at least five copies of *Pride and Prejudice*, all their covers battered and worn. I flip through one, but see that he's written things in the margins, faded highlighter decorating entire passages.

I put it back down quickly. That feels too personal, almost like I'm peeping into his diary. The rest of the books range from fantasy to contemporary stories. I can even recognize a few of them.

There doesn't seem to be any sort of organization though. Not by series, or author's last name, or title. Even the heights of all the books are off. His desk is neat, at least, the screen saver of his laptop playing in the background.

There's a calendar with nearly all the days crossed off as we get closer to the end of April, and a handful of pictures have been pinned to the corkboard that hangs on the wall. Ones of Nathan and his mom, another one of all three of them downtown. They remind me so much of the pictures Mom took. Photos of a happy family at play.

Except when I look at Nathan and his parents, I feel like I see an actual family.

"Hey."

I jump at Nathan's voice. Oh God, what if he thinks I was looking through his things? I mean, I guess technically I am, but just the pictures. I wasn't going through his drawers or anything.

"We took that last year." He motions to the wall of photos, and it's hard to tell which one he's really talking about before he walks over, his fingers brushing it. It's one with him, Sophie, and Meleika in the water. "They couldn't believe I'd never been to a beach. Those aren't exactly common in Colorado."

"Is that where you lived before?" I ask.

"Yeah." He chuckles. "It was weird. Never actually been to one before, but the sand was really warm, and it felt nice under my feet."

"That's before you get in the water," I say. "After that it just starts sticking to you and you'll never get it all off."

"Fair enough. Can't say I've really felt the urge to go back."

I feel the brush of his fingers, and I'm all too happy to take his hand again. We don't acknowledge. Neither of us look down, or tighten our grips, or say anything.

Because we don't have to.

———

Monday comes and Mrs. Liu needs an answer.

"I know I keep pestering you about this, but the show is Friday night and we really need an answer if you—"

I stop her. "I'll do it."

To be honest, I hadn't walked into school with a definite answer. I kept thinking about what Nathan said, about being scared. I don't really know if it helped. I actually think I just said whatever came to mind first.

Which was apparently a yes.

Mrs. Liu's face brightens and she starts bouncing up and down. "Oh, Ben! I'm so excited! Okay, we've got a lot to do. I made sure to plan for your space, so you'll just need to pick the work you want to showcase. We're limiting each student to five pieces, okay?"

"I'll just show the paintings I've already done," I say.

"Like the one of Nathan?" Her voice sort of trails off.

I nod. "That one too."

"Ben, that's fantastic. I'm asking everyone to stay after school Friday to help with the setup. It should definitely leave enough time for you to go home and get changed."

"Okay. I'll be here."

Except when Friday finally comes, I am not ready.

All day at school I'm a nervous wreck, hardly talking, and I can't quit shaking. At lunch, Sophie gives me this cube toy she says helps her when her ADHD gets really bad. And it helps a little, but only so much.

"Any clue what we're supposed to wear?" Nathan asks.

I shake my head. "None at all." I've been thinking about the floral shirt, the one Hannah bought me. But what if that's too formal? Or too casual?

"Excellent, I'll just break out my birthday suit." He tries to get me to laugh, but it's not happening.

"Yeah, didn't need that mental image," Meleika says.

"I think I'm emotionally scarred for life," Sophie mutters.

After school, I head to the art room. There isn't much to set up since all the partitions to hang the art are already up. We just have to pick our stations and move our work. The second I step into the art room I'm surrounded by a bunch of people. Some I've never seen before, others I've seen in passing.

For a few seconds everyone just stares, but then they go back to whatever conversations they were having before. Mrs. Liu tells everyone who's ready to go to the front of the school and pick their spots. Those of us who have to get work hanging in the back have to take turns with the ladder to get it down.

"That's amazing." This girl glances over my shoulder at the painting of Nathan. "Nathan's so freaking cute, oh my God."

"Oh, um, thanks," I say, like I can take credit for his cuteness. Can't argue with her though.

I pick a place near the back, that way I might not attract a ton of attention. And once I'm done, Mrs. Liu dismisses me.

"Just be here by eight, okay?" she says.

Thomas doesn't really have to change, and Hannah's almost done by the time we get home, but I waste nearly an hour trying to decide what to wear, and now I stare at myself in the mirror, and *really* consider just not going to this art show at all.

I pick the floral shirt Hannah bought me, the black one with the pink flowers, and I guess I look fine, but there's just something weird about my body tonight, and I've got this gross red bump on my chin that I asked Hannah to cover up, but we don't really have matching skin tones, and I'd rather have a bump than this random streak of slightly darker skin.

"You ready, sib?" Hannah definitely looks better than I do. Hell, even Thomas looks more comfortable. I'm just a weirdly shaped, awkward body. Always have been, probably always will be.

"I don't really know." I give myself another look, but I still hate what I see. Back home, I'd just wear whatever Mom bought me. She had good taste, and the clothes fit, and they were close to what everyone else wore so I felt less self-conscious.

"Want to talk?" she asks.

"Nothing to really talk about."

"You sure?" Hannah walks over to my bed and takes a seat on the edge, patting the spot next to her. "Come on."

I sigh, but do what I'm told, resting my elbows on my knees.

"What's up?" Hannah asks.

"Just nerves," I say, knowing that it isn't just that.

I already know my answer to Mom and Dad's question. There's no way I can go back to that house, not after everything they did. I want to believe they've changed, but I truly don't think they have. I think this sort of change is beyond them. They aren't mature enough to have grown on their own.

Then there's the idea that I've kept this all from Hannah. I don't think I could ever tell her about meeting with them. It seems like a total betrayal on my part, and I don't ever want to see her face if she finds out.

I tried to talk to Mariam about all this, but it still feels like this oddly private thing; I can't really explain it. Besides, I can't always shove all my problems on them and expect them to solve it. That's not fair.

"Hey, nerves can be a good thing," Hannah says.

"How so?"

"Well . . ." She opens her mouth. "Damn, I don't have any advice."

"See?"

Hannah pats my knee. "Just pretend that tonight's gonna be the best night of your life."

"Really setting the bar low, aren't we?"

"The best night of your life, so far?" she corrects.

"Better," I say, rocking back and forth a little. "I can do this." I breathe in and out slowly. "I got this." For just the briefest of seconds I think about telling her. About the message and the meeting. But that won't help anyone.

I already have my answer, my home.

"You got this," she says.

I hear Thomas coming down the hallway, still rolling up the sleeves of his shirt. "Everyone ready to go?"

Hannah glances at me out of the corner of her eye. "Well?"

"Yeah, let's go."

———

North Wake at night is sort of odd. All the lights are off except the ones in the main building where the show is. And the parking lot is packed with cars, so I guess any chance of this being a small show just flew out the window.

"Are your friends going to make it tonight?" Hannah locks the car behind us.

"I think so." I check my phone, but there are no new texts. We talked about it at lunch today though, and everyone seemed excited.

"Ben!" someone yells from across the lot, and suddenly two people are running toward me. Well, Meleika is running, Sophie's stumbling. She can't do much in her heels.

"You guys made it." I let Meleika wrap me in a hug.

"Why wouldn't we?" Meleika asks.

"You weren't answering your texts." I don't mean for it to sound like some kind of accusation.

"Oh, I was driving," she says.

"And I have absolutely no service." Sophie taps on her phone angrily.

"It's okay," I say. "Do you know where Nathan is?"

"I think he was going to try and get here early," Sophie says.

Meleika's phone gives a little *ding*. "Yeah, he's inside already."

"Well, since Ben isn't going to introduce us, I will." Hannah offers her hand to Sophie. "I'm Hannah, Ben's sister."

"Sorry," I say. "This is Sophie, and Meleika."

"Hey, girls." Thomas gives them both a wave.

"Hi, Mr. Waller." Meleika digs around in her purse for a second. "Ready to kick this art show's ass?" she asks.

"Totally," I say, following them into the school.

There isn't much you can do with a school lobby, but with the partitions and everyone's work hanging up, it looks like a real gallery. And people are already walking around. I'm guessing it's mostly parents, but I recognize a few faces. I even see Stephanie. Thankfully Todd seems absent.

"Where is your stuff?" Sophie asks.

"Around here." We walk by rows and rows of different student's paintings. They all seem to be standing to the side, ready to talk to people at a moment's notice. When we round the corner to my spot, right at the very end of the row, I finally see Nathan.

And he's staring at my work. More specifically, he's staring at the portrait of him.

"And you must be Nathan!" Hannah says, holding out her hand. "Ben and my husband have talked about you quite a bit."

"All good things, I hope." Nathan takes her hand. A perfect gentleman, as always. "I only hope I can live up to their glowing recommendation."

"Oh wow, Ben." Meleika stares, her mouth wide open. "You painted this?"

Now all five of them are staring. Well, Thomas not so much, since he's already seen these.

"Yeah," I say, trying not to blush.

"Someone's already asked me if I painted it," Nathan murmurs. "Told them there's no way I had this much talent."

"This is so cool." Sophie glances from one painting to another. "Oh my God, that's Nathan!" She leans in real close.

"Hey." Nathan pulls her back. "Don't breathe on my gorgeous portrait, you'll lower the value."

Sophie rolls her eyes. "Oh God, Ben, this was a mistake. His ego's already too big."

"We'll talk about it when your portrait hangs in an art gallery."

She flips him off, but they're both smiling.

Art shows are sort of surreal, even if it is just a student show. At least this one is. I can't speak for the other ones.

People keep phasing in and out, a few stopping to talk to me or look at the paintings. According to Nathan, Hannah and Thomas are taking a lap around the gallery. Mrs. Liu finds us a few minutes later.

"Oh, Ben, isn't this amazing?" She hugs me again. "The turnout is better than I hoped!"

"Yeah." The spot I picked isn't too busy, but people filter by, some stopping, asking me questions about how I did the paintings. But most will just smile, nod, and move on. After another ten minutes, Meleika and Sophie head off to find the food table, and Mrs. Liu gets caught up talking to someone else.

So now it's just me and Nathan.

"Still can't believe you did that," he says, turning around to look at his portrait again. "I like how you can see the details of the paint, like the paint isn't lying flat? If that makes sense."

"It's just the brushstrokes, nothing fancy."

"I still like it. It makes me feel warm."

"That'd be the yellow," I say.

"Why *did* you pick yellow?" he asks.

I'm answering before I can stop myself. "Because it's bright and hopeful." I wait a beat. "Like you."

Nathan glances at me out of the corners of his eyes and gives me that sly grin.

I feel my face go hot. "Sorry, I mean . . . It's nothing special," I argue, hoping he'll forget what I said. "Look." I let my finger hover over the painted version of his face. "The lines here aren't really right."

"Oh, please."

"And I should've added a darker tone here to make it seem more like a shadow."

"Ben." He sighs.

"What?"

"Tell me one thing you like about this painting."

"What do you mean?"

"You always point out the flaws in your work, but what's one thing you like about this painting? Or that one?" He points to the one of the cardinal, which seems like it's from such a lifetime ago.

I think for a moment. "I like that I could make it up, the space around it, I mean." Sure, I got the bird accurate, but the rest of the void was my playground. A blend of blues and purples with the small red bird providing the contrast.

"And the Pollock thing?"

"Drip painting," I correct.

"The drip painting," he says with a grin on his face. "What's one thing you like about it?"

"I like how the purples still come through, even under all the blue."

"And this one." Nathan points back to his portrait.

"I like that it's about you," I say quietly, and he doesn't seem to hear me at first, or I think he doesn't.

Then he says, "That's a pretty good feature." He lets out a long sigh. "You always point out the problems with the paintings or the drawings. But what about the things you got right?"

"What about them?"

"Don't they mean something?"

His words make my stomach drop. I don't know, maybe he's right. But I don't think he realizes how difficult it can be to forget all the mistakes when I know they're my fault. When I know I should've caught them. "It's hard to be proud of something you messed up, even if everything around it is perfect."

"Don't ignore the problems," he says. "Learn from them. But also, don't knock what you get right. Every success deserves a celebration."

I feel sort of speechless, before I can manage to spit out a "Thank you."

"It's what I'm here for. Emotional support. Being a model just narrowly comes in second."

"I think Sophie's right. This hasn't done much for that ego."

"Whatever. So, we need to discuss modeling opportunities. I'm thinking I go full nude next?"

"Not on your life," I say, laughing him off, and trying *really* hard not to think about Nathan being naked. "What about you?"

"Hmm?"

"What do you like about my work?"

Nathan glances toward me, but he doesn't answer.

"That day we got the paint from the art room, you acted like you were going to say something. What was it?"

"You remember that?" He chuckles.

"I think it was the only time I've seen you speechless." I nudge him. "Come on." I make my voice deeper, sounding as serious as I can. "What do you feel when you see them?"

"That's a terrible accent."

"I sound scholarly," I argue. "Now stop avoiding the question."

"Your paintings seem . . . complicated."

I freeze; okay, not really expecting that. "What do you mean?"

"It's . . . nothing," he says, and then he starts to laugh for no reason. "Nothing, I swear."

"No," I say. "Tell me."

"I don't know, I feel like I can see you in them. That probably doesn't make any sense."

Not really. But I want to hear him out on this. "Keep talking."

"Like the Pollock one, I don't know, it seems bright and active. But, like, really dark at the same time. If that even makes sense." He takes a slow breath. "I think it's the painting that feels most like you."

"That one was just some assignment. Mrs. Liu wanted me to show her freshman class how Pollock painted."

"Still, it feels like you." He laughs again. "Like a very 'Ben-ish' painting."

"'Ben-ish'?" I say. "Huh."

"Sorry."

"No, no, no." I glance toward him, and then back to the painting. "I get it." At least, I think I do.

"The one of the bird feels lonely," Nathan keeps going. "Like you've got all this empty space, even though it's this huge canvas."

"You should critique art," I say.

"Or maybe I'll just critique you." He winks.

"That might be your worst line yet." But I can still feel my face getting a little hot, and I can't hold his gaze for more than a few seconds.

I wait for him to keep going, to say something about his portrait, but I guess he's already told me everything he needs to say about it. The bright colors, the angle. "Do you want to walk around?" I ask him.

"Yeah, why not?"

But the second we round the corner, my eyes find the front doors of the school. And the two people walking right through them.

"Fuck," I whisper under my breath.

Mom and Dad are here.

TWENTY

"No. No, no, no, no."

Nathan freezes. "What are they . . ."

I have to think fast. "Listen, please find Hannah and Thomas," I say just low enough so that only Nathan will hear me. "Distract them, keep them away from my section, okay?"

"Got it." Nathan nods and runs off, glancing down the aisles.

"Hi, honey, where is your friend going?" Mom asks.

"To get something to drink," I murmur. "What are you two doing here?"

"Well, we were looking at your school's website," Mom says with a smile. "And we saw that there was an art show, and that your name was on the list of students!"

"So, we thought we'd stop by." Dad folds up a flyer he was given at the door.

"Don't y'all think you should've messaged me first? To see if I was okay with this?" I ask.

"Oh, honey, don't be silly. We wanted to support you." Mom bats at me with her hand.

"Now, where is your stuff? I'd love to see it."

"I think you two should go."

Dad scoffs. "So now we aren't allowed to view our own child's work? You used to talk about your art all the time, I thought you'd be excited!"

I catch the word use, no "sons" yet. Maybe they're trying now? "Hannah's here, and I didn't invite you. I don't think this is a good idea."

"Oh, stop, Ben." Dad brushes past me. "We'll take one quick look and then leave, okay? Maybe we'll go out to dinner to celebrate."

"Yeah, sure. Maybe." I'll say whatever I need to, as long as they leave as quickly as possible. I duck in front of Mom and lead them both toward my little section. "Here you go."

"Oh goodness, these sure are something, Ben."

I keep myself from asking exactly what kind of "something" they are. "Thank you."

"You really painted these?" Dad asks, leaning in for a closer look. "I'm surprised; you're more talented than I thought."

Maybe if he'd actually bothered to look at any of the things I showed him back home he'd be less surprised. "Yep." I glance around, hoping that Nathan's found Hannah and Thomas.

"Oh, get in close, sweetie." Mom pulls out her phone. "I want to take a picture!"

"Fine, then you guys really need to leave," I say, standing beside the drip painting.

I hear Mom whisper, "I do wish you were wearing a different shirt." But I choose to ignore her. No point in getting them riled up.

"Is that your friend?" Dad asks. "Nate?"

"Nathan," I say. "And yes."

"Looks just like him." But it doesn't sound like a compliment. I'm sure the pieces are coming together in his head. I painted a portrait of a boy, a boy I seem very close with. In his head it's simple addition.

"Thank you," I say, maybe just to spite him.

"Are you getting paid for these?" Dad asks.

"No, Dad."

"Well, we should talk to someone about that." He starts to look around, but I have to stop him.

"No, Dad, it's okay. This is a student show. No one's getting paid."

Mom snaps a few photos with her phone. "Well, this was just fantastic. These really are amazing, Ben."

"Okay, now please, leave."

"Benjamin, there's no need to be rude, we came all this way." Dad wraps an arm around Mom's waist.

"Guys, I'm begging you. Listen—"

"Ah-ah." Dad lets out a low chuckle and eyes Mom, but she isn't laughing. "Now who's misgendering someone?"

Un-fucking-believable.

And he's just going to keep laughing in my face.

"That was one of the things we found, when you use the wrong words for someone," Mom explains.

"Well, then maybe you understand how it isn't a fucking joke?" I say just loud enough so they can still hear me.

Neither of them acknowledges it though. In fact, they start looking around at all the other students like they're purposely ignoring me.

"You know, this really is a nice school," Mom says. "Very modern."

"Yeah, it's perfect." God, why won't they just leave? "Now, please—"

"Oh, great," Dad whispers under his breath.

Oh no.

Fuck me.

Hannah's coming right for us, Thomas on her heels, and Nathan's behind Thomas. A fucking conga line of disaster.

"Ben, I'm sorry, I—" Nathan tries to say, but he's blocked out by Hannah.

"What are you two doing here?" Hannah doesn't waste any time, getting right in Mom's face.

"Hannah, listen—" I try to beg her to calm down. "Please don't do this here."

"Stay out of this, Ben," she pushes back.

"Hannah, honey, come on." Thomas takes Hannah by the shoulders and tries to lead her away, but it's no use. "Let's just go outside."

"I'm going to ask you again." She points a finger right at Dad's face. "What are you two doing here?"

"We came to see Ben," Mom says calmly.

"We wanted to support him," Dad says.

This can't be real, this can't be happening. Not here, please God, not in the middle of the freaking school lobby.

"Oh, so *now* you can support them? After you kicked Ben out of the goddamn house?"

Not here, not here, not here.

I feel Nathan step closer, his arm wrapping around my shoulder. All I want to do is pull away, run out the door away from the place. But I can't. I'm frozen where I stand, my stomach churning as that nauseated feeling takes over.

"Hannah Marie De Backer," Dad tries to say, but Hannah isn't having any of it.

"Do you understand what you've put Ben through, the panic attacks, the anxiety? You kicked out your own child, for god sakes."

"This is none of your business," Dad huffs. "We've realized our mistake, and we're working to fix it. Ben's even agreed to come back home after he graduates."

Oh no.

Hannah turns on me. "What?"

This isn't happening, this cannot be happening. "No, no, no, that's not what I said!" Where did he even pull that from?

"We met up the other day and discussed him coming to stay with us once he's done here. That way he can properly pursue a college education." Dad keeps talking.

Hannah starts to laugh. "You met with them? After what they did?"

I have to wrestle my way out of Nathan's grip, and it's not until he's let go that I realize he was basically the only reason I was still standing upright. "Hannah, please stop. I swear to you, I'm not going back there." I stumble, nearly falling to the tile. "I *never* said I'd go back there."

"Ben." Dad actually looks surprised. "You said you'd come home after graduation."

"They aren't going anywhere," Hannah says.

"Listen here, you little bitch—" Dad almost raises his hand. I can see the twitch of his wrist, stopping himself when he remembers we're in public. He never hit Hannah. *Never.*

At least, as far as I knew . . .

But maybe he's at his limit with both of us. Maybe this is proof enough. He'll never change, neither of them will.

"I wasn't serious." I raise my voice without meaning to. "I said what I thought would get you off my back."

"We thought that you'd be a little more understanding." Dad's getting louder with every word.

And suddenly, I'm hyperaware of everyone gathered around us. Like this is some kind of fucking fight in the hallway.

Mrs. Liu's just standing there, staring at me, her face full of pity. Meleika and Sophie found Nathan, and all three of them look like they're ready to actually brawl or something. Hell,

Sophie's even got her heels in her hands, ready to go. Stephanie's staring at the disaster in front of her, alongside every other North Wake student here. Their parents, and friends.

Everyone.

"I . . ." I feel myself start to shake, and I can't stop it.

I can't stop it. Any of it. I can't make them leave, I can't make Hannah calm down, I can't do anything.

"Ben." Nathan's voice is so distant. His hands on my shoulders, they're almost enough to tip me back over the edge.

"I can't do this."

"Ben?" Concern washes over Hannah's face, the anger gone in an instant. "Ben, come on, let's get you home."

"No. I'm not going anywhere with you." I shake my head and turn to look at Nathan. "Can we leave?"

"Yeah . . ." he says after a second. "Sure, come on." Nathan's grip tightens, and he leads me around the corner. Right to the door.

"Ben!" someone shouts. I don't know who, and really, I don't care.

I let Nathan lead me to his car. It's in its normal spot in the student parking lot. Before I can crawl into the passenger seat, I hear the *click* of heels behind me on the pavement.

"Benjamin!"

Mom. And Dad's right behind her.

"Stop right now, young man!" Dad shouts.

"Leave me alone," I try to say, but when Mom grabs my wrist, I can't help but seize up.

"Ben, we're sorry. We just wanted to support you . . . to prove to you—" Mom's stammering, and I realize she's actually scared.

Maybe because for the first time in a while, she isn't getting what she wants from me. And for a second, I see the woman

I loved. The woman who might still love me. "Just come home, okay? We can talk this through. We'll go meet with that doctor, and maybe he can help you through some of these things."

Her nails quietly dig into my skin.

"No," I say; my voice sounds strange. Even to me. "I'm not going anywhere with you."

"Ben, you'll come home with us right—" Dad starts to say, but I cut him off.

"I'm not your son. If you ever come near me, or Hannah's house again, I'll call the police." I open the door to Nathan's car slowly. "I'm not joking. Don't ever talk to me again." I climb into the passenger seat, feeling the lurch of the car as Nathan backs out of his spot.

I catch a glimpse of Mom and Dad in the rearview mirror, staring at the car, mouths open.

And I honestly hope it's the last time I see them.

TWENTY-ONE

When we get to Nathan's house, I walk up the stairs to his bed-room, like I own the place or something.

"I'm going to talk to my parents real quick," he says. "I'll be right up."

I almost go with him, because the second his hands leave me, I miss his touch. But I can't let his parents see me like this. I climb the stairs slowly, but when I finally make it to his room, I'm lost. I don't know where to go, if I should lie on the bed or throw open the window and crawl out onto the roof.

Before too long I hear the sounds of his footsteps coming up the stairs, the creak of the hardwood floors underneath his feet.

"Want to lie down?" he asks.

"Sure," I say, and I get that ache in my jaw. I know if I keep talking, I'll just start crying.

Nathan sits against the wall and grabs a pillow, laying it in his lap. "Come here," he says, patting it.

I'm not in the mood to argue or question it, so I crawl up the bed and lay my head down. He says, "My mom did this for me when I was younger. It always made me feel better." His hands move to my hair and begin threading through the curls. It's a sort of relaxing I've never felt before.

It's taking everything in me not to fall apart right now. "I'm sorry you saw that."

"It's not your fault," he says. I listen to his breathing. "Is there anything you want me to do?"

"Can I stay here? Just for a little bit?"

"Of course, as long as you need to. Anything else?"

I shrug. I'm not exactly partial to anything right now.

"I know what we need." His fingers don't stop, even as he leans over to his nightstand to grab something.

The press in my ear surprises me, but Nathan slides the earbud in smoothly. He hits play on his phone, and there's this really haunting sound, almost like a horror movie. Then this acoustic guitar kicks in, and a guy starts singing with a voice that sounds just as sad.

"Who is this?"

"Troye Sivan." Nathan chuckles.

It's nice, but not what I'd expect from Nathan. This seems too somber, but the closer I listen to the lyrics, the happier they seem.

I close my eyes. I don't want to, but my eyelids are getting too heavy to keep open. "Nathan?"

"Hmmm?"

"I'm glad we met."

"Me too, Ben."

"You've made these last few months suck less."

"Same here."

"I'm sorry."

Nathan's fingers brush my neck. "It's not your fault, Ben. None of it is."

My eyes finally close, and I let myself cry.

———

I don't get out of bed much over the next few days. I just lie there under the sheets, my fingers tracing the faded crescent shapes on my wrist Mom left behind. They still sting if I press hard enough.

My phone keeps vibrating from its spot on the nightstand, the lock screen filled with unanswered messages. I stare at the way the screen lights up, Nathan's name flashing again and again. I pick up the phone and stare at the texts. Every single one he's sent over since Saturday morning.

I stayed in his bed, stayed with him, as long as I could. And if I had my choice, I wouldn't have left. But I knew if I didn't go home, Hannah would probably have filed a missing person's report or something. When I came back, she and Thomas were home. They both tried to talk to me, but the second I saw Hannah, I got angry all over again.

I went up to my room, slamming the door behind me. And I hardly saw them for the rest of the weekend. They made sure I ate, and that was it, I didn't leave a lot of room for them to stick around and talk to me.

At least they didn't make me go to school today.

Nathan: *Good afternoon!*

Nathan: *Just want to see how you're doing!*

Nathan: *Missed you today, I got your homework from the office.*

Nathan: *Mel and Sophie wanted me to check in, see if you're okay.*

Nathan: *Did you know it's male peacocks who have all the colorful plumage? the females are sort of bland looking.*

I can't help but laugh at the last one because it screams Nathan. I really don't deserve someone like him.

No one does.

Nathan: *I can keep sending random facts if you want!*

Nathan: *Or videos of puppies!!!*

He's sent five, and I watch all of them. I want to reply, to let him know that I'm at least safe. But something in me is just keeping me from typing the simplest of messages.

I am okay.

For some reason, it's easier to text Mariam. The words come easier with them.

Me: *hey*

Mariam: *Hey Benji, what's up???*

Me: *Something happened...*

Mariam: *uh-oh*

Me: *I met with my parents.*

The little bubble beside Mariam's name appears and reappears over and over again for almost a full minute.

Me: *you okay?*

Mariam: *me? Okay? Ben are YOU okay????*

Mariam: *sorry, I just...*

Mariam: *Couldn't even think of what to say to that*

Mariam: *Ben... what happened?*

I tell them everything. The message, meeting with Mom and Dad, them showing up at the art show and the fight with Hannah. The texting already feels easier. Maybe it's because Mariam isn't actually here. I can't see their face while I tell them this, and they won't run over from their house to come and try to comfort me or whatever.

Mariam: *Are you safe?*

Me: *Yeah, they're gone.*

Mariam: *Ben... I don't even know where to begin...*

Me: *They wanted me to go back home with them.*

Me: *I told them no*

Mariam: *THE. FUCK.*

Mariam: *Send me their address, I'm going to go kick their asses*

Mariam: *What can I do?*

Me: *keep me company?*

Mariam: *You got it, want to Facetime?*

Me: *Not right now.*

Me: *Just keep talking, not about them.*

Mariam: *Well...*

Mariam: *me and Shauna made it official, which sucks because my tour will take me out of California next week and she can't come with me.*

Me: *That's great! The official part, not the separating part.*

Nothing feels faker than typing out false enthusiasm while I feel like I'm rotting from the inside out.

Me: *I don't think you told me how you met.*

Mariam: *The usual way. I kept seeing her at a Starbucks and I melted slowly into a puddle of anxiety until she actually came up to me and we started talking.*

Me: *Love at first anxiety attack*

Mariam: *That's how I roll.*

Mariam: *What about you, what's going on with your boy troubles?*

Me: *I don't know... he was there, like he saw the fight and stuff.*

Mariam: *Please tell me they didn't out you*

Me: *They didn't*

If there was a silver lining in all of this, I suppose it was that.

Me: *But I…*

Me: *I think I like him. Like really like him. Maybe more than that.*

Mariam: *That's great, Benji! I'm so happy for you*

Mariam: *Now how do we make the grand declaration of love? I've got those cannons that shoot t-shirts.*

Mariam: *Or a flash mob? We can all dance to a Carly Rae Jepsen song and then you pop out in the middle with one of those 'Will You Go Out With Me' signs*

I want to laugh. I want to laugh so badly, but I can't make myself do it.

Me: *It'll never happen*

Mariam: *Why?*

Me: *I'm too messy*

Mariam: *Messy?*

I take deep breaths. There's that weird feeling in my stomach again.

Me: *He deserves something simpler.*

Me: *And I'm not that*

Mariam: *Don't you think that's his call to make?*

Me: *I don't want to hurt him*

Me: *And I don't want him to hurt me.*

Mariam: *sometimes it's worth it*

Mariam: *Never know until you try right?*

Me: *maybe.*

"Ben?" Hannah's voice almost makes me jump. "You okay?"
I don't answer.

I want to, but I can't right now. It's too much. And in all honesty, Hannah's one of the last people I want to talk to right now.

———

I miss an entire week of school. Which isn't smart since it's getting so close to exam season, but I don't care. It feels like I can't move half the time, and there's no way I can face everyone at North Wake yet. The only time I get up is to use the bathroom. Every other free moment is spent watching something on my phone. One of Mariam's new videos, or Bob Ross painting something. Anything to take the edge off.

Thomas brings me food, but I can only nibble at it, even though it feels like my stomach is trying to digest itself. I don't have much of an appetite. "Hannah made an appointment with Dr. Taylor tomorrow. She has an opening after lunch."

I notice that it's not a request. I'll be going to this appointment, even if they have to drag me out of bed. I'll have to tell Dr. Taylor I've been neglecting my meds. I know not taking them is only making things worse, but I just can't bring myself to take them, I don't know why.

"Can you talk to me, Ben?" He reaches for my hand, but I bury it under the sheets. "Or at least talk to Hannah?"

"Not right now." I'm not angry with her, except that I am. I know it wasn't really her fault, that Mom and Dad lied, just like they always did. Trying to make themselves the good guys. But it still hurt. "Just leave me alone."

"Do you think you want to try and go to school tomorrow? Hannah can pick you up for the appointment."

Nothing. My answer would be no. I can't face everyone after

all of this. I just can't. I know I need to, and I know the actual probability of anyone giving a shit about what happened at a student art show over a week ago is slim. But I can't get over the feeling.

———

Despite everything, I force myself to go back. It's the end of the year, and while I'd love nothing more than to wallow in my own misery for the next month, the idea of repeating a year is not something I find appealing.

Nathan doesn't try to talk to me in Chemistry. Maybe he knows I'm not in the mood. When the bell for lunch rings, I hang back for a few seconds.

"Hannah's waiting for you in the office, Ben." Thomas waits for me to grab my bag. He even follows me the entire way to the office. No worries, Thomas, I don't feel like running anywhere. Or I don't have the energy, at least. I'd really rather do nothing but go home and crawl back under the sheets until I have to repeat all of this again tomorrow.

"You feeling okay?" Hannah asks when we're in the car.

"Yeah," I mutter.

"I want you to tell her about the show, okay?"

I really don't want to talk about it again, but I think I should. Or I *know* I should. My guess is that Hannah's already mentioned something to her. I hope she has. Maybe then I won't have to.

"Ben?" The way she says my name makes it feel like I'm a thousand miles away. I just stare out the window as we drive past the bright walls of North Wake. She doesn't try to strike up a conversation again. I'm sure she knows it's pointless. It takes every bit of effort I have left to crawl out of the car and make my way to the elevator. Hannah goes to her usual spot in the corner of the room.

"Good morning, Ben." Dr. Taylor's already holding the door open for me. "Or should I say good afternoon?" She chuckles and glances at the clock on the wall. "My, where does the time go?"

I look back at Hannah. She gives me one of those half smiles that I think is supposed to mean she's trying to be supportive. "Can Hannah come in?"

They both look sort of surprised, but I just really don't want it to be me and Dr. Taylor.

Dr. Taylor just nods. "Of course. Hannah?"

"You sure, sib?" Hannah asks, grabbing her bag.

I nod and walk into the office, taking my spot on the ugly yellow couch. Hannah sits at the other end.

"So, how're you doing, Ben?"

I shrug and listen to her write something down.

"It's been awhile since we've met. Has anything happened?" She asks it in a way that I can tell she's referring to the meeting with Mom and Dad. I just shrug again. Apparently, it's all I'm good for at the moment. I can feel the frustration in the way Dr. Taylor sighs, and I want to apologize.

"Can I speak?" Hannah raises her hand and looks at me, like she needs my approval or something.

"Of course," Dr. Taylor answers for me.

"It's been over a week and they've just been . . ." Hannah looks at me. "Like this, like . . ." She trails off like she's searching for the right word.

Has it really been over a week? I try to lay the time line out in my head. Days of lying in bed, not showering or eating or bothering to talk to anyone.

It couldn't really have been a week . . . could it?

"Unresponsive?"

"They haven't been doing anything. No talking, barely eating. I checked their journal and I don't think they've been taking their medication either."

Checking my journal? I want to tell myself that means Hannah cares, but all I'm hearing is that she's been going behind my back, looking into things that aren't her business.

"What happened to cause this?" Dr. Taylor asks me. But Hannah does before I have a chance to.

"Our parents," she says. "They came to Ben's art show."

"Oh. You met with them, didn't you?" Dr. Taylor writes something down.

"You knew about this?" Hannah asks.

"I did," Dr. Taylor says quietly. "Ben and I discussed it at our last meeting."

Hannah opens her mouth, but then she just huffs and sinks back into the couch. "I can't believe you thought it was a good idea."

"I never suggested Ben meet with them, I simply gave my opinion."

"Yes, but—"

"Hannah." Dr. Taylor holds up a finger. "I let Ben make their own decision. Now please." Wow. I stare at Dr. Taylor, a little dumbfounded. And if I'm being honest, I'm a little jealous of the way she shut Hannah down. "Ben, would you mind starting from the beginning, so Hannah knows the full story?"

"It started with a message." I glance toward Hannah. "Mom sent it a few months back, but I didn't see it until recently." Then I turn back to Dr. Taylor. "We met and they . . . they wanted me to go home with them, claimed they'd learned and wanted to try."

"Try what, Ben?" Dr. Taylor asks.

"To be a family again, I guess."

Hannah still isn't really looking at me. "Why didn't you tell me, Ben?"

"Because I knew you'd overreact."

"Well, I don't really think that's a reason." She crosses her arms. "You should've shared that message with me. I could've gone with you."

"Because the reunion at school went so well, didn't it?"

"Ben," Dr. Taylor chimes in. "Why did you think Hannah would overreact?"

"She always did when it came to Dad. I think she proved that at the show."

Dr. Taylor jots something down. "Okay, now *that* I don't know about."

"I had an art show at school. And everything was going great until—" I start to say.

And Hannah interrupts me. "They showed up."

"I see," Dr. Taylor says. "And what happened?"

"They made a scene." Hannah pouts. "Embarrassed me, Ben, their friends."

I snort. "Yeah, *they* made a scene."

"Well, they did!" Hannah actually looks surprised. Like, really? She can't be serious right now.

"Hannah, none of that would've happened if you would've just stayed back. That's why I sent Nathan to keep you away."

"They shouldn't have been there, Ben."

"You think I don't know that?" God, she's really going for it. "I was handling it. They were going to leave before you saw them and started a fight. Just like you always used to." I can hear my voice getting louder, but I can't keep it back anymore.

"Oh, so I started the fights?" Hannah growls.

"Most of the time? Yeah! Were Mom and Dad kinda shitty? Of course, but you didn't have to fight with them every chance you got. That's what they wanted, Hannah. They thrived on that shit and so did you!"

"Ben . . ." Hannah's eyes are wet.

"You always used to do that. You'd keep fighting with them even though you knew it was no use, that it was just a waste of time. And that's what you did at school. Started a fight for no reason."

"No reason? Ben, they abandoned you—"

"Well, they weren't the only ones who've done that, are they?" I can't keep it back anymore. It's all about to flood over, the waves are lapping at the edge, and I can't keep it back. "Ten years, Hannah. Ten years."

"What do you mean?" she asks, but she already knows. There's no way she can't.

"For ten years you left me with them. With a note and a phone number, which might as well have been a big 'fuck you, I'm done, you're on your own now, kid!'" I collapse back into the couch, my shoulders lurching.

I don't feel any better. In fact, I feel like I'm going to be sick. And then the tears come.

"I was just a kid. I didn't have a phone or anything. How was I supposed to call you without them knowing?"

"I didn't . . ." Hannah runs a hand through her hair.

"But that was it. A phone number I couldn't call, and an address to a place I couldn't get to. I understand that you had to leave. That you couldn't take it anymore, I'm not mad at you for that." I wipe my eyes with my sleeve, and Dr. Taylor slides the box of tissues toward me. "But I was alone. I was alone and scared, and I didn't really know what'd happened to you. You knew how bad they could get, and you just left me to fight for myself."

For a few seconds, the room is totally quiet, save for my quiet sobs. Hannah's staring at the place on the floor, and Dr. Taylor's looking between the two of us. I guess maybe waiting for the next explosion.

"Ben?" Dr. Taylor's voice is surprisingly calm. "Are you okay?"

"I'm sorry, I just . . ." I shake my head. "I didn't mean that, Hannah, I'm sorry."

"No." She still isn't looking at me. "No, I get it." Then she buries her face in her hands and lets out this long groan. "Oh God, I can't believe this."

"I'm sorry," I say, and then again. And again, like they're the only two words left. "I'm sorry, I'm sorry, I'm sorry."

"Why are you sorry?" Hannah asks, her voice made up half of laughter, half of sobs. "I'm the one who should be fucking sorry. The first chance I got I left that house and never looked back." Her eyes finally meet mine. My eyes, our father's eyes. "I fucked up."

"Well, to be honest, in the sort of situation you two came from, there are rarely winners," Dr. Taylor says. "Tell me what you're feeling, Hannah."

Hannah blows into a tissue, not the most graceful sound. "That I messed up."

"Yes, well." Dr. Taylor chuckles. "That I understand, but you must be feeling something deeper than that?"

"I'm just sort of confused, and angry with myself."

"About?"

"How right Ben is." She plucks another tissue, and wipes under her eyes. "When I left, I still thought about them, almost every day. Until, I guess . . ." Hannah's voice falters, and she starts to shake her head. "My husband, Thomas, he didn't even know about Ben until we'd been dating for a few years."

"You didn't tell him?" Dr. Taylor asks. "How did he find out?"

"We were unpacking. He found a photo album I took, and he saw Ben's pictures."

"So, you really did forget about me?" I stare at her. I don't know why I'm shocked. This was a truth I already knew. Maybe I thought she could prove me wrong. That she'd admit to fighting for custody of me or trying her best to mail me letters only to have them intercepted by Mom or Dad.

But no. My own sister forgot about me.

"I didn't forget about you, Ben," Hannah says. "I just . . . had other things on my mind."

"Ah." I stare ahead. "Because that makes everything better."

"Ben, tell me what you're thinking." God bless Dr. Taylor. If she wasn't here to mediate this whole thing, I think we might've started tearing each other's hair out. "Are you angry with Hannah?"

"I'm not angry," I say. I don't think I am, at least. "But it still hurts."

Dr. Taylor nods. "And that's perfectly valid. Do you ever think she could make it up to you?"

"She has, hasn't she?" All the things she's done for me. Jesus, I don't have any right to be angry at her. The clothes, the food, getting me into school, giving me a bed.

"You're still hurt, aren't you?"

I nod.

"It's a hard thing to forget, isn't it? Even harder to forgive." Dr. Taylor asks, "Hannah, do you think that's where your willingness to help Ben comes from?"

"Well, they're my sibling," Hannah says. "I'd do anything . . ." Then she stops. "I like to think I'd do anything for them."

"Except make sure they're safe?" It's odd how Dr. Taylor can keep something from sounding like an accusation. Her words don't sound mean or directed at Hannah in some sort of personal attack. They sound like the truth. Simple and easy. "I'm sure it'd be easy to help Ben now, you two have reconnected, and you've been able to have an actual relationship. But back in January? After a decade apart, was it really so easy?"

"No." Hannah breathes. In through her nose and out through her mouth. "Thomas and I, we didn't sleep that night. After I went and got Ben."

"Really?" I ask.

"We weren't sure why you'd been kicked out. Neither of us wanted to assume the worst, but for a little bit, we actually considered calling the police. We didn't, obviously." Hannah cracks a smile. "By the time the sun came up, we knew we had to help you, no matter what had happened."

"Hannah." Dr. Taylor straightens in her seat, notepad and pen forgotten. "When you took Ben in, when you bought them clothes and necessities, when Thomas got them into a new school, what was your goal?"

Hannah answers without hesitation. "Protecting them."

"Do you think a part of you was trying to make up for your absence?"

This one's less easy. Hannah's mouth hangs open for a few seconds, her eyes unfocused. "I . . . maybe."

"Ben." Dr. Taylor looks right at me, like her sharp eyes can see right through me. "Do you feel better? Now that you've told Hannah how you feel?"

"Not really," I say. There's just a bigger void between us now, and I don't know what could possibly fill it.

"Do you wish you'd stayed quiet?"

"No. I *am* glad I said something, but I don't know." This has all just been really confusing, and I'm not really sure what we were trying to accomplish here.

"What do you want from Hannah now? What can she do to make you feel better?"

"I don't really know." I don't want anything else from her; she's done so much for me. "She's the only reason I've made it this far."

"There's nothing that you can think of?"

I look at Hannah, her red-rimmed eyes, her messy hair. I'm guessing I look about the same right now. There really is no mistaking us as anything other than siblings. We have so much of our parents in us, sometimes too much.

But we can't help it.

"No."

TWENTY-TWO

"Can we talk, just for a second?" Hannah asks me when we're back home.

"Didn't we just do that?" I say. I don't want to be an asshole, but I just don't have it in me right now.

"I wanted to tell you something. Something I didn't want Dr. Taylor to know."

Oh.

Already my mind is racing with whatever it could be. Something so bad she wouldn't even want to say it out loud to anyone but me?

"Is that smart? Shouldn't we do it with her?"

"If I wanted her to know I would've told you both at the appointment." Hannah's voice is surprisingly short, but then she closes her eyes and takes a deep breath and starts walking toward the kitchen. I follow her, the air between us feeling more poisonous with every step. "Sorry."

The entire ride back home, we didn't speak to each other. It was weird, and I was starting to feel like this wasn't something we'd be able to fix.

"Sit down." Hannah points to the chair at the table in the corner, the exact spot where I'd come out to her. "I haven't told anyone this, except Thomas, and I only told him a few years ago, after we were married."

"Okay."

"I want to tell you about why I left the house."

"I thought it was just because Mom and Dad were so

suffocating," I say, even though I feel like right now isn't *my* time to talk.

"That was part of it, but there's more." She clasps her hands together.

"Okay . . . What was it?"

"So, about a month before I graduated, I was seeing this guy, and we decided to sleep together."

"You were dating someone?" I ask her.

Hannah nods. "That's a part of the story."

"Oh, sorry." I had no idea, but that was probably on purpose.

Hannah takes a long sigh, like she's thinking of what to say next. "We were safe, used a condom and everything, but that doesn't always work. A few weeks later when I was supposed to get my period, I didn't."

Fuck.

"You were . . ."

"No, no." Hannah shakes her head. "Just my cycle, it was weird. I think I was syncing up with some of the other girls in my class. That's not the point." She takes another breath. "I *thought* I might be pregnant though. So, I bought a few tests, did them, all negative."

I notice her hands are shaking.

"I thought I threw them all away. I was so careful." Hannah shakes her head, almost like she's talking more to herself than she is to me. "But I guess I forgot one or maybe Mom was snooping in the trash but . . . she found out."

"Hannah . . ."

"She freaked, obviously. I told her they were all negative. That's when she figured out I was dating Mark, the boy I'd slept with. I asked her to keep the secret from Dad, because I knew he'd blow a fuse. And she told me she would."

Hannah swallows, and it feels like it takes forever for her to start talking again.

"Except she didn't. She told him at some point, and he exploded. Told me I was a disappointment, that he 'didn't raise a whore.' That was the only time he ever hit me, and that was the night I decided that I couldn't be there anymore, and I figured after graduation was as nice a time as any."

"Hannah, I didn't—"

"I know, you didn't know. I didn't tell you for a reason. But that was why I left. And it hurt me for so long to know that I was leaving you with them, Ben. Part of me hoped they'd get better, or maybe they'd go easier on you." She lets out this pitiful little chuckle, if you can even call it that. "Maybe all this is my fault. Maybe I should've called child services, told them where you were. But I was only eighteen, I couldn't take care of a kid. So, I thought you'd end up in the system. And if that happened . . . I knew I'd never see you again." The tears fall quickly down her face. "I'm sorry, Ben, I'm so sorry."

"I . . ." I can't move, and there are no words for what I'm feeling right now. This mix of helplessness, guilt, the betrayal, the bile rising in the back of my throat. I get up from my seat and I walk over to her, pulling my sister into the tightest hug I can manage. I don't care if it's hurting me, or her, I just want her to be close to me right now, and I never want to let go of her.

"I'm sorry, Hannah. I'm so sorry." I start sobbing, the room filled with nothing but the sound of us crying while we hold each other.

"I'm sorry, Ben." Her arms wrap around me. "I felt like it was my fault for so long, that I left you there with them. I should've done more."

"It's not your fault," I tell her. "It's them . . . it's no one's fault but theirs."

We pull away from each other, and for a second it's awkward silence, but then we start laughing when we see each other. Red, puffy faces. Hannah's makeup has run a little.

"Don't laugh," she says, walking over to the counter to grab some paper towels. "It's not funny," she says while trying to keep back another laugh.

And I can't stop myself from giggling. "It's pretty funny."

But then we stop, and it's awkward again. Hannah balls up the paper towel and eyes me, stepping a little closer. "I love you, kiddo. You're the best sib a sister could ask for."

"I love you too." We hug each other again, and there's this feeling that sort of washes over me. Because it actually feels like things might be okay again.

Maybe not right away, but they'll get there.

One day.

———

School's helping keep my mind busy, which isn't really something I ever thought I'd be grateful for. It's officially the start of exam season, and May is pretty much nonstop for seniors. The semesters at North Wake are shorter than Wayne's, so instead of the school year ending in June, it ends in May. And the whole month is going to be spent getting our caps and gowns, rehearsing for graduation, signing yearbooks, preparing for senior night, and getting ready for prom.

Which means that no one really has the time to care about what happened at the art show. Maybe they wouldn't have cared anyway. There's still the feeling that everyone is watching me, or laughing at me behind my back, but maybe that's normal. And

Meleika and Sophie haven't really brought it up. Maybe Nathan talked to them. Or maybe they just know not to talk about it.

Mrs. Liu hasn't talked about it either, which might be what I'm most grateful for. She's very good at acting like nothing's happened. Bless her.

At least I can knock prom and senior night off my list of things to handle. I'd even skip graduation if I could, but North Wake won't let you graduate unless you come to all the practices and attend the actual ceremony. Apparently, they hold your diploma hostage until afterward. So that's sweet of them.

There are nights I know I should be studying, or reviewing, or doing the practice quizzes. But I can't. Because what's the point? When all's said and done, I'll barely scrape by in English, and if I never have to write another essay in my life, I'll be very happy. I actually thought about maybe getting Nathan's help, but we haven't really talked much over the last two weeks.

Actually, he's talked to me plenty, I've just been too selfish to respond.

That probably isn't how I should be thinking of it, but I can't stop myself. I have no idea what I'm going to say to him.

The rest of my classes will be easy enough. We have to take an actual exam in Art, which sucks, but I know enough about the "history" aspect of the subject to pass. Chemistry will be the real kicker since Thomas can't give me the exam. Something about nepotism, and it not being fair. Luckily, the test is made by the state, so all I really have to do is take it in a different room than everyone else. Just three weeks.

Three whole weeks.

Three weeks to get ready to never see Nathan ever again. He brought his letter from UCLA to lunch the other day. He got in, with a pretty big scholarship too, so he's not even going to worry about his other choices. In three weeks he'll be getting ready for school. In two months he'll be touring the campus, a month after that, he'll be one of UCLA's newest students. And I'll be nothing but a memory.

———

"Hey, kid." Hannah knocks on my door.

"Hey." I try my best to sound casual.

"Do you have any plans tonight?" She takes a seat right on the edge of my bed. Her usual spot.

"No." Besides wallowing in a pool of self-pity and anxiety? I don't know what's hit me lately, maybe the art show is still at the back of my head, and everything that Hannah told me after. It feels like my parents aren't the people I knew anymore.

I mean, my opinion of Dad hasn't changed that much but Mom . . . I thought she was different. It makes me think about everything I ever told her. If she really went behind my back like she did to Hannah.

"Do you want to do anything?"

"Not particularly."

"Come on!" She hops off the bed and pats at my legs. "Let's party, let's get loose. It takes two, come on!"

"Why are you quoting Carly Rae Jepsen to me?"

"Okay, first of all she only covered that song. Secondly—" Hannah shakes her head. "Never mind, come on, you've sulked enough." She reaches for my hand before she remembers the whole touching thing.

I put down my sketchbook. Not that I've been working on much anyway. All my Art assignments are done, and I've basically been painting at school nonstop since I won't have the art room soon. "What's gotten into you?"

Hannah sighs and runs a hand through her hair. "Okay, guys, I tried!" she shouts to no one. Or at least, I think it's no one, until Nathan and Meleika come down the hallway.

"You call that trying?" I hear Meleika mutter.

"What are you two doing here?" I ask.

"Well, you've been so down lately," Meleika says. "So we figured we'd kidnap you and take you to senior night!"

"No, thanks," I say.

"You mean I brought this pillowcase for nothing?" Nathan eyes the thing balled up in his hands.

"I thought it might be a good idea for you to get out." Hannah sits back on the edge of the bed. "Go have fun, be a kid for one more night."

"Yeah, no." I roll over on my side.

"Come on!" Nathan hops on the end of the bed. "It'll be fun."

"There's bowling." Meleika says this like it adds some kind of incentive for me to get out of bed. "And skating." Strike two. "And everyone's going to be there." Strike three.

"Okay, I'm going to talk to Ben, y'all wait downstairs." Hannah shoos them both out of my room, closing the door behind them.

"I'm not going," I say again.

"I heard you."

"Good." I'll apologize to everyone on Monday or something.

"Ben . . ." Hannah huffs. "I know this hasn't been the easiest time for you."

Understatement of the freaking year. "Yeah, and right now I just want to be alone. Okay?"

"You've been alone for the last month, Ben." A month? I guess it has been that long. "You've hardly talked to me, or Thomas. Nathan said you've been unresponsive at school. And the second you get home you crawl into bed. I know you're feeling a lot of things, with Mom and Dad and—"

"I'm allowed to feel sad about this, Hannah." I'm trying not to be frustrated with her, but everything she says sounds terribly close to her telling me just to get over all this even if she doesn't mean for it to.

"I didn't say that you shouldn't feel sad. I'm just saying you need to prove them wrong." Her words echo for a bit, settling in my ears. "Be sad, hell, sit in bed all weekend and just watch Netflix. I've had those times too. But don't stop living your life for them." I feel her drop back down onto the bed. "I know it's hard, and I know that you need help, but you've got some amazing friends who are there for you, and amazing opportunities. And an amazing sister, if I can toot my own horn. But you can't let them control you like this, Ben."

"Easy for you to say."

"No, it isn't." She sighs. "There are still days I feel like they're right behind me, waiting. I'm always sort of scared it'll never go away."

I try my best not to breathe, not to move a muscle.

"Because even when I finally got out of that goddamn house they still had a hold on me. And it's breaking my heart to see you going through the same thing, Ben."

"I . . ."

"I want you to have a good life. I don't want you to waste years trying to forget about them like I did. You've got this amazing support system of people who care about you. I mean, when I moved out I hardly had anyone. People I'd talked to in Goldsboro maybe once or twice. I'm actually jealous of your friends, if I'm being honest. They seem pretty awesome."

I let myself smile. "They are."

"I know . . . I know none of this has been easy. But I think you owe it to yourself. Lying in bed, you've got nothing but time to sit here and think about every little thing they did."

"I don't think you really know what's going on, Hannah."

"I don't," she says. "Not really. Only you can know that." She sighs. "But I was in a similar spot when I finally got out from underneath them."

"And what helped you get out of it?" I ask.

"Putting myself out there. Making friends, doing things. It kept me from thinking about them all the time."

I let her words sink in. And I know she's right. I can't just sit in this bed for the rest of my life. But right now, it's all I seem capable of. The universe has crashed down around me and all I can do is lie in the aftermath.

Maybe I'm being dramatic.

And maybe I'm not. I don't know.

But what I do know is that Hannah's right. And I think it's time I made a decision for myself.

"I'm going to tell Nathan and Meleika you aren't coming. Maybe we'll order takeout tonight or something." She pats my leg, and I feel the bed relax as Hannah stands up, her footsteps inching closer to the door.

"Hannah?" I say, my voice hoarse.

"Yeah?"

I sit up, catching sight of myself in the mirror behind my dresser. God, I look like death. "I'll go," I say. "Tell them I'll be down in fifteen minutes."

"So, what do we do first?" Sophie pulls her car into the parking lot of this huge sports complex. Reading off the list of things we can do already makes me regret my decision to come here. But it's too late now.

"Bowling!" Meleika shouts. "I'm going to kick all your asses."

"Pssh." Nathan rolls his eyes. "If they let you put in the kiddie rails, maybe."

"Ben?" Sophie asks.

"Bowling is fine." I'll probably just sit there and watch anyway.

We show our student IDs at the door, and it's already pretty chaotic in here. "Come on." Nathan leads us to the side of the complex with the huge "Bowling" sign. It must not be the most popular sport in Raleigh, because five of the twelve lanes are open.

Thankfully Meleika picks the one right at the very end. We both sit down at the center console seat, eyes bouncing from the screen in front of us to the one hanging from the ceiling.

"Oh, you don't have to put me in," I say when I see her typing in my name.

"Come on, you've got to do at least one game," she says.

"I'm not that good at bowling."

"Last time we were here, Nathan bowled a forty." She keeps her voice low. "You'll be fine."

"How is that even possible?" I ask.

"Hey, no whispering." Nathan goes over to the machine that cranks out the balls and fiddles around with a few before settling on one that fits his long fingers. Sure enough, the second it lands, the ball drifts to the right, sinking into the gutter.

I can't stop myself from laughing. "Oh my God."

Nathan's giving us such an evil look while he waits for his ball to return. His second try goes marginally better, but he only knocks down two pins.

"Are you, like, trying to be bad on purpose?" Sophie asks.

"No, no, he is not," Meleika says under her breath before looking right at me. "Your turn."

Besides birthday parties as a kid, I've never bowled before, and back then we *did* have those rail things, so I was sort of, accidentally, the best one there. I don't even know what sort of ball I'm looking for though, so I take the light pink one. It seems to fit my fingers all right, and it's not too heavy.

I throw the ball down the lane, scared for a moment that I'm going to go along with it, but it slips right off my fingers and glides smoothly, striking the pins right in the middle and sending all of them toppling. The big screen above me flashes with a huge red X.

"That's good, right?" They should probably find a better way to show off a strike. The three of them are all clapping for me when I take my seat again.

"We'll say it's beginner's luck." Nathan pats my shoulder.

"And we'll say it's you being a sore loser." Sophie takes her turn.

It's actually pretty fun, as much as I hate to admit it. Nathan's as terrible as Meleika promised, barely scraping by with a 60. According to Meleika, that's the highest she's ever seen him get. At first the strike is just beginner's luck, but after a while I get the hang of it and end up with 200.

"Are you sure you aren't some secret professional bowler, and you just want us to feel bad about ourselves?" Sophie drops off a basket of fries in the middle of the table. More and more people have begun to flow in, meaning there is a line for the lanes now. So we only get in one game before we have to take a break.

"I promise." My phone buzzes in my pocket.

Mariam: *officially landed in NC, gonna nap for 15 hours. Don't ever fly, Ben, it's not worth it.*

I laugh to myself and send them a few kissy emojis.

Me: *sleep well, see you tomorrow.*

"Who is that?" Nathan leans over my shoulder. "Texting quite a few kissy faces."

My first instinct is to throw my phone across the room. "No one," I say, sipping my drink.

"So, what do we do now?" Meleika bites a fry in half.

"What are we supposed to do?" I ask.

"It's just whatever we want to do," Sophie says. "The school rents out the whole place until like six in the morning, so we've got plenty of time."

I check my phone again. It's only nine. "We don't have to stay the whole time, right?"

"Oh, hell no." Sophie laughs. "I'm putting on the strict one a.m. curfew for all of y'all. Unless you want to walk home."

"We could do laser tag." Nathan reads down the list again. "Or skating?"

"I can't skate," I say.

"Oh, then we definitely have to go skating." Nathan chuckles. "I need to see that."

"No way in hell," Meleika says, winking at me. "I can't skate either."

"Fine." Nathan groans. "Putt-Putt?"

"I'm game," I say.

Meleika kicks ass at Putt-Putt, but the course is outside, and it's getting pretty chilly, so after a few holes we just head back inside. There's this whole room near the arcade rented out for dancing. Nathan and Meleika run right in, but Sophie and I hang back, just sort of standing there, staring at the entryway.

"Come on." Sophie hooks an arm through mine, and we head toward the arcade. I've been waiting all night for her and Meleika to say something about the art show. But they haven't. They didn't even say anything at school yet, but maybe they were waiting to get me alone.

Or maybe they aren't planning on saying anything at all? Maybe they're just trying to be as normal as humanly possible with me because they think that's what I need right now? I hope it's the last one. Because I don't want to talk about it anymore.

I want to forget that night ever happened.

"What do you want to play?" Sophie asks.

I look around, and nothing seems all that interesting, and ever fewer games are two-player, so we end up in front of the claw machine game. And Sophie's pretty amazing at it. Like, ridiculously amazing.

"My dad taught me a few tricks." Sophie aims the crane just right, so she picks up this cat from an anime I've never seen. Her tenth win in under half an hour. "Here." She hands the cat to me.

"You sure?"

"Yeah, I've already got one of him." Then she starts to wrestle with the bundle of plushies on the floor. "Mind helping me?"

I take most of them, trying to balance them all in my arms. It really should not be this difficult to carry around a bunch of stuffed animals.

"So, this is where you two ran off." Nathan's laugh makes me jump. "Aw, cute." He taps the nose of the pink Yoshi at the top of the pile.

"Shut up." I almost throw one of the plushies at him, but I think I'll drop them all if I do.

"Mel wants to do laser tag next. Y'all game?"

"Yeah." Sophie wrangles her keys out of her purse. "Here, you want to go put those in the car?"

"Come on." Nathan grabs the keys. "We'll meet you two over there."

"Just don't take my car on a joyride." Sophie winks and walks off in the direction of the arena.

We brush past our classmates, Nathan waving to people every now and then. I try to tell myself they're staring at Nathan, or the bundle of stuffed animals in my arms. Because that's what they're doing. No one cares about the art show; no one cares about what happened there. I just have to keep telling myself that.

"Having fun?" Nathan nudges me.

"Yeah," I say. "Why?"

"Just wondering." He huffs. "I was worried about you there. After everything happened. You weren't really answering my texts, and you seemed so distant at school."

"Oh," I say. "Sorry."

"Don't apologize. I can't even imagine what you're dealing with." I feel him get closer, like he wants to take my hand or something. Maybe dropping all these plushies wouldn't be such a bad thing?

"It's been . . ." I start to say, but I don't even know how to finish that statement.

"Rough?" he finishes.

"That's probably the nicest word you could use." I see Principal Smith across the room. I don't think she was at the art show. No doubt she heard all about it though. She gives me a half smile and a short wave when she catches me looking.

I try to wave back.

It's weird to think this really all happened because of her. She could've said no to me, denied me a spot in North Wake. I never would've met Mrs. Liu, or gotten to paint as much as I have, or met Meleika or Sophie. Or Nathan.

"Well, if you ever need me for anything just tell me, okay?" Nathan says.

"Okay," I say.

"Anything," he repeats. "I mean it, Ben."

I stare ahead and try not to think too hard about what "anything" implies. "Thank you."

———

I actually don't sleep well that night, which isn't good because Sophie drops me off at home around one thirty. Laser tag ran a little long.

But it has more to do with the fact that in less than twelve hours, I'll be meeting Mariam. At least I hope it's because of that. I've still got time to kill when I do finally decide to get out of bed. Mariam's got a tour of State's campus scheduled, and some kind of special lunch, but after that we're totally free to do whatever we want.

"You want to use my car?" Hannah asks.

"Is that okay?"

"Here." Hannah reaches over the counter and snatches her keys. "Don't be too late, okay? I'll see you at dinner."

"Okay."

"Just don't run over any hydrants, please?" Hannah pleads.

I look at her, and smile. "I mean, I can't exactly promise anything."

"Ha." She takes the keys back. "Funny, kid. Now promise."

"I'll be careful, I swear."

Except when the GPS tries to lead me down a one-way street, I nearly run into someone. And *then* I nearly run over a fire hydrant while I try to get into a parking lot to turn around. This is why I let Hannah drive me everywhere. Eventually I make it to the coffee shop, but when I look around I don't see Mariam, or anyone who could maybe be Mariam from behind.

Oh God, what if I'm so late they left? It's only been ten minutes, but maybe they think I stood them up. I have to double-check my phone to make sure it's even the right day. Definitely Saturday, definitely the time we agreed on. So where are they?

There's a tap on my shoulder. "Ben?"

"Oh my God!" My first instinct is to wrap Mariam in a hug, because they're *here*, they're actually, really here. But then I don't remember if that's haram for them, so I keep my arms to my side and just sort of awkwardly shuffle my feet. Better safe than sorry.

"Oh, please." Mariam throws out their arms. "I'm sorry I'm late. You'd think I'd be used to traffic."

"It's okay." Their arms wrap around me. "I was worried I'd missed you or something." We hug for what feels like forever, because they're here. They're really here.

"Sorry," I say, finally letting go. "Guess I got a little excited." I almost want to cry.

"It's cool."

"So, um . . ." I rub the back of my neck.

Great. It only took point-five seconds for me to get awkward. That must be some sort of record.

"Oh, don't get all flustered on me." Mariam nudges me with

their elbow. "Come on, we're getting coffee and you're showing me around."

"Can't promise you I'll be a good tour guide," I say.

"Excellent, you always find the best places when you get lost."

And lost is what we are after just ten minutes, but with Mariam it isn't so bad. We just sort of wander around aimlessly, picking any direction to go in. There's this weird used bookstore where everything inside has yellowed horribly, and the smell is unbearable. And once we're back outside and take in a few lungfuls of actual, sort-of-clean air, we head across the street to a frozen yogurt shop.

My iced coffee is still sitting heavy in my stomach, so I go with a plain vanilla and chocolate fudge. Mariam loads up though. I'm pretty sure at least half their bill is from toppings alone. I see gummy worms *and* bears, cherries, almonds, and Oreo crumbs. And that's just the top layer.

"How do you eat all that?" I ask.

"Listen, I didn't have time for dinner last night *or* breakfast. And the lunch at the school was a total bust, so I'm treating myself."

"That combination can't be good."

"You're right, but I don't care." Mariam picks off a gummy worm covered in chocolate and acts like they're going to throw it at me.

"Hey." I duck. "So where are we going?"

"Don't know. I want to see the water."

"Don't you live in California?"

"And?" They shrug.

"Fine," I say, and before I know it, we've both sort of automatically drifted toward this park. Not Pullen, this is a different one. But there's still a trail and plenty of places to relax in the shade.

"So, how was last night?" God, it still feels like they're going to vanish right before my eyes. "You were out with your friends, right?"

"Yeah, it was fun," I say.

"You got a date for prom yet? Or has that already happened?"

"No, and not yet. Next week, I think, but I'm not going."

"Why not?"

I shake my head. "Why would I?"

"'Cause it's a lot of fun. You shouldn't miss out like that."

"I don't have a date," I say. "Or a tuxedo." Not that I'd really want to wear one.

"So? What about Nathan? You two could just go as friends. Plenty of people do that."

"Yeah, that's so not happening." I don't think I could stomach that. We'd be so close, but we couldn't take that leap. That jump. It'd be a night of punishing myself with every look, every touch.

"Yikes, the crush has been crushed."

"I'm just wondering what the point is."

"Well, that's the real question, isn't it?" Mariam takes their last spoonful of yogurt. "The gummy bears were too much."

I take their empty bowl in the trash along with mine. "The hot fudge might've been overkill too."

"Hot fudge is always necessary. So, I'll pretend you didn't say that." They sigh and lean against the railing, looking down at the water beneath us. "So what, you'll pine over summer break, and then never see him again?"

"That's the plan. I'm sure he'll come back for holidays and

break." But it'll never be the same. He'll get new friends, find people he likes better. Hell, he might come back home one day with a boyfriend, or girlfriend, or partner. Someone who isn't as much of a burden as I am.

"Been there, done that, got the T-shirt. It's not fun, Benji."

"You say that like I don't already know." I let out a slow breath and stare down at the water. Much bluer in the daylight now, but still dark.

"You deserve a happy life, Ben." Mariam keeps going. "More than anyone I know. You're such a smart kid, and you're so kind, and you've got so much love to give."

"Sometimes the world isn't so fair," I say.

"I think you're a living testament to that. Don't you think you owe it to yourself to at least try?"

"I've been thinking about it." Last night, Nathan told me I could talk to him about anything, right? *Anything.* I wonder if that means he already knows something, or if he suspects I'm gay, or bisexual, or pansexual. Or if he's somehow figured out the nonbinary deal. I should be able to tell him anything. He's never given me a reason not to trust him.

"Good! You should do it, I think it's the right choice."

"Maybe." Because what have I done to deserve someone like Nathan? "What if he rejects me? Or doesn't want to be around me. I'll have to come out, there's no way I can't."

"If he won't accept you, then fuck him. But he doesn't seem like that kind of person."

"You don't even know him."

"True. But I know you. And you're so in love with him it isn't funny. It's time to make your grand declaration. I'm sure we could find another T-shirt cannon around here."

I can't help but laugh. "Oh, that's so easier said than done."

"I know." They sigh. "But it's the truth. And you've only got two more weeks of school, and after that, you've got three months with him. What is there to lose? Be brave."

"The last time I was brave I got kicked out of my house."

"Sometimes it's worth it to try again," Mariam adds. "And Nathan isn't like your parents."

"I know."

"You ever dream of just driving back to their house and telling them off?"

"I'd be happier if I never had to see them again. That'd be the real gift."

Mariam giggles. "Damn, kid, you're cold."

"I'm done with them." I shrug.

It's odd. Before all this, I don't know what I believed about them. Even that night on the roof, I told Nathan I might still love them. I don't think I did then, but there's really no telling what I thought exactly.

Now I know for certain. They don't deserve my love.

And I sure as hell don't need theirs.

"Good call."

Deep down, I know Mariam's right. And I know Nathan won't hate me, he can't, but there's still that fear.

And maybe it is worth the risk. I've never felt like this for another person. Ever. When I'm with him, it already feels like I'm out, that he knows. Because he makes me feel more like myself than anyone I've ever known.

Then there's that urge. The one I felt before I came out to Mom and Dad. When I first realized I'm nonbinary, it was like this secret. One that I only I knew. Part of me wanted to keep it that way. But as the months passed, I felt it all bubbling over. Every comment at home or at school. Every time I was called Mr. or sir.

It just kept rising and rising until I just knew I had to tell someone. I had to get it out of me, like it was some sort of poison. And Mom and Dad were who I chose.

That's what this feels like. Every time Nathan uses the wrong pronouns for me, it feels like a stab to the gut. Even if Mariam and Hannah and Thomas know to use the right ones. His words are the ones I care about the most right now.

I need him to know. For my sake.

For his.

"I want to tell him." I say those five little words and they feel like they could end the world. "That I'm nonbinary."

"Yeah?" I can sense the confusion in their voice. But this is the first step. The first logical one anyway. A declaration of love can come later.

"I'm scared, Mariam." It's like it's all catching up with me, and it feels like a dream. I'm going to try and come out to Nathan Allan. I *want* to come out to Nathan Allan.

"I was too." They put their hand over mine. "It'll be worth it."

"How do you know?"

They shrug. "What answer makes you feel better?"

"That you have a hunch? That it'll all go amazingly, and he'll love me for who and what I am. That he won't hate me."

Mariam laughs. "I have a hunch, galbi."

"Galbi?" I look at them. "What's that?"

"It means 'my heart.'"

I lean in closer to them, shoulder to shoulder. "I love you."

"Love you too, Benji."

━━━━━

We walk around for another hour, thankfully avoiding the topic of my parents, or Nathan. It's weird to finally be here with

Mariam. And we've only known each other for about a year and a half now, but when you owe someone your life, can you really call them anything but your best friend?

If it wasn't for them, I'm not exactly sure where I'd be. Probably still at home, wasting away under that roof all by myself, not really understanding who I am. Or if I did understand who I am, I probably wouldn't have figured it out until much later.

"You should come and see me speak tonight," Mariam says while we're walking back to their hotel. Whatever organization they work for really shelled out. It's not the *nicest* place in the city, but even just a night here can't be cheap.

"Maybe." It's like the word rolls around in my head for a bit, and the second it's out there, I hate it. Why am I not more excited about Mariam's speech?

"Come on, smaller crowd, and if I just tell them you're my friend, then no pressure, right?"

"Right." I mean, I've been worried about the group this entire time, running across someone from school or just in general having to come out to an entire group of people. But this is for Mariam. For my best friend. For the person who probably saved my life.

I can't believe I was thinking about not going.

God, I'm an asshole sometimes.

"I'll be there." I make the promise to them, and to myself. "Just have to do the most difficult thing I've ever done first."

"It's going to go amazingly, I promise." Mariam reassures one. "Want to grab dinner when I'm done? There's something I wanted to talk to you about, a new project."

"New project?" I ask.

Mariam just gives me a mysterious smile. "Yeah, I think you'll like it."

"Okay, I'll be there."

"Starts at six thirty. I'll text you the address."

I check my phone. There's still plenty of time to get ready. Maybe I should ask Nathan. Maybe it'd answer any question he has. God, I can't believe I'm doing this. I'm going to come out to Nathan Allan. It might not even be the actual coming out that scares me. It's what he's going to think of me after.

TWENTY-THREE

I try to waste time walking around the park, but that just makes me more nervous, so I sit in the car, slowly typing out a text one letter at a time, until it makes some sort of sense.

Me: *Hey, can you meet me near the Wake County Community Center?*

I need to talk to you.

I close my eyes and hit send.

There, out of my hands. I have to tell him now, right?

Nathan: *Sure, everything okay?*

Me: *Yeah, just need to tell you something*

Nathan: *okay... be there in ten*

Ten minutes to decide how to tell him. Just being up front would be easiest. In theory, at least.

Just say the words. I've said them before, and it's gone well, mostly. Maybe the odds are with me here. Or maybe I can just hand him my phone with an article on being nonbinary, let him read up on it. Then I can answer any questions he'll have.

Maybe I won't do it at all. And I'm wasting his time. And mine.

Time crawls at a snail's pace while I wait for Nathan, the perfect view of the community center right across the street from me. With my luck, he won't even show up, he'll call and cancel, and I'll have worked myself up for nothing.

I glance at the clock on the dashboard. 5:40. Maybe we'll have enough time to make it to Mariam's talk.

"You can do this," I whisper to myself, trying to will my heart to beat slower, my hands to stop shaking around the wheel. "You can do this. He isn't going to hate you, or try to hurt you. That's not who he is."

Wouldn't be the first time I've been wrong. Certainly won't be the last.

A knock on the window pulls me out of this trance, and for a split second I don't even recognize Nathan. But then he gives me that familiar smile, and I roll down the window just enough to tell him to get in. Maybe doing this in the car will be better, less chance of a scene, and if he gets angry enough, he'll just leave himself.

"What's up?" He stretches his legs out, leaning against the door.

"Hey." I try to breathe as calmly as I can.

"Hey. You okay?" He leans in a little closer. "You look like you need help hiding a body."

"Yeah, I just . . . There's something I need to tell you."

"Okay."

"And it's pretty big, and I really don't want you to hate me, but I need to tell you."

"Unless that whole body thing is true, I don't think there's anything to hate about you." He tries to get me to laugh, or even crack a smile, but I can't. I just can't. Because it's taking everything inside me not to break down right now.

I'm doing this.

"I just . . ." I stammer. "I need you not to be you right now."

He leans back in the seat, his mouth a flat line. "Deal."

"And I know it's not totally fair, but you can't ask any more questions, okay? Not until I'm done."

"Pinky promise." He offers me his pinky finger.

And I take it.

"The reason I left home, the reason I was kicked out of my home . . ." I breathe. "Is because I'm nonbinary." I watch his face, and to his credit he doesn't seem surprised or shocked or angry. And he doesn't ask any questions. I can tell he wants to, but he doesn't.

I start with New Year's Eve night, a lifetime ago, and I tell him everything. Calling Hannah, moving to Raleigh, the car outside the house, the appointments with Dr. Taylor and the medication, and everything with Mariam. I'm shaking the entire time, and I'm still shaking when I'm done talking, but I did it. It's done. And there's no taking it back.

And when I am done, and when he can tell I'm done, he finally opens his mouth. "Wow."

"I'm sorry I kept this from you for so long."

"I don't know what to say." I watch him do that thing where he rubs the back of his neck.

"Listen, if this a deal breaker and you don't want to be my friend anymore, then I—"

The way he looks at me, it's as serious as I've ever seen him. "That's not what's going to happen. Why would you think I'd want to lose you like that?"

I shrug, fighting back tears. "I don't know . . . I'm sorry."

"Come here." He pulls me in. At first, I don't want to move, but he's so warm, and I'm desperate for a touch right now. His touch. He rocks us both back and forth a little. "If anyone should be apologizing, it's me." He's sniffling. Is he crying too? "I just spent the last half year misgendering you, and you're apologizing to me?"

"It's not your fault."

"I wish I could've known." His voice breaks, and I feel his tears fall on my hands. "I'm so sorry, Ben, I'm so, so sorry you had to put up with it. And I'm so sorry I did that to you for so long." He's full-on crying now, and it's making me cry more, and we're both blubbering messes.

"I forgive you," I choke out.

I'm sure there are people walking by who can see us, or maybe hear us weeping because we are *not* holding it back. But neither of us care. Or I don't at least.

"I'm sorry I didn't tell you." I breathe. In and out. "I was just scared, I guess."

"You really need to stop apologizing." He lets out this weird sound between a cry and a laugh.

I can't even help myself. "I'm sorry."

"You're the worst."

"I know."

We sit there for a few more minutes, and I just relish in his being here, the warmth of him, the comfort. I can't believe I waited so long to tell him this, I can't believe I ever thought he could hate me.

"We're both messes." Nathan tries his best to wipe away the tears.

"Yeah, we are." I try to relax. Because it's over, it's done. I did it. That weight should be gone, but it isn't. It's still hanging there, pressing on my heart. But it feels lighter, at least. Small victories. Small celebrations.

"I wonder how many people are staring at us."

"Probably a lot," I say.

"So how does this work exactly? What sort of pronouns should I use for you?"

I try to swallow. "I use they and them."

"Okay. I want you to correct me if I use the wrong ones, okay? Promise me."

"Pinky promise," I say. We may only have months left together. But right now, I just want to pretend like we've got an eternity.

"So, what about things like 'dude' or 'my man'?"

"I don't think I've ever heard you say 'my man' before."

"I'm trying out something new."

"Well, please don't use that for me, or 'dude.'" It's gender-neutral enough for most people, but not for me.

"Got it." He looks out the window to the community center. "I do have another question. Why here?"

"Oh, that. My friend Mariam, the vlogger? They're speaking here tonight, and I wanted to come see them." I glance toward the community center, and then back to Nathan. "Would you want to come with me?"

"Why, Benjamin De Backer, it'd be a delight," he says with a smile.

———

The group meets on the fourth floor of the community center. I'm actually glad Nathan agreed to come with me, because I don't really think I can do this by myself. Not right now. I would've waited for Mariam, but I have no clue when they're supposed to be here.

"So, this is your first time here?" Nathan asks.

"Yeah."

"Great, so I'm not the only one that's totally nervous, right?"

"Not at all." I press the button for the elevator.

"Good." Nathan sighs as the doors slide open. "Are you going to tell Sophie and Meleika?"

I shrug. "Don't really know. Do you think they'd be okay with it?"

"I think they'd be fine with your being a ten-foot-tall lizard person in a skin suit."

"Let's not test that theory." I feel the familiar brush of his hand against mine.

"Thank you," he says. "For trusting me with this."

Our palms press together, fingers dancing. "I was scared out of my mind to be honest."

"I hope I didn't make you feel like it wasn't safe or anything."

"It wasn't really you, it was . . . the after. Like what was going to happen when I finally did it. I really didn't want to lose you either."

"I'm very proud of you, Ben."

"Thank you," I say.

"I'm getting kind of excited." Nathan stares at the numbers above the door, watching them rise slowly. "For the meeting."

"I'm glad you're here," I offer.

I have to push away the idea that we're in the wrong building. I doubled-checked all the addresses and the group's page says they meet in the community center. This has to be the right building. I breathe a sigh of relief when the elevator door opens because right there on the list of offices and their room numbers is "Project Safe Space—Room 414."

The directory just outside the elevator says that's to the left, so we follow the arrows, counting down the rooms until I see the one labeled 414. For some reason I'm expecting a big rainbow banner that says "All Are Welcome Here!" or flags hanging all around the door or something, but it matches the rest of the rooms. In fact, the only "decoration," if it can even be called that, is the poster that lists the meetings, naming them "Project Safe Space," and giving the dates for the meetings underneath.

"Ready?" Nathan pulls on the door handle.

"Yeah."

Mariam's already being called to the front of the room when we step in. They catch us, and a smile lights up their face before they refocus on the papers in front of them.

There are only a few stares from other people when we decide to burst in, taking a spot at the back. Mariam doesn't miss a beat though and just keeps going. The actual talk itself lasts about an hour, but then there's another half hour of people asking Mariam questions, and it seems like with every one of them, Mariam falls down this rabbit hole of explanation. They never told me what the subject of the talk would be, but Mariam delves deep into the need for more queer safe spaces. Specifically ones geared toward queer minors, places that don't focus on dancing or drinking, like most clubs do.

And it's not like I didn't know it before, but sitting here, listening to them talk, it hits me just how brilliant my best friend actually is.

"Okay, everyone. I'd love to keep going," they say. "But unfortunately, that's all the questions for now."

The applause is immediate. People even give them a standing ovation, which coming from a smaller crowd is sort of odd. But maybe Mariam deserves that sort of reaction. Nathan and I sort of hang near the back, but since we are new faces, we still catch some attention.

"Hi!" This guy walks up to us.

He's cute, or I guess *they're* cute. I shouldn't be assuming anyone's pronouns. The chances of me screwing up are probably higher here. I shouldn't do that anyway, honestly; I know the pain all too well. "Are you here for the group?" they ask.

"Kinda." I clear my throat. "My name is Ben."

"I'm Nathan." He gives a wave.

"Micah." They don't reach to shake my hand or anything, which I appreciate. "What are your pronouns?" they ask.

"Oh, um." I don't really know why that catches me off guard. "They and them, please."

"Awesome. I use he and him," he says before he looks Nathan's way.

"Oh, I use he and him, I guess. Sorry, not used to the pronoun thing yet."

"It's cool."

Nathan falls into easy conversation with Micah, and then more people sort of crowd around. There's Camryn, who's nonbinary like me; Ava, who's pan and gender-fluid; Cody, who's bisexual; and Blair, who's an aromantic trans girl. They all sort of get caught up in Nathan's gravitational pull, and I'm envious. He just slides right into the conversation, as if he's known everyone for years. Like we're one big happy queer family. I guess that's sort of the point of the whole group really.

I try to chime in here and there, answer any questions I'm asked. But really, I can't help but watch Nathan. He seems so happy.

But eventually Micah has to go to the front of the room and make an announcement that the building is closing. People start running up to Mariam, getting in last-minute questions and pictures.

"Maybe we should just wait outside," I say.

"I was thinking the same thing."

We sit in that silence outside. The comfortable one that comes when it's just the two of us. Well, the two of us and the few people walking around downtown so late at night, but it feels like just the two of us, the cool air of the night keeping us comfortable.

"You know prom tickets go on sale Monday," he says out of the blue.

Why on earth is he telling me this? "Oh yeah?"

"Yeah. You want to go?"

"I don't have anything to wear." Or the money to rent something. And I can't ask Hannah to do that. Not on such short notice.

"We can find you something," he offers.

"I'm good." My eyes fly from the floor to his face.

"You sure?"

"Yeah." I can feel my heart beating faster, and that sweaty feeling in my palms. Because did he just ask me to prom? That's what it sounded like, right? I just thought it was going to be him and Meleika and Sophie all going as friends. Meleika already said they'd made the reservations for dinner and everything.

So even if I say yes, there's really no room for me.

"So, did you like it?" I ask Nathan, desperate for a subject change here. Anything to get us far away from prom. "The talk, I mean."

"Yeah," he says. "She seems pretty popular."

"They," I correct.

"Right, sorry. They, they, they," he starts repeating under his breath. "What's their channel name again?"

"Just search Mariam Haidari," I say.

His eyes go wide when he hits enter and sees all the places Mariam's name is popping up. "Oh my God. You're totally friends with a famous person."

"I guess." I don't know if Mariam's ever seen it that way.

"Come on." He keeps scrolling. "Wow, they've done a lot." Then he sees the picture. *The* picture. And I can tell it's *the* picture because he grips my arm and his eyes go wide. "They fucking met Beyoncé?"

"Yes, I have, and she's lovely." Mariam's voice surprises the both of us as they round the corner. "It's nice to meet you. Nathan, right?" They hold out a hand.

Nathan takes it all too eagerly. "I'm guessing this one's been talking about me?" He nods to me.

"You're such a pain in my side it's sort of hard not to," I say, and Nathan grips his chest and pretends to be wounded.

"Ouch."

"Okay!" Mariam wraps their arms around my shoulders. "Where are we going for dinner, because I don't know about you two, but I'm starving!"

Nathan's already up and walking down the street. I swear, he could be best friends with anyone if you just give him enough time. "If we head down a block, you'll have the best pizza in town. It's still terrible, but in Raleigh, it's the best you'll find."

"I'm game." Mariam glances over their shoulder. "You coming, Ben? We've got that thing to talk about," they say with a wink.

"Yeah." I follow them both closely, watching these two worlds of mine collide. It still feels like a dream.

But if it is, I really don't want to wake up.

TWENTY-FOUR

Prom week might be more of a nightmare than exam week.

Scratch that.

Prom week is *definitely* more of a nightmare than exam week. Student council probably should've spaced things out a little more, maybe started selling tickets at the beginning of April. But nope, they waited until the week of. So now there's a line at the entrance of the cafeteria, stretching all the way down to the front office.

And since Meleika and Nathan are a part of the student council, they have to spend all their time after school decorating, hanging flyers, and making sure everything is to Stephanie's standards. Luckily, it seems like most of the pieces from the Spring Fling can be reused.

I actually thought about coming out to Meleika and Sophie when we got back to school on Monday, but I want to tell them at the same time, and with the way Meleika's stressing, that time definitely isn't now.

"I got two just in case." Nathan comes back to the lunch table with the two tickets in hand.

"I told you I'm not going."

"Just in case." He winks at me and slides the ticket over.

"Well, thank you." I slide the ticket back. "But I won't need it."

"Fine." He folds it up and stuffs it into his wallet. "So, what *are* you going to do Friday night?"

"Probably Netflix and pizza," I say. Thomas and Hannah

officially called it a date night since he hasn't been dragged in to chaperone this year, so I'd have the whole house to myself. I wish I could just ask Mariam to hang out again, but their flight to Florida left this morning.

I watch Nathan's face carefully. We haven't really talked about me being nonbinary much since I came out. He's asked a few questions, tried to learn some things online. He even said he started watching Mariam's videos.

"That's the dream." Sophie sighs. "Did I show you guys my dress?" She flips her phone around.

"Oh my God, they're animals." Meleika runs right for our table and collapses into her seat. "Look, I chipped a nail! And they stepped on my shoes."

"Did you get them?" Sophie asks.

"Yes, I did, Sophie, thank you for being concerned about my well-being." She hands Sophie her ticket.

"Thank you." Sophie takes it, sliding the ten dollars over to Meleika. "You sure you aren't going, Ben? It's going to be fun."

"I think I'll survive," I tease.

"Okay!"

That week I stay after school pretty much every day. Thomas has to come up with a way to spend the last two weeks of class, which seems like a waste, but he says he's got a few cool experiments planned. I pretty much spend the rest of that extra time in the art room. It's going to be hard to leave this place behind. I'll have to ask Hannah if it'll be okay to buy my own supplies. My birthday is in October anyway, and a paint set might not make such a bad gift.

The day of actual prom is a lot more relaxed, especially since half the senior class decides to skip, probably to get ready.

None of the teachers really care either. Thomas just throws on *Planet Earth*, but it somehow manages to enthrall the entire class, except the part where the fungus infects the ant's brain. Everyone pretty much has to turn away from that scene.

"Hey," Nathan whispers, and when I look over at him he slides a piece of paper. It's easy to hide it in the dark, but when I try to read it I have to angle it toward the movie.

My place, tonight, 9 o'clock? is written in big blocky letters. And underneath that he's got Y/N with my extra prom ticket taped to it.

"I told you I'm not going," I whisper.

"Just humor me?" He slides over a marker.

"What is it?" I look at the note again and then back at Nathan. There's something odd about the way he's looking at it, and he won't quite meet my eyes.

"Just answer."

"Not unless you tell me what's up."

Nathan rolls his eyes. "Yes or no?"

I'll never win an argument with this boy. I read over the five words again as if they've changed somehow. I stare at the ticket, the black-and-red font, the clip-art disco ball. What on earth could he be planning to do with it? I circle Y and hand the note back to him.

"You'll need the ticket," he says, and I swipe the note back from him and yank on the ticket, keeping it folded in my pocket until I get home.

If I go over there and he's rented me a tuxedo and tries to drag me to prom, I'm not going to make it easy for him. According to the ticket, the dance starts at eight, so if he wanted to dress me and push me into a limo he'd probably want me there earlier, right? Why does he even want me to go?

———

"Ben? Can you come here for a moment?" Mrs. Liu calls from her office.

"Huh?" I've been thinking about the ticket in my pocket since Nathan gave it to me. Thinking about it so much, in fact, that I haven't been able to focus on drawing or painting anything. So I've just been cleaning up my workstation in the back, which has really suffered lately. "What's up?" I ask, peering into her office.

"Well, this is awkward, but I'll need my key back."

Oh. "Of course." I reach into my pocket and grab my ring of keys, carefully sliding off the one to the art room. As I hand it to her, it feels like I'm giving away this piece of myself.

Good-bye, art room.

"I also wanted to say how proud I am of you."

"I . . . thank you," I say.

"In all my years of teaching, rarely do I get students with the same drive and ambition I've seen in you, Ben." She rests a hand on my shoulder. "I'm really going to miss you."

I hold out my arms and Mrs. Liu is all too eager to take my hug, squeezing me so tight I can hardly breathe for a few seconds. "Whoops, sorry. Don't know my own strength."

"Thank you," I tell her. "You have no idea how much everything you've done means to me."

"Oh, Ben." God, she's actually crying. This is why I don't get sentimental. "How much do I have to pay you to stay?"

Well, I'll still be in Raleigh. "A few thousand?" I offer.

She laughs, wiping the corners of her eyes with her apron. "Deal."

When I get home, I try to make myself busy all afternoon, but I can't focus on any shows, or even Mariam's newest vlog. Georgia is their next stop. I try to talk with Hannah while she gets ready, but I'm so antsy and I can't sit still. I take my second Xanax of the day, making sure I mark it down in the journal, but it's not really helping this weird bubbling in my stomach.

"You okay, kid?" she asks.

"Yeah, just . . ." I drift off without even meaning to.

"Benji?" She snaps her fingers right in my face.

"Would it be that note Nathan passed you in class today?" Thomas asks.

I stare at Thomas, who's leaning over the countertop and typing something on his phone. "How did you—"

"Don't ask, kid," Hannah tells me. "I can't get away with anything around here."

Thomas points at me and then at his eyes. "I see everything. Teacher superpower."

When they've left, I waste the rest of my time pacing back and forth in my room, staring at the time on my phone. I swear it's going slower. I check it once at 8:15, and even though it feels like an hour's passed, it's only 8:17 when I check again.

I fall on my bed facedown, setting an alarm for ten till. Maybe I can just sleep away the forty minutes. But nope, not happening. I just stare at my ceiling until the alarm comes. And when it does, I feel stuck.

It's time, but I'm still not sure what he's doing. I double-check that the ticket is still in my pocket, right where I put it this afternoon.

When I make it to his door, I nearly just run back home and forget the whole thing. But this is obviously important to Nathan. I ring the doorbell and wait a few seconds, listening for the sound of footsteps. But there's nothing. Not even Ryder's barking. I knock again and wait. Still nothing.

Then my phone starts to ring, Nathan's name flashing on the screen.

"Hello?"

"Come on inside, it's unlocked," he says.

"Okay." I open the front door slowly. "Where are you?"

"You're getting warmer."

"Nathan."

"Play along? I spent all week planning this. Now, where are you?"

"The hallway by the kitchen." I think I can hear his voice. Somewhere around here.

"Okay, you're still lukewarm at best. Like when you warm up chili in the microwave and it's hot on the outside but cold in the middle?"

"That's a gross metaphor."

"A simile, my dear Watson."

"Did I tell you I passed my English exam?"

"No, that's great!"

"Yup. Well, I barely passed the class with a C, but I did it."

"Oh, Benji, I knew you could do it."

"No help from you," I say, and I can almost hear him smiling. "You know you could save me some time and let me know where you are?" I keep moving through the kitchen, ducking into the living room. Still nothing.

"That, my dear friend, would spoil all the fun."

"Should I go up the stairs?"

"Maybe."

"Nathan."

"It'll be worth it, I promise."

I climb the stairs slowly, almost afraid of what I'm going to find up here. The hallway is mostly dark, the only light coming from the crack in his door. And is that music? "Nathan?"

"Warmer."

I open the door to his room slowly. It's empty, looking the same as it usually does except his bed isn't made. And there's a blazer thrown over the back of his desk chair. "You aren't here," I say.

"Where else would I be, then?"

My eyes automatically go to the window, which is sitting wide open. "Outside?"

"Warmer." Then he ends the call. I slip my phone back into my pocket and try to climb outside without injuring myself. Which is easier said than done. But he's waiting for me in our usual spot with that white blanket laid out under a pile of pillows.

"You're here." He looks up at me, and there's that smile.

"I'm aware," I say. "So why aren't you at prom?" He even looks like he was getting dressed for it but stopped halfway, with his black slacks, and white dress shirt that's only about halfway buttoned up. I try not to think about that last point too much.

"Because you aren't there."

"I don't really . . ."

"I tried to ask you to prom, and you turned me down, so I thought this might be a bit more up your alley."

"Oh, I thought . . ." Am I really that clueless? "I didn't know you were *asking me* asking me."

"It's okay. I like this better."

"So, you wanted to ask me to prom?"

"Yeah, for a few weeks now, I thought it might be the perfect time."

"For what?"

"Maybe you should sit down." He rubs at the back of his neck.

"Is Nathan Allan speechless?" I tease. "This has to be a moment for the record books."

"You know how, when you came out to me, you said you needed me to not be me?" And the way he looks at me, it wrecks my heart.

"Oh, okay." I take the place beside him. "I'm sorry. Is something wrong?"

"I wish I'd written this down." He fakes a laugh; it's so unlike him that I really don't want to ever hear it again. "Do you remember that day in the park? When I took you to see the movie?"

How could I ever forget it? "Yeah."

"And you asked me if I had a secret. A secret that there was no reason to be ashamed of, but you still felt like you had to hide it?"

I nod.

"What was yours?"

I swallow hard. "That I'm nonbinary."

"Right." He shakes his head quickly. "That's what I figured. I mean, not at the time. But you know, now I can see that. So that's why I wanted to tell you mine."

He's so flustered, and it's so cute. "You know you don't have to."

"I know." He looks at me, his lips spreading. "I want to." Nathan takes my hand, running his thumb over the skin. "I've been really scared to tell you this, but since you trusted me, I'm going to trust you. Okay?"

I nod. "Okay."

"Okay," he says again, and he breathes in and out. "For a while, I've sort of been thinking about the way I feel about you." Then he starts shaking his head. "God, I *really* should've written this all down."

"It's all right. Take your time." I can feel his pulse getting faster.

"I knew I should've just copied Mr. Darcy's speech." Nathan breathes. "I, um . . . I've been trying to find out a way to tell you how I feel. For months now, really."

Months?

"And I know I picked the greatest time, since I'm going to be moving across the country in a few weeks, but I figured that if we could have three months, it'd be better than nothing, right?"

"Nathan, I—"

"I really like you, Ben. I really, really, really like you," he finally says, and I can almost see his shoulders relax. "I'd use the other L-word, but if I'm being a hundred percent honest, it scares the absolute shit out of me." He takes a deep breath. "And I've spent months trying to figure out how I could tell you without scaring you away, or making you hate me, but yeah."

"Nathan." I can't even think of anything to tell him. Because I still can't believe this is happening. I just stare at him, at how goddamn beautiful he is. With that bright smile, and those brown eyes, and his deep brown skin, and those freckles that are so unfair I can't stand it. I never want to do anything but stare at him.

"If you could say something besides my name, I'd really appreciate it." He lets out this exasperated laugh. "At least a 'fuck off' or something."

"I, um . . ." I try not to giggle too much. It actually feels like I'm high on happiness right now. Is there even such a thing? "I really like you too," I say. "More than like, in fact."

"Really?" His voice strains a little.

"Really. I have for a while, actually."

His smile falters for a split second. "You have?"

"Yeah."

"Since when?"

I don't even have to think about it; I've known the answer for so long. "That night, here, after the party."

"I've been torturing you with my good looks for that long, huh?"

I shake my head. "You have no idea."

"I . . . I want to kiss you," he tells me. "Can I do that?"

"Yeah," I whisper.

He leans in, and well, it's sort of terrible. Our lips meet, but we move too fast and bump noses, and Nathan catches my bottom lip. It's rushed and wet, and really messy. But the good kind of messy.

There are no fireworks. Time doesn't stop. And I don't mind; I don't think he does either. Because this has been in the making for so long. And like he said, if we have three months of this, I'd rather spend those three months practicing this with him.

"That was sort of bad," he says.

"I'm kind of new at this." I rest my forehead against his. "You want to try again?"

He nods. The second kiss is better. I move my arms so they drape off his shoulders, and both of his hands are on my back now, pushing us as close as possible. Then he grabs me by the collar of my shirt and we slowly fall back on the pillows, the music echoing through the night. God, I can feel the way his body is moving underneath his shirt, and it's pure magic.

This boy is such a work of art.

"That one was better," I say when I pull away, trying to catch my breath.

"Much better."

"They say that the third time's the charm." I reach up again and feel his lips against mine. He tangles his fingers in my hair, and we sit there. I don't know for how long, and I don't care. Because right now the world is so quiet and so peaceful that it might as well be just the two of us here alone, the only company we have with each other. I don't think I mind that, actually.

But eventually we have to go inside, because even for May, the night is getting chilly. I don't hesitate to crawl into the bed beside him, my head on his stomach, rising and falling to his calm breathing.

"I'm glad I met you, Nathan," I say, because there's nothing else to say. I'm so happy right now, so ridiculously and terribly happy that I don't think I'll ever be able to accurately describe the feeling.

"I'm glad I met you too." His fingers find my hair again. "I guess we need to talk, huh? Because I can't exactly call you my boyfriend, can I?"

I hadn't even thought about that. "I guess not," I say. "Is partner a little too cowboy for you?" I tip an imaginary cowboy hat. "Yee haw."

He tries not to laugh, but he fails miserably. Good, I don't want him to hold back. "Seriously though what can I call you?"

"Is 'my kissing friend who isn't on the gender binary but who I love very much' a little too wordy?" I say.

"Who said 'love'?" There's that smirk.

"I did. I'm planning for the future." I stretch up to him, giving him one more kiss. "And maybe 'partner' is a little too . . . square dance-y."

"Yee haw." He can't stop laughing while he tips the invisible hat, and then his face settles. The way he's looking at me warms me from the inside out, and part of me wants to cry and the other part wants to laugh and all of me wants him to look at me this way forever. Then he opens his mouth again. "What about my person?"

"Your person." I like the way the words sound. On his lips and to my ears.

"My Ben." Nathan leans in, kissing the top of my hand, and all at once my heart feels so full. Maybe we'll only have three months of this, but it's going to be a damn good three months. "Things might be hard, when I go to UCLA. Do you still want to do this?"

"Yes," I say, and I've never been more sure of anything else.

I take a deep breath and relax into his touch. God, I can't even have a night with this boy without worrying about the future, can I? "Is that what you want this to be? Us together? For however long it lasts?"

"I'm not going to be perfect. With the pronouns. I'll go ahead and admit that, but I'm going to try my hardest to remember."

"Thank you." He's been nothing but perfect so far though.

"I don't want you to be afraid to correct me, okay? Please. I don't want to hurt you. Never again. Not if I can help it."

"I will." I don't make myself any promises, but for him I think I'd do almost anything. "And we'll figure it out. When you leave in August. Maybe I can visit you." If this project with Mariam pans out, I can probably afford to go every few months.

"Guess that's why you're my person, huh?" He wraps his arms around me and pulls me in as close as he can. "We'll figure it out," he repeats.

"We'll have to figure a lot of things out, won't we?"

"Yeah." His grip on me tightens. "But at least we can do it together, right?" He leans in and kisses me again, and I never want him to stop.

EPILOGUE

THREE MONTHS LATER

"Come on, lovebirds!" Meleika screams from across the parking lot. We should hurry. It's the last day of summer break and everyone knows it, because the parking lot is flooded with cars. I can't even imagine how the beach looks right now.

But I don't want to move, because I don't want this to end.

"What's wrong?" Nathan asks me, his hands moving to the back of my head, playing with the tie that's keeping my hair up.

I swallow. "I'm going to miss you."

"Please." He rolls his eyes and leans in close to me. "You're Ben-ing again."

"I'm 'Ben-ing'?" Since when am I a verb?

"Hey, you got that right." He laughs, the corners of his mouth poking up, and my heart flutters. Every single damn time. "You're worrying about nothing."

I glance toward Sophie and Meleika. They're waiting at the ramp that'll take us down to the beach. The God-awful sand. But Nathan wanted to go. Just as one last hurrah, we'd driven down to Emerald Isle in the hopes that the crowds might've died down a little.

Different oceans, I guess. Technically. Definitely different sand.

"What are you smiling at?" he asks.

"Nothing." I look over at him, at that grin I fell in love with, and those brown eyes. "I'm still going to miss you," I say again.

He rolls his eyes, grinning like a fool. "Come on, it's one day."

"I know, but it's one day I won't see you. An entire day without Nathan Allan."

"Ben-ing," he repeats. "Though I suppose I'd be sad too if I had to go a day without this face."

"Hate you."

"Love you too." He leans over and kisses me. "It's your fault, anyway. It's what you get for booking your flight late."

"Shut up." I kiss him again. "You're the one who distracted me, so really it all goes back to you."

Nathan sighs and rolls his eyes. "Just like everything else."

There's a tap on the window that makes us both jump. "If y'all don't hurry up, we're dragging you out of that car," Sophie huffs.

"I didn't spend three hours in a car to watch you two make out." Meleika's standing behind her.

"Come on. Our party awaits." He grabs the huge white blanket out of the back seat and pops the trunk so I can grab the umbrella. No way I'm flying to Los Angeles red as a lobster. I still can't believe it's happening, that I'm leaving this place. January feels like such a lifetime ago.

But when Mariam asked me to help them with a new project they're starting, there was no way I was going to turn them down. Even if it meant leaving Hannah and Thomas. And Meleika. And Sophie. All while providing a little emotional support for my boyfriend, while he spends long nights writing papers and drinking way too much coffee. Of course, he has to live in the dorms for the first year, but Mariam and I have worked something out.

My boyfriend.

That still feels weird to say. But the good weird. The weird that I never want to stop. Because Nathan Allan is my boyfriend.

It's taken us both some time to really get used to it. Because dating wasn't exactly different from being the kind of friends we were before.

Nathan had suspected that he's bisexual for a while. And when he started going to the safe space meetings with me, everything sort of clicked for him. His parents took it well. Honestly, they really didn't care who he was dating as long as whatever we did involved condoms, a talk neither of us was really too thrilled to have. Hannah and Thomas weren't all that surprised, but we did have to leave the door open anytime Nathan was over.

I sink in the sand, and it's already burning the bottoms of my feet. "Sand should be illegal." I try to shake it from between my toes.

"Quit whining." Nathan leans over and kisses my cheek.

Meleika mimes sticking her finger down her throat to Sophie, and I flip them both off.

"Jealousy isn't a good color, girls."

"Whatever." Meleika rolls her eyes. "You're gonna let me repaint those today, right?" She waves around the bag of nail polish she's holding. "I'm thinking polka dots, for your big day."

"Of course," I say. My nails are looking pretty rough, the black paint chipped in a few spots. This is the first time I've been able to wear it long enough for it to chip away.

I'll have to find YouTube tutorials or something. I don't think it'll be very lucrative to fly back and forth between California and North Carolina just for Meleika to do my nails.

The beach is as crowded as I thought it would be, but we find a spot that isn't too far from the entrance. I hammer the umbrella stand into the sand, going a few rounds so I know the wind won't blow it away. I'm already hot and sweaty when I'm done, but I don't feel like taking off my shirt. I collapse beneath the shade of the umbrella and look up at Nathan, and even though I've seen his bare chest a dozen times now, I still can't stop myself from staring.

"Take a picture, it'll last longer." He balls up the shirt and tosses it to me.

"Funny boy."

"You aren't even going to *try* and get in the water."

I shake my head. This is why I brought the sketch pad. "No way."

"Come on, it's your last chance." Nathan holds out his hands.

"They have oceans in California."

He does that weird eyebrow wiggle thing that he knows drives me up a wall. "But not this ocean." I sigh and take his hand. "You might want to leave that here." He pulls at the hem of my shirt.

"Is this some elaborate plan to get me to take my shirt off?" Wouldn't be the first time we've both been shirtless around each other. Won't be last. At least, I hope it won't be.

"Come on. It's a science."

"Okay, you'll have to explain that one."

"Your shirt gets all wet and you're uncomfortable for the rest of the day because you've got this gross heavy thing weighing you down."

"Yes, all science." I slip my arms through the gaping holes of my tank top and leave it on the towel next to Meleika and Sophie. They both already look like they're asleep in their chairs, but the sunglasses make it hard to guess.

"Have fun." Sophie waves at us. "Don't cut yourself on a seashell."

"I regret telling you that," I say before Nathan drags me down the sand and toward the water.

We wade around for a few minutes before I'm ready to sit

back on dry land, but I tolerate it, at least for Nathan. I can do that for him. But eventually he gets tired too, and we head back to our spot, the sand sticking to the bottoms of my feet. It's terrible. But for once I don't mind.

The beach starts clearing out after a while, the sun slowly setting until it's this huge ball in the sky. That's when Meleika and Sophie decide to head into the water, never going more than thigh deep.

"Hey." Nathan's hands wrap around mine. He's sitting behind me, his legs stretched out around me, his stomach pressed to my back, so his chin can rest on my shoulder.

"Hey." I squeeze. I really can't believe I'm this lucky.

"You look like you're thinking about something." Nathan pulls on the hair tie and the curls fall to my shoulder, his fingers threading through them to try and untangle them. Good luck.

I try to laugh. "Am I Ben-ing again?"

"A little bit."

"Just nervous," I say. "Just Mariam, and Hannah, and moving, and I don't . . . I don't know." There are actually a thousand different things to worry about. The things I am going to take to California, finding another psychiatrist as amazing as Dr. Taylor, worrying about Meleika and Sophie and hoping our friendship will survive two of us moving across the country.

Over the last three months, Mariam and I worked from the second we both woke up to when we both passed out in front of our webcams on ideas and things we could do. Mariam wants me to join their channel, to speak with them at conferences and events.

To build something that could continue to help kids who are like us.

It'd taken a lot for me to say yes, mostly because I didn't feel like I deserved it. My track record with talking about my identity wasn't the best. But I had Nathan there with me.

Eventually I worked up the courage to start going to the group therapy sessions. It was difficult at first, but I got used to that. Especially with Nathan there beside me. And, with his help, I was able to come out to Sophie and Meleika. They both had a few questions, but they seemed to understand and apologized for the months of accidental misgendering.

I thought about making a big Facebook post or something, but I decided against it. Just didn't seem right.

"You're going to do great, I know it," Nathan tells me, and I feel his skin against mine and the way he's relaxed against me. And for the first time in a while, it really does feel like things may be okay.

"What about Hannah?"

"It feels like we sort of *just* fixed things. And now I'm the one leaving her." It hadn't dawned on me until I told Hannah and Thomas about the project. But I'd be moving across the country.

They were both happy, but I could see the look on Hannah's face, that split second before she was congratulating me. "I'm a terrible sibling."

"Except you aren't," Nathan says.

"But I—"

"Hush, hush, hush," he whispers in my ear. "Just hush. This isn't the same kind of situation, you both know that."

I sigh, tucking my knees close to my chest. "You don't think she hates me?"

"I think it'd take a lot for her to hate you."

"You promise?"

He nods. "You know as well as she does that this isn't the

same situation. You'll be talking to each other every day. You both actually have cell phones now, and you can FaceTime. Believe me, Ben, she doesn't resent you for moving."

"It feels like we just became siblings again."

I feel Nathan's skin against mine. "And this isn't going to ruin that. Don't you think she's proud of you? This project . . . It's important, babe."

"I know." I feel my chest unclench a little. And deep down, I do know that. Nathan's right, anyway. Hannah made me promise we'd talk every day. Over the summer, things have gotten better. Slowly but surely, we've come out the other side. Together. "And did you just call me babe?"

"Trying something new, schnookums." He kisses my neck again. "No good?"

I relax against him. "Let's stick with 'babe' if we have to."

"I can. Besides, you should be more nervous about that meeting next week."

"Please don't remind me."

"I'll be right there in the audience, cheering you on."

I angle myself so I can kiss him. Those soft lips have quickly become my favorite part of Nathan. "No audience in this kind of meeting."

"I'll just sneak in. I told you, emotional support comes before modeling." He lets out a deep sigh and we both stare at the sun, slowly but surely sinking beneath the surface of the dark ocean. "I wish you all the best, Benjamin De Backer."

They aren't the same words, but I know exactly what he means.

"I love you too."

AUTHOR'S NOTE

I started writing *I Wish You All the Best* when I decided I wanted to tell the story that I needed when I was younger. This book is what I needed when I was fifteen, when I was eighteen, and it's still the story I need in my twenties. This is how a lot of stories are born: out of necessity.

Writing this book helped me confront my anxieties, my depression, and, ultimately, it helped me confront myself. I realize it may be harder for some readers to understand this, and for others, it'll be an all too relatable reality. For a long time, I struggled to realize who exactly I am, and in a lot of ways I still do. I struggle believing myself when I tell people that I'm nonbinary. I still have a hard time correcting others when they use the wrong pronouns because I don't want to make them uncomfortable or make them feel bad. Some mornings I look in the mirror and hate what I see because I feel as if my body isn't up to the standard as other members of the queer community.

Some days are better than others. Days where my confidence is off the charts and I feel perfectly comfortable in my body and my incredibly tacky style. And as I've gotten older and have surrounded myself with people like me, I find that those days happen more often than not.

When I set out to write this book, my one hope was that it would help people feel less alone, no matter how or why they related to Ben—or even Nathan, or Hannah, or anyone else in this book. I wanted for readers to be able to see a piece of themselves in these words.

And remember: Whatever happens, I wish you all the best.

ACKNOWLEDGMENTS

So yeah, *I Wish You All the Best* is out, it's here, it's in your hands in some form or another. It's been a journey. A weird, long journey through which I discovered that I am terrible at writing emails, a tad impatient, and apparently incapable of not working on *something* while the waiting eats at me from the inside out.

But I survived, mostly thanks to my amazing support system and friends who kept me going by encouraging me, even when I was at my lowest.

Robin, one of my dearest friends and to whom this book is dedicated: Without you, this book would not exist. Literally. Our texts and late-night calls helped pull me out of writing funks. You've been there since the start of Ben and Nathan, when they were two kids in college, staring up at the night sky and denying their feelings for each other. Seriously, it might not sound like it, but this book went through a lot of changes, and you were there for all of them. Start to finish.

Mariam Haidari, who let me borrow their name for this book: You've been the best parent to Ben and Nathan, and your support has meant the most to me. The way you talked about these kids, the way you loved them and supported them. It made me believe they would one day be real. And now they are. Your status as their #1 parent is cemented in these words. And here is where I'll apologize for all the mysterious notes I send you that cause you to worry over the well-being of all your future fictional kids.

Shauna, Cam, and Hương: You three are some of my best

friends in the world, and I can't imagine going on this journey without the three of you there to share the experience with.

Becky Albertalli for her priceless help during the editing stages and for her books that kept me going. For her kind words and optimism about the future of this story, and her help along the way. Seriously, I owe you so much. Besides, you gave me my first piece of Ben fan art!

My agent, Lauren Abramo, who left me absolutely speechless during our first phone call. A lot of people believed in Ben and Nathan, but Lauren was the first person who I felt truly understood what I wanted to do with this story. I knew from the first call that we'd be great together, and I'm glad I trusted my gut.

Jeffrey West, who has been an absolute dream editor and has seen things where I haven't and helped me make this story into something truly fantastic. I've been lucky to find two people to work with who truly understood the story I was trying to tell.

To my early readers who gave me their sound advice and careful eyes. But mostly, you guys kept me going during hard times. Ava, Cody, Camryn, Kav, Fadwa, Megan, and Sarah.

Roseanne Wells, who first proposed a huge revision and made this book all the better for it, even if you are team pancake.

To Caleb, Kari, TJ, and Alice, who helped bring Ben and Nathan to life with their stunning artwork, which I love with all my heart.

And to all my amazing friends online who gave their constant support through this whole journey. Through the writing and the editing and the waiting. Jonas (who gave me the name De Backer), Claribel, Sabina, both Jays, Nic, Olivia, Sandhya, Meleika (who also let me borrow their name!), Kimberly, Janani, Meredith, Sona, Zoraida, and anyone else who has followed this book since it was nothing more than three hundred poorly written pages with the name #EnbyLoveStory. Seriously, you all kept me going through this entire journey, and your support means the world to me.

In the words of Andrew Gold, though preferably sung by Cynthia Fee: Thank you for being a friend.

Lastly, to my mother, who is one of the bravest people I know and the person I love most in this world.

And to my father: You never got the chance to see these words, to know about this book in all its detail. Truthfully, I don't know if you would've liked it, and I don't know if you would've liked me, but we'll never really know, will we? You only told me that you wanted me to be the next J. K. Rowling. And while I'm not sure I'd want that, I hope this is close enough.